# VEIL OF ASH

## ASCENSION TRILOGY: BOOK 1

### J. L. WILLIS

WILLIS PUBLISHING

*In honor of my brother, Sean.*
*See you again on the other side.*

# ACKNOWLEDGMENTS

The concept of this story has lived in my head since the age of ten. I always knew it was going to be the first book I wrote. I just didn't know when. After years of stewing on the idea, I finally decided it was time.

This manuscript made its rounds, and I received wonderful feedback from friends and strangers alike. Thank you to every person who took the time to read my work. I'm especially grateful to those of you who read the rough drafts... Don't worry, I figured out how to use an Oxford comma!

I had the privilege of working with artists I know personally, and it made this project even more special. The cover was done by a gifted painter, Corinne Mikulik. She produced a stunning piece of art that I'm in awe of every time I see it. My wonderful illustrator and amazing father, Craig Willis, took time away from crafting guitars to spend countless hours creating the perfect map.

Finally, I would like to give special thanks to my grandfather. He kept me writing even when I wanted to stop. This book exists because he coerced me into sending him more chapters, and then made me feel bad when I didn't have any written.

All these people assisted me in taking the world that had once only existed in my head and making it available to you, the reader.

With a full heart,

Jess Willis

# CONTENTS

# Content Warning

The following content is mentioned and may be difficult for some audiences:

Conversations Surrounding Suicide

Kidnapping

Sexual Content

Murder

Descriptions of Depression

Trauma

PTSD

Bullying

Depictions of Medical Experimentation

# Pronunciation Guide

Ethoria (ee-THOR-ee-uh)
Ravaryn (ruh-VAR-in) / Ravarie (ruh-VAR-ee)

Aeta (AY-eh-tuh)
Anam (Uh-NAHM)
Elspeth (ELZ-beth)
Oren (OR-in)
Netali (neh-TAH-lee)
Mavis (MAY-vis)
Kaven (KAY-vin)
Alona (uh-LONE-uh)
Grandmother Alma (ALL-muh)
Rowan (ROW-in)
Renata (rih-NAH-duh)
Balor (BAY-lore)
Marcum (MAR-kum)
Corsica (COR-sih-kuh)
Talia (TAH-lee-uh)
Naia (NIGH-uh)

# PROLOGUE

The following excerpt has been translated from Old Ethoric to the Common Tongue. It is the only verified translation in circulation.

*"In the beginning, there was nothing and no one, for Ethoria had yet to be. Aeta and her twin brother, Anam, were born of pure starlight. Anam formed Ethoria from the lifeless rocks in the Sky, and Aeta planted the first seed. From that seed, life was created. After creation, Anam took to the Ground, and Aeta stayed true to the Sky, becoming known as Our Lady of the Stars.*

*"Our Lady craved more kin, children to bless with life and love. With three tears, she created three celestial children: Elspeth, Oren, and Netali. Each celestial child was gifted a portion of Her power. Elspeth: Bender of Wind, Seer of Fate, and Courier of Death. Oren: Keeper of Knowledge, Bearer of Seasons, and Father of Beasts. Netali: Mother of Salt and Sea, Enchantress, and Lady of Love. The celestial children protect the balance of Ethoria; that is their purpose.*

*"Aeta took from both Ethoria and herself to create mortals. Their lives are brief, yet full of hope—something no god possesses, for they do not need it. Mortals are a reminder to all that time is fleeting and must be exalted. Being of the Ground, mortals must also answer to Anam. His price for their life is judgment upon their soul after death."*

-The Old Book

# CHAPTER 1

*"Be righteous in this life,*
*for it is not Our Lady you meet after—it is Anam,*
*the Keeper of Names and Reaper of Souls.*
*He is your judgment."*
*- The Old Book*

T he shutters shook fiercely, rattling like teeth in a fever.

A cold draft coiled down my neck, and my skin prickled before I understood why.

Beyond the second-story window, oak branches bowed in the gusts, their brittle leaves torn free and whirled into the night. The sound wasn't the playful rush of autumn, but a low, hollow cry that seemed to carry its own warning. My pulse matched its rhythm.

"Mavis, what's wrong?"

Kaven's voice was behind me, warm and familiar, but I couldn't turn away from the glass.

"The wind is blowing from the west," I replied, my voice quieter than I intended. "It never blows from the west."

The hair on my nape raised, acutely aware of the *wrongness* in the air.

I was taught that the Sky watched, and the Ground remembered. Each belonged to the gods. Something was amiss—and the Sky was watching us closely now.

"Mavis, the wind is just wind." His words were flat and tired, as if we had done this song and dance more than he could count.

I put a finger to the glass, scraping at the condensation. "It isn't. Can't you feel it?"

The cold seeped through, making me tense.

"No, because there's nothing to feel. You're scaring yourself again."

"I'm not scared. I'm concerned," I bristled. "There's a difference."

"Well, I'd rather not spend my life bothered by shadows in the corner."

"Shadows move. Maybe you *should* be wary of them."

I turned at last. Kaven was slouched across his bed, a battered book in hand, his rich mahogany skin catching the quick flicker of lightning through the shutters. His shadow flashed in the light, showing itself to me. It made me realize that anything could hide in the dark.

"Do you ever get the feeling," I asked, "that you aren't alone? That someone is only a breath away, watching?"

His brow knit. "You mean the gods?"

The skepticism was thick.

"Or something else."

His eyes widened, a flicker of unease quickly masked with mischief. "A ghost?"

The word clung to the air. A shiver rippled through me, and I froze. Mother always said sudden chills were caused by the touch of a spirit. Of course, Father dismissed it as superstition, but the thought persisted. Maybe we weren't as alone as we thought.

Kaven broke into a wide grin. He knew exactly where my mind had gone, and he thought it amusing.

"Relax, you're not being haunted."

"It's not a joke."

He folded his page and set the book aside. Then, he pushed up from the squeaking mattress and sighed, "I know it's not a joke." Brushing a strand of hair behind my ear, he asked, "Are you ready to go downstairs? We've hidden up here long enough."

My shoulders tensed.

Sensing my hesitation, he gave me a pointed, chastising look. "Mavis, it's her name-day. She'll want you there."

We stared at each other for a few moments in a quiet battle of wills. Seconds of squinting through prolonged eye contact passed before I finally let out a sigh of defeat. He won.

He smiled in victory and placed a quick kiss on my lips. Lacing his fingers with mine, he tugged me toward the door.

I grunted. Crowds made my skin itch. I felt every stare as if I were naked, every accidental brush of skin as if it were a burn.

We descended the staircase together, the chatter and clink of glasses growing louder with each step. Candles flickered in metal sconces, scattering light across the oak floor.

Grandmother Alma stood in the corner of the dining area, muttering to herself and looking worriedly out the window. I squeezed Kaven's hand with a pleading look.

Kaven glanced at Grandmother Alma and back at me. He rolled his eyes. I smiled and pushed at his chest—but he didn't budge. He groaned, mouthing, "Five minutes."

I nodded, and he bent down to press one more kiss on my cheek. He passed through the archway, leading to the sitting room, while I made my way to Grandmother Alma. Upon hearing my footsteps, she twisted toward me. Her gaze relaxed as it met mine.

"Is everything all right?" I asked.

Her frown tilted upward into a wavering smile.

"Oh, I'm alright, dear."

There was a slight tremor in her voice. Her eyes wandered back to the window, glinting with interest. Did she share the same ill sensation I did?

Without looking back, she asked, "What can you feel?"

I searched the storm's chaos for words to capture exactly how I felt. There were none.

"The wind is fierce tonight, and it's blowing from an odd direction," I said.

"That's not what I asked."

A moment of silence passed. I put a hand to my stomach and pressed my fingers inward, as if I could dig out the discomfort. Nausea threatened to overwhelm me as bitterness coated my mouth. It was acrid, reminding me of ash on my tongue.

"There's something in that breeze that doesn't sit right in the pit of my stomach."

"Good."

I furrowed my brow. "How is that good?"

"It means you are no fool. You see this storm for what it is."

"And what is it?"

Her eyes snapped to mine. "A warning."

My chest grew tight, and my breathing turned into short pants.

"Can you sense omens, Grandmother Alma?"

"Elders have always had a knack for sensing the weather, but omens are a different beast." She hesitated. "Not everyone shares the beliefs I do. Whether it be salt on the front stoop to ward off evil, or the chirping of crickets signaling good fortune. But I know this wind carries an off-putting scent in the air. I can smell it—something wicked."

I fidgeted with the hem of my tunic as she studied me, forehead wrinkling.

"Lately my dreams have been filled with flashes of something I can't make out, like smudges of charcoal over painted canvas. It's mixed with a feeling of helplessness I can't shake. Then, just as I'm about to pierce the haze, I hear screams and wake up."

"How long have you been having these dreams?"

"A week."

I trusted her with my secrets. She was the only one I didn't fear judgment from. The last time I told Kaven about my dreams, he dismissed them, saying that they were just nightmares. My dreams then had been suffocating, like I was holding my breath.

A few days later, a little boy drowned in the river.

Kaven held me while I cried over the boy, but he didn't understand the depth of my sorrow. When I told Grandmother Alma what happened, she believed me. I have gone to her ever since.

"What do they mean?" I asked.

"In truth? I do not know. It is something you will have to discover yourself."

Another shiver racked my body—but it wasn't from the cold.

Grandmother Alma lifted her shaky hand and lightly patted my cheek, lingering to cup my face.

"Now, if you'll excuse an old woman, I believe it is time I retire for the evening."

She dropped her hand, but her worried expression remained. After she left, I stayed still, lost in thought. All I wanted was normalcy, structure, and security. But I knew my destiny was to have none of it.

The shutters groaned, and the candles guttered low. Then, in the silence that followed, I swore I heard it—my name, whispered in the wailing wind.

# CHAPTER 2

*"The gods leave crumbs for mortals, so be quick to follow.*
*Lest they blow away."*
*- The Old Book*

I slipped into the sitting room, joining Kaven on the sofa. Alona was unwrapping her name-day gifts. With the same smile and laugh, she was Kaven's mirror, just eight years younger.

She tore through the paper and gasped at the leather-bound journal she uncovered. She flipped through its thick, deckled pages with her jaw slack.

"For your watercolor paintings," I said, trying to keep my voice steady.

"I love it!" Alona jumped up and ran to me. She threw her arms around my stomach and hugged me a little too hard. "Thank you!"

"Happy thirteenth name-day, Alona." I kissed the top of her head. "Go finish." Without hesitation, she dropped back onto the floor and resumed unwrapping.

The next gift she unveiled was a stunningly vibrant paint set and an array of new brushes. Only one person would have known to get her that.

I whipped my head toward Kaven and narrowed my eyes. Sure enough, he was beaming with pride. It had probably cost him an entire week's worth of earnings from work at the forge. More than my measly stipend as a leather maker's apprentice.

It was a perfect paint set for a journal he should have known nothing about.

"How did you know?"

I had kept it hidden at my mother's house, away from Kaven's wandering eyes.

"You hide things in the same spot every year," he teased.

"Can't you suppress your disdain for surprises just once?"

"Hmm," he hummed, pretending to ponder my request. "No."

I rolled my eyes and pinched his side. He flinched back, mock-offended.

His scent of spearmint enveloped my senses, and I sank into it.

The storm and my conversation with Grandmother Alma had rattled me. Nestling further into Kaven's embrace soothed my nerves. His warmth cloaked me, and the sound of his heart steadied the racing pace of my own.

"Hey." His voice was curious, but not prying.

I tried to keep the waver out of my voice when I replied, "Hey."

But I failed.

His eyes glinted with suspicion, and I wordlessly cursed myself for being so obvious. I didn't want him to worry about me like he often did. He had his sister and Grandmother Alma to take care of. My burdens were mine alone.

"What are you thinking?" he asked.

I considered telling him what I was really thinking. But he wouldn't understand. Kaven wasn't as attuned to his spiritual side as I was. He often poked fun at it all. So, I settled for a half-truth.

"I want to go upstairs."

It wasn't a lie. I needed to get away from the crowd of people who were magnifying my anxiety. I longed for a quiet place to unwind. My body felt far too tight.

Kaven grabbed my hand and squeezed; our way of saying we understood.

"Well, we showed our faces. That should be enough."

He helped me stand, supporting my nervous legs. I followed him up the stairwell to his bedchamber. He quietly closed the door and clasped his hands behind his back, watching me with intense focus.

I stared at his barren walls, attempting to evade his intrusive gaze.

Kaven kept his room clean of clutter and displayed very few personal items. It looked more like a guest room than someone's bedroom. The only true sentimental item he showed was a portrait of his parents on his nightstand. They had been gone since an illness swept through our village years ago.

That's when Kaven and I grew close. Well... Kaven, me, and Willam.

We three were always causing trouble in some form or another—like stealing Arger Brook's crops, or swimming nude in the drinking spring. I think everyone looked past most of our actions because they pitied what had happened to Kaven and his family.

A year later, I knew exactly how Kaven felt as a recipient of everyone's pity. A year later, Willam was taken in the Culling of our village.

I didn't let myself linger on the portrait of his parents for too long because I knew the wound was deep.

"Today has been exhausting." I sighed, letting myself collapse onto his bed.

"What did you and Grandmother Alma talk about?"

I kept my eyes glued to his ceiling as I spoke.

"She feels it too. Something isn't right."

"You know how she is. She used to bore the three of us all the time, incessantly quoting *The Old Book*. The woman loves to be ominous."

I picked my head up to look at him.

"Hey, that's your grandmother. Be kind."

He sighed. "You don't know what it's like. All she does is talk about the gods and our role as the creator's children. I just want to live my life without wondering if Our Lady is listening, watching, and approving of every decision I make."

I laughed and rested my head back down on the sheets.

"Be careful, or she'll report back to Anam. I don't think you'd fare well eternally drowning in the Sea of Sorrow."

Kaven chuckled and took his seat on the bed next to me. The laughter quickly dissipated, replaced with unspoken tension. When I looked back at him, he was picking the skin off his thumb.

"This town is so small," he muttered.

I sat up. "What?"

He stopped picking.

"I want to leave Oak Hollow," he admitted. "With you."

My eyes widened, and a glimmer of panic shone across Kaven's face.

"Kaven—" I started, but couldn't finish. I didn't know what to say.

His brow shot upward, and tense lines formed across his forehead. His eyes locked with mine, pleading and impatient.

"Mavis, please just listen." He gripped my arm. "You have been taking care of your mother for eight *years*. I have been taking care of Alona and Grandmother

Alma for eleven. We have become so accustomed to taking care of others that we have forgotten about ourselves, about our own lives."

He held me firmly in place. I might have been shaking. A mixture of frustration, panic, and confusion whirled within me.

"We deserve something better. That's what I want, and, gods... I hope that's what you want too."

"Where would we go?"

Kaven scratched the top of his head. "I'm not sure yet. Maybe the capital?"

"But you love Alona and Grandmother Alma. Why would you leave them?"

"You know I love them, and so do they. They appreciate everything I've done for them all these years, but they know that staying here in Oak Hollow isn't what's best for me—for us."

Something inside me bristled at the idea of others gathering around to talk about *my* future, as if I wouldn't want to be part of the conversation.

"And they know what's best for me? You think *you* know what's best for me?" I stood and faced him, crossing my arms over my chest. "Please tell me what that is."

It was a challenge, making him roll his shoulders back.

"I know that spending all your time working, or reminding your mother to eat, wash—"

"You are drastically overstepping, and I caution you to choose your next words *very* carefully." My words were calm but clipped.

Kaven groaned.

"You can't keep doing this alone," he said. "It's killing you."

"You would have me leave her then?"

"There are people—caretakers—who specialize in these types of situations and can look after her. We could leave and send money back for her care." He threw his chin back in exasperation.

"You make it all sound so simple, but do you know what you're saying? Do you understand what led to all of this? She couldn't take it! Willam was taken, my father..." I paused, unable to finish my sentence. Swallowing the lump in my throat, I continued.

"She broke under the stress of it all. How do you think she would fare if the last member of her family were to abandon her as well? It would kill her. I will *not* kill my mother!"

Kaven rubbed hard at his temples as if trying to soothe a nagging migraine. Then, he looked back at me and squeezed my hand, begging for understanding. But I couldn't give it to him.

I couldn't believe he'd say that—as if he didn't know what my family meant to me. It was something I thought we had in common. My duty to my family was far more important than some half-concocted dream. Chasing after another life wouldn't make my current one disappear.

Kaven ran his hand down my arm, handling me like one would a wounded animal.

"Please, just think about it at least? That's all I ask." His words were a broken whisper.

"I... I have to go."

Kaven stood. "Mavis—"

"It's alright," I assured him. "We'll talk about it tomorrow."

I had nothing left to say on the topic. I needed to think.

He nodded, concern lacing his features. I stood on my tiptoes and planted a brief kiss on his cheek. With that, I turned around and left.

When I stepped out into the night, the torrent of rain had stopped. Crumbs of moonlight filtered through the swift current of clouds above. The Sky was making haste, and I could smell the change in the air.

I shook my head, silently cursing myself for being so superstitious. Perhaps Kaven was right; I had just been scaring myself for no good reason.

That's all it was.

It had to be.

# CHAPTER 3

*"Do not linger in your sorrow.*
*Your tears do nothing but muddy the Ground."*
*- The Old Book*

I walked into my mother's house, and dust immediately rose, stinging my throat. What once was a beautiful home, filled with laughter and light, was now a house in shambles. The roof leaked, the windows were broken, and the floors rotted. All things that should have been resolved years prior. But it wasn't my home anymore, and it hadn't been for a long time.

"Mom?" My voice echoed.

No answer. But then again, there never was.

I walked into the kitchen and observed the dishes I had yet to wash. They were next to a moldy loaf of bread I had forgotten to throw out.

Going further back into the hall, I walked to her bedroom. The door was open.

Inside, Mother was sleeping in her moth-eaten armchair. The one she refused to let me get rid of.

I paused, waiting for her chest to rise and fall just to make sure. Then I moved closer.

"Mom?"

She startled awake, eyes half-closed. "Willam?"

"No, Mom. It's Mavis." I pressed my hand gently to her sternum, easing her back down.

"Oh."

Not the child she wanted to see.

"Just sleep," I cooed.

She made a noise of agreement and closed her eyes again.

She was taking far too much valerian root. But it was a moot point; she wouldn't have wanted me to interfere. She didn't like being awake; it made everything real.

I went back to the kitchen and opened a jar of soup. I didn't care to heat it; it wouldn't matter to her. It was just something for her to eat when she woke up.

Once I put the soup on her side table, I took a walk through the rest of the house. I mentally cataloged all the tasks I needed to get to, but probably wouldn't. There was only one room I didn't enter, and that was my childhood bedroom. The room I had once shared with my brother.

Another shiver ran down my spine, and I instantly decided I didn't want to spend any more time there. Kaven might not believe in spirits, but I did.

I hated my mother's house. It felt like an empty shell, one I didn't want to be in more than I had to be. I often spent the night with Kaven. I spent the night only at my mother's house on her bad days. Those were the days I slept on the couch and covered my head with a pillow while she sobbed.

I worked most of the time to keep away. It was a terrible job that made me barely enough money to survive on my own, let alone with a dependent. So when I wasn't working, I was hunting.

After I completed my walk-through, I went back to check on Mother. She hadn't moved.

I bent over and placed a kiss on her cheek. When I stepped back, her eyes were open and sharp.

"You look so much like him."

"I know," I whispered.

Her eyes fluttered closed once more.

She could have been talking about Willam, or perhaps Father. I couldn't be sure of which. Emotion burned my throat.

I slowly stepped back until I was in the hallway again. Covering my mouth with my hand, I let out a muffled sob. I needed to contain myself, otherwise it would make things worse. It was time to leave.

I ran out the door toward Kaven's house. Tears rimmed my eyes, but I refused to let them fall. I quickly wiped the moisture away with my sleeve. Everyone knew my pain. It was clear as day, but that didn't mean I enjoyed showcasing it.

Maybe I shouldn't have been so quick to turn down Kaven's offer to leave.

I pinched myself for thinking that way. I could be free of Oak Hollow if I wished, but I could never remove its imprint.

It was too much.

The rain drizzled once more. It was almost as if Our Lady was listening and grieving with me.

Once I reached Kaven's house, I picked up a pebble and threw it at his window. A few seconds passed, and then I threw another.

Kaven opened his window, and when he looked down at me, no words needed to be spoken. He understood. He always did.

"Come on up," he shouted.

I nodded and made my way into his home, my only anchor left.

Kaven met me on the stairs and laced his fingers with mine in a quiet show of support. Even when we were children, his presence was always comforting.

Once we reached his bedchamber, we both silently moved to his bed and lay down.

I lay there with his arm thrown over my waist for hours. I stayed perfectly still until I heard his soft snores.

As I moved my hips to exit, he twitched. Kaven grunted and then shifted to his other side, freeing me from his hold. I quickly got out of bed and went into the attached bathing chamber. After relieving myself, I discarded my clothes to change into my nightgown.

By accident, I glimpsed my foreign body in the mirror.

The candlelight was dim, but it still exposed every curve and crevice.

Years had passed since the last time I had properly looked at myself in a mirror. I had been too scared to see the changes taking place, so I avoided them altogether.

My hair was the same, midnight waves that fell to my shoulders and contrasted with the piercing blue of my eyes.

However, I looked more hollow, my face thinner. I wasn't too frail, though. While I would be no match for someone as broad and strong as Kaven, the subtle muscles from my hours as a tanner were visible.

I was careful not to make any noise as I climbed back into bed. Kaven seldom rested well, so I didn't want to chance waking him. Too often, he woke screaming from dreams he didn't dare to tell me about. Dreams I never asked about.

I got under his sheets and felt his hard chest press firmly into my soft back.

Kaven's arms tightened around me, as if afraid I might slip away. My chest ached at the thought.

He deserved so much better.

# CHAPTER 4

*"Death is not the only end.*
*Ascend from ruin and rejoice in being made anew.*
*One must both choose and be chosen.*
*For hidden in flesh and accessed through spirit,*
*a pure soul may find its light at last."*
- The Old Book

I awoke from my dreamless sleep to panicked screams seeping in from outside. The sound reverberated through my body. I shot upright, air bursting from my lungs, leaving me gasping. Turning my attention to the bedchamber window, I noticed flickering lights below.

The distant roar of chaos sent ice down my spine. I knew that sound. I had lived that sound before. A memory surfaced unbidden—screams, fire, bodies dragged into the night. I was right back where I had been ten years ago.

The Culling had begun.

"Kaven!" I shook him fiercely. "Kaven!"

He jolted awake and looked at me in a confused daze, which quickly turned into a fear-twisted rage. We heard pounding on a door a level below and the sound of a latch breaking. Our heads immediately spun in opposite directions.

Jumping out of bed, I threw on an overcoat and rushed out of the room.

Out in the hall, Alona's door hung ajar. When I opened it further, I found the inside of the room cold and empty. Kaven's voice barely registered in my mind as he yelled after me to wait for him. I ran instead.

With my mind racing, I sprinted across the landing. My hand latched onto the banister, slick with a cold sweat, as I slid down. I half-leapt, half-fell down the stairs, the slap of my bare feet echoing on each step. Once I reached the bottom of the stairwell, I searched for Alona in the main rooms, but I couldn't find her.

A hand gripped my wrist hard from behind, and I whipped around to meet the eyes of Grandmother Alma. They were full of tears.

Her words splintered as she spoke, "Don't let them steal my grandchild."

My gut clenched.

"I won't. I promise."

I was resolute in my word.

Kaven soon appeared, panting and looking disheveled, with the top laces of his tunic undone. I hurried out the door. He could catch up.

The outside world was pitch black. The only light came from frantic torches roaming the village like specks in the distance. I heard the shrieking screams of women and children echoing alongside the guttural yells of men. Families were dragged from their homes and separated. Those who fought back were beaten bloody.

The Veiled Ones had come once again in the night, looking the same as they did ten years ago. They were shrouded in black, a plague come to claim us once more. My fists clenched as Veiled Ones—or Veilers—swarmed the town like flies.

I stood in the center of the cobblestone street and watched the scene unfold in disbelief. I begged my body to move, but it refused. My feet stayed rooted in place as my mind raced, each thought fighting for dominance.

A firm hand seized my shoulders with bruising force, and then my side was jerked into an unfamiliar chest—a Veiler. He smiled, his crooked teeth sharp and protruding. The smell of his breath made me gag.

"Caught you," he snickered.

Instinctively, I slammed my elbow back into his face. He let go of my shoulders to cover his bloody lips and curse me. His words dripped with menace.

"I'm going to gut you!"

He spat blood from his mouth onto the Ground and unsheathed a knife from his side. I stared at the blade and froze. I wasn't a skilled fighter, and fights had one outcome when only one person was armed. A second before he reached me, the Veiler suddenly fell forward with a grunt. I met Kaven's determined eyes as he stood in the Veiler's place, frying pan in hand.

"We need to find Alona," I choked, swallowing back the bile threatening to rise. Kaven only nodded. His steely demeanor almost fooled me, but his trembling hands betrayed just how terrified he was. We both were.

I thought of Willam, what had happened to our family, and that was all it took for my bitterness and hatred of Veilers to consume me. The adrenaline resurfaced, fiercer and more profound.

I plucked the knife from the motionless Veiler's hand. Staring at his still body, I hoped he stayed down. Veilers were stronger and more ruthless than the average mercenary. The fewer we had to face, the better. I signaled for Kaven to go one direction, and I went the other.

I darted, scouring every dark corner and listening to every heart-wrenching cry. As the minutes went by, I grew more and more desperate. When I finally spotted her, my feet stumbled. Alona was fighting against a Veiler's hold as he lugged her down the road. She kicked and screamed, but it was to no avail.

I used every bit of stealth learned from my years of hunting to follow and remain undetected. I watched with quiet pride as Alona bit the Veiler's arm—hard. He grunted and wrestled to regain control of her.

It was exactly the distraction I needed. I crept up behind the Veiler, focusing on silencing my heavy breathing—and I struck.

I placed the tip of the knife against his neck. Hard enough for him to feel the pressure of my threat, but not enough to draw blood. My lungs stuttered and my pulse rioted, but I held the knife firm.

"You're quiet, aren't you?" he grumbled.

I was about to command him to let Alona go, but then he moved. With lightning-quick speed, he grabbed the sharp blade with his free hand and pried it away. Blood streamed down his arm, but he didn't flinch. He endured the pain as if it were nothing.

Even after prying it from his neck, his fingers remained clamped around the blade. I dropped my hold on the knife and staggered back. The Veiler scoffed and let it fall. The clatter of steel hitting cobblestone made me wince.

Slowly, he turned toward me.

"The moment you see blood, you cower. I'm not surprised."

He sounded almost disappointed.

"I'm not afraid of you." My words were far too soft to be believable.

"But aren't you? Aren't you afraid of the power I currently wield over your friend's life?" He squeezed Alona's throat harder, and I saw her eyes widen and her mouth fall open.

"No! Please don't hurt her! She's just a child!"

The Veiler loosened the headlock, and I heard Alona wheeze as oxygen made its way back into her lungs. But he didn't look at her—he kept his gaze locked on me.

"Mavis!" someone bellowed in the distance.

Out of the corner of my eye, I registered the figure sprinting toward us at full speed. It was Kaven. His presence drew the attention of the Veiler, and I muttered a curse. I wanted to yell at him in protest, to tell him not to put himself in danger. But I knew he would never listen. He was far too stubborn.

Willam's face flared in my mind for a second—and I knew I couldn't let that happen again. Kaven had already lost too much. I wouldn't allow him to lose more—not when I could prevent it.

Perhaps I was a reckless fool, but I didn't care.

"Take me instead!" I shouted.

The Veiler's eyes flicked from Kaven to mine, and surprise flashed there.

The Veiler loosened his grip just enough, allowing Alona to squirm free. Once she was out of his arms, I pulled her into mine. She was frantic and sobbing, and when Kaven arrived moments later, she dashed over to him. He wordlessly enveloped his sister in an emotional embrace that made my throat burn.

I had kept my promise. Alona was safe, and Kaven would not lose a sibling.

Strong arms surrounded me, but the scent of spearmint never came.

"MAVIS! NO!" Kaven bellowed.

I pushed at the Veiler's chest, attempting to pivot and break free. But he was too powerful.

There was no escaping this time.

# CHAPTER 5

*"The mother watches and waits for her children to learn.*
*Rarely does she interfere."*
*- The Old Book*

The Veiler clamped my hips tightly and stepped closer.

Far too close for comfort.

His hair fell to his chin in dark waves that stuck to his face, damp with what was probably a combination of sweat and blood. I wanted to retch at the thought.

I saw him roam the features of my face, then start below. Without thinking, I slapped him, shocking both him and myself.

Of course, my courage would pick now to appear.

He yanked my hair, forcing my head back. His brown eyes threatened to swallow me whole, but I met them head-on. It was a challenge that I accepted. I refused to cower.

"How old are you?"

His voice was thick and edged like a knife.

"Twenty."

"It is not righteous to lie."

"Yet it's righteous to steal us from our homes in the night?"

"Watch that tongue carefully, Miss. You are not required to keep it."

"Zealot," I spat out.

"There you go again."

His grip on my hair tightened, nearly ripping out the roots.

Through gritted teeth, I continued.

"You are nothing but a pawn who murders innocents at the whim of those who control you."

Fury lit in his eyes. Good, I'd struck a nerve.

"No one controls me, Miss. You'd be wise to remember that," he growled.

He was a fool if he truly believed that. Veilers were puppets. They executed the will of the king, whatever it may be, on the grounds of protecting the faith of the realm. I lived in a kingdom that didn't care about causing bloodshed, as long as it maintained control.

The Veiler suddenly released me from his grip, staring at me as if he were looking for something. I should have run, self-sacrifice be damned, but I didn't. My body felt glued in place. He squinted, almost confused. Then, his eyes widened just as I noted the outline of a faint scar through his short beard, cutting across his upper lip.

"What's your name?"

I rolled my shoulders back. "My name is Mavis Ashbone, sister of Willam Ashbone," I declared.

"Should I know who that is?" he asked, bored.

"Yes. He was taken in the last Culling of Oak Hollow. It is in his name that I seek justice for my family."

He smirked. "I don't know if you'll succeed, but I'll enjoy watching you try."

A sudden scratch of coarse fiber grazed my skin. My gaze flicked down—but I was too late. The Veiler had already looped the rope once, twice, his movements quick and practiced. The strands bit into my wrists.

I jerked back, but his body pinned me in place. Each pull tightened the cord until my fingers tingled. The knot was cinched with a last tug, and the tail-end coiled in his hand like a leash.

"There now, no running away."

Nearing footsteps sounded, and in the corner of my eye, a woman with hair the color of flame approached. She wore what all Veilers did: a black tunic, pants, and mask with narrow slits for the eyes. Her ginger hair hung in one messy braid that fell over her left shoulder. Even in the dim torchlight, her eyes were an unmistakable spring green.

She shook her head as she glanced over my body, not once, but twice. I shifted uncomfortably under her brazen appraisal. She put her hands on her hips and shook her head at my captor.

"You know the rules. We don't take martyrs."

"I know, but—"

"I can see why you want to keep her," the woman teased.

"Renata," my captor scolded.

They spoke as if I were some object they were debating keeping.

"What difference does it make if you take me instead?" I asked, tired of being talked around. "Is it important that your victim be unwilling?"

The woman unsheathed a medium dagger strapped at her thigh and pressed the tip to my chest.

"So quick to speak when you have not been spoken to." She trailed the blade up to my jaw like a dangerous caress. "Not that I, or anyone I ride with, owes you an explanation for our actions. The work we do is of royal and divine merit." She paused briefly, as if weighing her next words carefully. "We pray to Our Lady of the Stars. She shows us who is *chosen*."

"Lies," I hissed.

"Careful," warned my captor.

"You are all murderers who hide behind masks because you're too cowardly to face the truth!"

The woman leaned in closer.

"And what is the *truth*?" She asked with a glint in her eyes.

I met her gaze unflinchingly.

"The prophecy you believe in—the one you burn, pillage, and slaughter for—doesn't exist. It's all a delusion, and you follow it blindly."

"Hmm," she hummed. "You think you know the scripture better than I do?"

I scoffed, "I know I do."

She tilted her head to the side and assessed me once more with a renewed sense of interest. Stepping back, she drew her blade. Then, she snatched my hand and examined the palm. When I tried to rip my hand away, she slashed it open.

I cried out in pain as blood quickly pooled. My knees buckled and threatened to give out. All I could do was clench my fist tight and try to keep the wound as sealed as possible while watching crimson seep between my fingers.

My captor stiffened. "Was that necessary?"

"Look at the Ground," she demanded.

I ignored the pain radiating through my arm and joined their gaze downward. It was dark, and I could barely see the shadowy stone. I blinked, nearly stumbling when I finally saw it. I stared for several moments before accepting it wasn't a hallucination.

The blood that dripped from my hand was being absorbed into the Ground. Not just being absorbed, but disappearing without a trace. It wasn't possible, yet I couldn't deny the sight of it.

"She is blessed," whispered my captor in astonishment.

"Take her," said the woman.

"Mavis!" Kaven yelled from off to the side, bringing me back to reality.

I had forgotten he was there; he had been so silent. The relief I expected to come from hearing his voice never did.

Kaven started toward my captor, frying pan in hand. The woman, Renata, stepped between them and swiftly bludgeoned Kaven with the hilt of her dagger. There was a loud thud as his body hit the Ground. I covered my mouth with my non-bloody hand and screamed.

"He'll live. He just might not like it when he wakes." She grinned, sheathing her dagger, and sauntered off.

"Alona!" I cried. She was crouched down next to her brother, holding his bleeding head in her lap.

My captor leaned in close to my ear and whispered, "Come with us, and no harm will befall the girl. That is a promise."

"I don't think you can keep promises," I sniffled, my composure breaking.

"Then you will just have to see, won't you?"

"I don't have a choice."

"No, you do not," his words resolute, echoing what I already knew.

I looked at Alona, at her small frame hovering protectively over her brother, and my throat tightened. I had so much to say and such little time to say it.

"Alona, listen carefully." She looked up at me tentatively. "Tell Kaven when he wakes to take care of my mother while I'm gone. Don't let him come after me. I will return."

Alona nodded, tears streaming down her face. I opened my mouth to say more, but then I felt the sudden jerk of the rope.

"Time to go." My captor tugged the rope away, pulling me from Kaven and Alona. I followed his lead without a fight, looking back only once to take one last glance at them. They were as much my family as my flesh and blood were, and now I was losing them, too.

I told myself that it wouldn't be the last time I saw their faces. It couldn't be.

I would fight with everything in me to get back.

I decided in that moment that there was a benefit to my new situation—a purpose. I would finally learn what happened to Willam. And maybe, if the gods were merciful, I could bring him home with me.

The Veiler hauled me through the streets. I had no choice but to obey—for now.

When we reached the village square, I saw families grouped and lined up in rows. Mothers clung to their children, and fathers clutched their wives. I counted fifteen Veilers in the square. Some held swords, while others merely stalked around looking bored.

"Do not fight us, and you will not die. We do not wish to see more bloodshed," boomed a hauntingly graveled voice addressing the people.

I searched for the source of that voice. When I found it, I stiffened. The speaker was Crooked Teeth, the same Veiler that Kaven had knocked unconscious. I was shocked to see him alive—he had taken quite a blow to the head. And from the way he scowled at me, I could tell he remembered who I was.

The Veiler who led me here suddenly shoved me to the Ground, earning a collective gasp from the villagers that watched helplessly. My knees stung with the contact against hard stone, and I winced. That would bruise.

"Our Lady demands two more to accompany us," Crooked Teeth continued. The bastard couldn't keep the glee from his voice.

"What?" Panic overcame me. "No, you have me! Please, I beg of you, just take me." I flipped my head up to my captor in a move of desperation.

"*It is always in three that nature likes to be*," he said, quoting *The Old Book*. "As much as you might like to believe that we make our own rules, we do not. We follow the words written in the sacred text."

"You mean you choose which words you follow. I distinctly remember reading that all of Our Lady's children contain a part of her, and so a crime committed against one of her children is a crime against her."

Unsurprisingly, the Veiler did not answer. Instead, he kept his eyes narrowed on the crowd before us.

"Those between the ages of thirteen and twenty, step forward!" ordered Crooked Teeth. "Keep in mind that if you attempt to trick us, it may very well be the last thing you do."

Slowly, people stepped forward. My stomach fell, and the feeling of bile rising inside returned. All I could do to keep it at bay was remind myself that Alona wasn't there. The Veiler had promised. While normally I would never value the word of a Veiler, I needed to believe that this was different. I needed to believe he meant what he said, and that Alona was safe; otherwise, I might break entirely.

I watched as the redheaded woman from before, Renata, walked intently by those who had stepped forward. She looked them over, searching. I wondered what she was looking for. Was she going to cut them like she had cut me?

Renata stopped in front of a young girl about Alona's age and then nodded to another Veiler. The Veiler then pulled her from the line. A woman sobbed, and a man cursed.

The girl stepped into the torchlight, and I recognized her as the baker's daughter, Serene. She was fourteen and one of the sweetest people in Oak Hollow. She delivered bread every Saturday and was one of the few people that my mother opened the door for. I mourned for her family already.

The second person Renata stopped in front of was Oliver. Oliver was sixteen and the son of the blacksmith, Duris, though he was drastically different from his father. He was a slender kid with a quiet and aloof demeanor. I saw him wield a sword only once—he dropped it on his foot and lost a toe. Oliver was often seen in the library with his nose in a book. That's where he seemed most himself.

When Oliver was pulled forward, Duris drew his sword. A Veiler quickly placed a dagger over Oliver's heart and spoke.

"Don't be a fool and stand in the way of fate. It would be a pity to end his life before it's really begun, wouldn't it?" threatened the Veiler, causing Duris to step back and drop his sword. "Wise choice."

Serene and Oliver's wrists were bound with rope like mine, and led over to where I still knelt on the Ground. Renata glanced at the Veilers that held us and communicated silently with a simple nod. I was yanked to my feet, and my knees throbbed as I wobbled to find my balance. Renata then turned to address the villagers.

"It is in Aeta's name that we execute Her will. These three have been divinely chosen to present their worth to Our Lady of the Stars. If they are found worthy, they will return to you. It is a great honor to be chosen by Our Lady. Regarding your few dead, bury them honorably as Anam demands it." Renata exited the square, and I was shoved in the same direction.

Serene, Oliver, and I were led out of Oak Hollow and into the thick brush of the surrounding forest. The rocks and twigs scraped the pads of my bare feet. Pain mixed with apprehension of what was to come was all that I felt.

The short hike ended when we approached a herd of twenty horses guarded by five Veilers. There were eight people mounted on the horses, but they didn't look like Veilers. They weren't dressed in black and wore no masks. Some even looked to be as young as Alona.

The understanding hit me then.

They were the others who had been taken in the Culling of their villages. They looked at us apathetically, exhaustion coating their expressions.

That was what we were to become.

The Veiler that held my rope tugged me toward a black horse. I could barely see the creature because it blended in so well with the night, much like the Veilers themselves. He reached into the satchel that was strapped to the back of the saddle and pulled out a small bottle and some gauze. The Veiler poured the clear liquid from the bottle, which smelled to be alcohol, over the wound he had gotten from grabbing my blade. He threw his head back and gritted his teeth. Then, he wrapped his hand in the gauze.

"Show me your cut hand," he commanded. When I didn't immediately give him my hand, he sighed. "Infection sets in quickly and kills even faster. Is that what you want?" he challenged. I reluctantly shook my head and offered him my cut palm. "It will hurt. But it's better than losing an arm."

He quickly poured the alcohol onto my cut before I could change my mind. I kept my eyes shut as tears welled up. The pain was searing, and I yelped as my knees gave out and I fell to the Ground.

"Stand. I need to wrap it."

I slowly stood and allowed him to wrap my hand so tightly that my fingers tingled. The Veiler put the materials back in the satchel and fastened its leather straps. He then lifted me onto the front portion of the horse's saddle, mounting behind me soon afterward. The sounds of whimpers and shuffling hooves filled the air.

A lone raven cawed, flying overhead, its ever-watchful eyes observing us from above. I was taught that ravens were the scouts of death.

Wherever they flocked, death followed.

The Veiler reached for the horse's reins, and we took off into the night.

# CHAPTER 6

*"I pledge my life until death or decree,*
*to serve the Kingdom of Ravaryn and the Ethorian gods in equal measure.*
*I recognize* The Old Book *as the one true holy script, and the Ravaryn Crown as its*
*enforcer.*
*In body and soul, so I swear it."*
*- The Order of the Veil's Oath of Servitude*

M y body was stiff and ached after so many hours in the saddle.

My bound hands were tied to the Veiler's saddle. His hands were on the reins, and my back was pressed against his front as we rode. It was my first time on horseback, and I prayed I wouldn't get trampled.

It was midday, and we had stopped only once to drink and eat stale bread with squirrel stew. It was enough to curb the hunger and thirst amassed from riding for hours. However, my body still craved more. Exhaustion was beating at my door, but the pain and discomfort I felt kept me awake.

My bare and blood-crusted feet dangled from the sides of the horse. My toes were numb, the pads of my feet twinging. I deeply regretted the decision I had made to forgo footwear.

My choice of clothing was also questionable.

My nightgown was sullied and ripped, exposing my bruised knees. The temperature was near freezing, and I visibly shook. The only fabric keeping me from falling victim to the elements was my lined overcoat.

"Stop!" my captor shouted.

The horse jerked to a halt, and I barely caught myself before pitching forward.

The cold air hit, making my limbs feel even heavier. Before I could take a full breath, my captor was dismounting.

He walked over to another horse carrying several satchels. Then he dug around and pulled out a pair of boots and two articles of clothing. When he walked back to our horse, he lifted me up and onto the Ground without warning.

"Here," he said, handing me the clothes. "Change. Before you freeze to death."

"I can't. My hands—"

Steel flashed. He cut the rope, holding the last fiber between his fingers. His eyes narrowed.

"Don't run."

"I won't."

The rope fell, and I unwrapped the bundle: a boy's tunic, black trousers, boots. Worn, but intact.

"Where did you get these?"

"Not everyone survives the road."

The breath caught in my throat. "You stripped a corpse."

I shoved the items back into the Veiler's arms, looking at my hands as if they were plagued with the smell and feel of death. I brushed my hands on my nightgown, trying to rid myself of that stench.

"He wasn't using them." He then shrugged as if it were nothing. "It's only going to get colder where we're going."

"Where are we going?"

"Just put the clothes on."

I grabbed the clothes from the Veiler's hands, letting my fingers rub the thick fabric. Disgust curdled in my stomach, but the cold bit harder.

"Turn around," I snapped.

"No chance. You'd bolt."

"I said I won't run."

"And I said I don't trust you." His smirk was icy, and it made my skin crawl.

I huffed because he was right. If I wanted information on Willam, I needed to survive long enough to find it.

I turned my back, stripping fast, one arm shielding my chest as I snatched the tunic from his lazy hand. His silence pressed on me heavier than his eyes.

The clothes fit well enough. The boots blessedly so.

It's one thing to wear slightly baggy or tight clothing, and quite another to trudge around in uncomfortable, ill-fitting footwear. That could cause blisters, and blisters pop and become infected.

"Are you done?" he asked impatiently. "I want to reach the prairie by evening."

"When will we stop to rest?"

"This was our break."

When I straightened, the Veiler was already holding another piece of rope.

"Is that really necessary?"

"You had five minutes unbound, be thankful." He caught my wrists before I could argue, tying them quickly, almost carelessly.

Then he lifted me back onto the horse.

"You seem sure of yourself, Veiler," I remarked, curling my lip.

He glanced up, his lip momentarily twitching upward before straightening again.

"Rowan."

"What?" I raised a brow at him.

"My name is Rowan," he stated, mounting behind me.

Why did he tell me willingly? If I ever made it home, knowing his name could endanger him. No one pitied the death of a Veiler, masked or not.

Names were weapons. Why hand me his?

I hated Veilers with a burning passion, and perhaps this Veiler even more so because of the harm he had caused Alona. However, I acknowledged that my traitorous body wasn't as repulsed by him as my conscience demanded.

He smelled of sandalwood and leather, and I had to shake my head to rid myself of the intrusive thoughts. I didn't need to learn all the little details about him. I didn't want to know.

He was a Veiler. Plain and simple.

Even if he wasn't personally responsible, he was the very representation of the people who took Willam and countless others. He was a murderer.

I had to remember that.

"Why would you tell me your name? Isn't your identity one of your most treasured secrets?"

The horse began moving again, and I fell forward in my seat. I promptly sat up and rolled my shoulders back. He chuckled.

"It's just a name."

"I suppose you believe that my death is inevitable, and hence knowing your name won't put you in any danger."

I felt him shrug again.

"Well, *Rowan*, unfortunately for you, I plan on surviving."

I would survive. I had to.

Silence lingered between us, broken only by the steady clop of hooves. Then, almost too softly to hear, Rowan muttered, "That will go away."

"What will?" I asked, my attention drawn back to him.

"Hope."

# CHAPTER 7

*"Hatred is a barren desert.*
*There is nothing for you there."*
*- The Old Book*

I must have dozed through the afternoon, because the grumbling of my stomach woke me to the setting sun.

My eyes opened enough to note the wisps of darkness in the Sky. My cheek was warm and my body relaxed as I breathed in the air's woody aroma. I closed my eyes once more and listened to the soothing, steady beat of the wind—until I realized that the wind shouldn't beat.

My eyes flared open, and I found that my head was resting on Rowan's chest behind me. I frantically sat up, almost falling off the horse. I would have fallen, too, if Rowan hadn't wrapped his arm around me and corrected my balance.

"Get your hand off of me!" I panicked, and he let go.

"I think the phrase you are looking for is 'thank you for saving me.'"

"Saving me?! You abducted me!"

"I recall a certain willingness on your part. Something about sacrificing yourself for that girl. What was her name again? Alona?"

"Don't speak of her," I bit out.

"No? What about the man who so *heroically* tried to save you? Was that your lover? He definitely looked at you like he'd seen you na—"

"Don't be crass. And don't speak of him either," I interjected. The jabs at me were one thing, but attacking those I loved was another.

"But he didn't save you, did he? No, he just stood there as you offered yourself up to the wolves."

"He tried to step in," I bristled. His accusations, coupled with my growing hunger, were eroding my remaining sense of reason.

"No, he watched and let you be taken. He stepped in at the last moment to preserve whatever shred of dignity he believed he had. Lies are easy to believe. The truth is brutal. I'm sorry to be the one to tell you this, but if he had wanted to free you, he could have."

That was the last straw. I elbowed his chest sharply. A sliver of pride filled me when I heard him release a low grunt. That pride was gone in an instant.

A deep chuckle vibrated against my back, and I froze.

That was worse than silence.

I clenched my fists and let myself feel the bite of my nails in my palms.

"You're psychotic," I muttered under my breath, but loud enough for him to hear.

We had reached the prairie, with faint light still left in the Sky.

I looked out over the grasslands, at the red and orange hues of the changing pastures. There was nothing but tall grass and withering wildflowers for as far as the eye could see. It was beautiful but completely different from the wooded area surrounding Oak Hollow that I'd grown up in my entire life.

When I was a child, I dreamed about exploring the continent and seeing all of Ethoria. My wanderlust had dimmed as I grew older and became more aware of my responsibilities. Kaven was right when he told me I was trapped in Oak Hollow. I didn't want to believe him. But it's true. I had become complacent, content to be stuck in a stalemate forever.

I had never been this far from home, and yet I felt no awe—only a dull ache in my chest. The longing for the smell of freshly cut oak stung my throat.

The horses stopped moving, and Veilers began dismounting alongside the culled. Rowan descended and turned to me. I prepared myself to be lifted, but he didn't touch me.

"As much as I would love to continue our back-and-forth repartee, I'm afraid it ends here for the night."

"Why? Are you afraid the others will question if you can handle me?"

"No, rather why I haven't. The others would expect me to punish you for speaking out of turn and in disrespect of a man of my stature."

I almost laughed. "A man of your stature?"

"Yes." He nodded affirmatively.

"What are you, their leader?"

"I am their commanding officer. Which means you've been bickering with the one person who might actually keep Balor from splitting you open like you did his lip." His eyes locked with mine, and I gulped at the threat. "Balor was not pleased with the little attack from you and your lover boy. He believes that women who talk over men—let alone fight—should be punished. He's old-fashioned like that."

"Are you old-fashioned like that?"

My gut clenched.

"Gods, no," he huffed.

I didn't know how to respond to that. So I didn't.

"I will lift you off the horse once you agree to temper yourself for the night. Do you agree?"

"He said he would *gut* me. I will silence my tongue if you agree to protect me from him."

"I will protect you from Balor. I swear it."

I nodded in agreement. Trusting a Veiler was dangerous and had the potential of getting me killed—but I didn't have a choice.

Rowan lifted me from the horse and planted me firmly on the Ground. He untied the rope knot on the saddle and lightly pulled me toward where the others were setting up camp. Dropping the end of the rope, he gestured for me to sit on a large rock.

Looking around at the culled, I noticed that none of them were bound. Even Serene and Oliver were no longer tied.

"I see that no one else is bound."

"They never threatened a Veiled One, and you have... on multiple occasions." I scoffed.

"That's ridiculous. You're idiotic if you think I could take you down."

"*No one* would ever think that. You couldn't even cut my throat when given the opportunity to do so."

"Then why are my wrists still bound if I'm not a threat?"

"I never said you weren't a threat. A fingernail scratch can still hurt," he taunted with a slight curve to his lips.

I wanted to scratch his eyes out—to show him a true fingernail scratch—but I could barely even see his eyes through the narrow slits of the mask that he *still* wore.

"Do you always wear that mask? It seems like it would be uncomfortable for long periods of time."

Maybe if I made light conversation, he would stop seeing me as a threat and cut me loose. The binding was chafing.

The heat of the fire that the Veilers had built hit me, and I inched further forward on the rock to be closer to it.

"No. Sometimes I sleep."

Rowan looked at me with a curious glance, as if I were the peculiar one. Another Veiler walked up to him and whispered something in his ear. Rowan's playful expression dropped. "I'll be back."

"Wait, what about Balor?" I asked nervously. "You said you would protect me from him!"

Anxiety blanketed me. I was an easy target out here, especially without full mobility.

"Balor won't dare try anything. Not if he values his life." His words lent me some relief, but not nearly enough. Rowan and the other Veiler roamed out of sight.

I sat on the rock and looked around at the camp. There were seven large tents pitched around the campsite. I counted twenty Veilers and eleven culled, including myself. Most of the culled sat around the fire in silence. Their eyes were lifeless. Rowan had warned me that my hope would go away, but theirs—it was long gone.

My wrists were still bound, but the tail-end that Rowan usually carried or tied to the saddle was lying in the grass. All the Veilers seemed to be busy either setting up the campsite or engaged in other tasks. I saw Oliver and another boy of his age sitting next to each other, quietly staring into the fire. I stood and moved toward them.

I crouched beside the fire, feeling its warmth brush against my skin. The flickering light cast deep shadows over Oliver's face, making the exhaustion in his eyes seem even heavier. He looked hollowed out, like a shell of the boy I had seen back home—always with his nose buried in a book, always somewhere else in his mind.

"Oliver?" I kept my voice low, careful not to draw attention.

He blinked, slow and unsteady, before finally turning toward me. It took him a moment to register who I was. When he did, something in his expression cracked.

"Mavis?" His voice was barely above a whisper.

I nodded and offered a small, reassuring smile. "Yeah, it's me."

His lip trembled. I could see the struggle behind his eyes—desperation warring with fear, trying to decide if he could be hopeful. I reached up, brushing away the single tear that rolled down his cheek with my knuckles.

"Don't let them see you break," I murmured. "I don't know what they want from us, but I know that we have to be strong if we want to survive it."

Oliver sniffed and wiped his face. It wasn't much, but I saw the faintest flicker of fight return to him.

Beside him, another boy shifted uncomfortably. His tawny skin looked paler than it should have, like the blood had drained from his face long before I sat down.

I placed a hand gently on his shoulder, feeling him startle under my touch. "What's your name?"

His throat bobbed as he swallowed. "Isaac," he rasped. "I'm from Dewwich."

Dewwich was about two weeks' travel from Oak Hollow. My father used to do trade in Dewwich all the time because of its proximity to the Corrish Sea and the capital.

Before I could say anything, Oliver stiffened beside me. His eyes widened in silent panic as he looked past my shoulder. Isaac followed suit, the color leaching from his already pale face. I stood and slowly turned, finding myself face-to-face with the woman of flame herself.

Her ginger hair was loose now, cascading over her shoulders in soft waves that fell to her hips. But there was nothing soft in the way she looked at me. Beneath her mask, her green eyes burned with something I couldn't quite place—*contempt? Intrigue? Disgust?*

Probably all three.

"Forming a coup, are we?" Her voice was smooth, but there was a dangerous undertone that caused goosebumps to form.

"Of course not. He's from my village."

"I don't care." She stepped forward, closing the already too-small space between us.

I resisted the urge to take a step back. She was close enough now that I could see the freckles dusting the bridge of her nose and the faint scar along her jaw. Close enough that if she wanted, she could grab me by the throat before I even had time to flinch.

"Let's clear some things up," she continued, "because you seem to be *confused* about your place here." She tilted her head, eyes flicking over me, sizing me up like a predator would its prey. "You may be *chosen*, but your being here was not *my* choice. If it were up to me, you'd still be rotting back in that little primitive village. Rowan may think that your behavior is entertaining, cute..." She let the words settle, and I felt my stomach tighten at her tone. "But I find it to be concerning. You are a risk to everything that we are doing."

I swallowed back down the acid creeping up my throat.

I lifted my chin. "I *am* a risk," I warned. "And yet, here I am."

Her eyes narrowed.

"There are some things," she murmured, "not even I get a choice in."

Before I could push further, the sound of someone clearing their throat caught both of our attention.

We turned to find Rowan standing with his hands in his pockets, deceptively relaxed. His face was expressionless, but then he flicked his gaze toward Renata. Something unspoken passed between them. A silent conversation that I wasn't privy to, but one that made Renata's posture stiffen.

She exhaled sharply and stepped back, brushing past me as she walked away.

"Making friends with everyone I see," Rowan teased, and his jaw flexed. I felt the unease in his tone slither against my skin.

"That wasn't my fault."

"I thought you promised to be silent for the night," he scolded.

I sneered. "I bit my tongue well enough. Trust me."

Rowan let out a hard sigh and pulled a knife from his pocket. My stomach twisted at the sight of it, and my pulse skipped.

The knife flashed.

This was it.

My throat seized. I closed my eyes and braced for the blade—but it never came.

Instead, the pressure at my wrists gave way, and the rope slumped into the dirt. I stared at my red, raw skin, and for a moment, I almost sobbed at the ache of freedom.

"Don't make me regret that," he cautioned.

"Thank you," I whispered in astonishment.

Rowan gasped. "She has manners!"

"I am polite to those who deserve kindness. Veilers are not on that list."

"Yet, you thanked me?"

"Don't mistake my words as kind, *Veiler*. This banter we have going on—it's not cordial. The hatred I have for you runs so deep that you could save my life tenfold, and I would still happily stake a blade into your heart. You're nothing but a monster to me, and you always will be," I vowed.

He needed to hear my words and let them sink in. I hoped it hurt, although I doubt it did. He was a Veiler, and Veilers were known for their apathy and ruthlessness.

"Then why didn't you?" His expression was blank, and his tone flat.

"Didn't what?"

"Stake a blade into my heart. You had a chance. I gave it to you."

I furrowed my brow. "That was a moment of weakness, and you *gave* me nothing of the sort."

"It takes only one moment to strike."

I opened my mouth to retort, but my stomach spoke for me. An earsplitting gurgle issued from it, then emptiness pierced me. I folded over and clutched my stomach. My cheeks burned with embarrassment, and I refused to look at Rowan.

"Hungry?"

"Obviously." I rolled my eyes.

"Stay here."

He was gone for less than a minute, and when he returned, he was holding two bowls.

"Here," he said, handing me a bowl. I looked inside and moved the spoon around. There was broth, chunks of carrots and cabbage, and some sort of meat.

"More stew, how wonderful," I said, my tone dripping with sarcasm. "What's the protein this time?"

"Rat."

"I beg your pardon?"

"Rat stew. The vegetables depend on whether local villages will trade, and the protein depends on hunting availability."

"I'm not going to eat this."

"That's fine. You can starve." His words were final and devoid of any emotion. He moved to grab the bowl from my hands, and I pulled away from him. "Seems tastier now, doesn't it?" he remarked smugly.

When I didn't reply to his comment, he continued.

"You're welcome, you know, for feeding you. Some captors aren't as generous."

"So you acknowledge that you're my captor?"

"I never said I wasn't. I just insinuated that you weren't entirely opposed to being taken. Which is true."

"I didn't wish to leave my life behind. I had little choice in the matter, given the situation."

I sipped the broth and savored its gamy taste. It was better than nothing, and anything to sate my stomach was welcome right now.

I moved to sit on the same large rock as before, and Rowan sat on another beside it. We ate in silence. My mind wandered to other things while I struggled to chew the tough meat.

"What happened to the boy whose clothes I wear?" I asked hesitantly.

"He caught a fever a few weeks back and went quickly. He didn't suffer."

"Good."

"The road is not for the weak. In fact, I suspect more will fall by the time we reach our destination." He shoveled a spoonful of the stew into his mouth.

"Where are we going? I know it's not the capital; that's in the southwest." I had been paying at least some attention to the direction we traveled.

"Somewhere you will need all your energy. Now eat."

I finished my stew and set my bowl aside. The Sky was dark now, and my eyelids were heavy with sleep. I yawned and rubbed my eyes. Rowan put his bowl down as well and stood. He gestured for me to stand as well, and I tentatively did as he requested.

I followed him to the outside of one of the larger tents. He untied the entrance, and I peered inside, glancing at a few of the culled huddled underneath blankets.

"This is your tent. Sleep. You will need it."

I stepped inside, too tired to criticize my accommodations. I picked up a wool blanket instead. It was slightly scratchy, but I knew it would keep me from freezing in the night. Just the thought of sleep had me nodding off while standing. I plopped onto the Ground and curled up into a corner, letting my eyes drift shut.

"Mavis," Rowan spoke quietly, and I squinted at him. "There will be a guard outside this tent all night. Don't try anything."

With that, he fastened the entrance shut and left.

I didn't have it in me to respond, so I let sleep take me instead.

# CHAPTER 8

*"All of Aeta's children dwell within Ethoria,*
*and each guards it in their own design."*
- The Old Book

I woke up half-expecting everything to have been a terrible dream. But when my eyes opened, the nightmare didn't end. It was only made worse when a Veiler threw a bucket of water onto Isaac because he didn't wake up on command. It soaked him and splashed onto several of the other culled, including me.

It was freezing. Even the few drops that hit me made me shiver. However, it was Isaac I was worried about. With the dropping temperatures outside, he could easily get hypothermia if not allowed to dry off.

"Everybody out! Of course, that's if you want to eat today," the Veiler sneered.

All eleven of us shuffled out of the tent, trying not to topple one another. I grabbed one of the wool blankets while exiting, hiding it between our moving bodies. Once out of the tent, I found Isaac and pulled him aside. He was drenched from the waist up, and his teeth visibly chattered.

"Take your shirt off," I ordered. He looked at me with a stunned expression, his shivering mouth agape. "Now. Or would you rather catch a cold? Which, I'll have you know, is a death sentence out here."

Isaac stopped glaring at me and closed his mouth. He peeled his tunic off without a word and trembled. He tried to warm himself by rubbing his hands along his chest and arms.

"Wring it out and let it air dry for as long as possible." I wrapped the blanket around him. A tremor surged through him, and he gripped it tighter.

"T-thank you," he stuttered.

"Just stay alive."

He nodded frantically.

When I turned to walk away, I caught sight of Rowan staring me down from across the camp. He was standing with his arms crossed and an indiscernible expression on his face. It was probably the fact that he was a Veiler, but he had an aptitude for lurking about. Rowan was never far, and I found it both comforting and a nuisance.

I could tell he had criticisms he wanted to spew by the way his eyes narrowed through the slits of his mask, but I wasn't interested in arguing with him today. I shook my head and steered clear of him, walking in the opposite direction. My plan was foiled when he dropped his arms and came toward me. Rowan was quick. He caught up with me in just a few strides.

"Don't become attached," he said sternly.

"That's rich coming from you," I scoffed.

He was the one who was attached. Rowan was almost always in the corner of my eye, prowling about like the predator he was. He wanted me to know that he was watching me, too—otherwise, I wouldn't have seen him at all.

"Oh, I'm not attached," he bit out defensively.

"Then why do you even care?"

"I don't."

"Really? Because it seems like you do, and I just can't figure out why. Is this some kind of game to you? If so, I'm not interested in playing."

The words slipped out before I could stop them. Reckless, but I didn't care. Rowan let me take many liberties in how I spoke to him. I didn't understand, nor did I care to ask why. As I left, he grabbed my arm, keeping me from going any further.

"This is not a game. People will die. And you'll sit there knowing you can't stop it."

"Then why help me?"

"Maybe I'm tired of watching death take everyone."

"You can't mean that. You're a Veiler."

Rowan leaned in, his grip tightening. His breath was warm against my ear. And when he spoke, it was low and dizzyingly grave.

"If you think you're the only one who's lost their freedom..." He let the words sink in before adding, quieter this time, almost like a confession. "Then you are sorely mistaken."

"Let. Me. Go." I bit out my words, over-enunciating each one.

Surprisingly, he did as I requested. Rowan dropped his hand from my arm and stormed off.

I rolled my shoulders back and mentally shook off the conversation that had just transpired. It added stress I couldn't afford to bear. Then, I made my way toward the Veilers who were handing out bowls of food. My guess was stew—again.

Once I was served my portion, I looked inside. I was right—it was leftover rat stew. I poked at it until I decided that starvation was probably worse than consumption. Scooping a spoonful into my mouth, I forced my jaw to chew the tough meat.

It was even worse than before. My mouth flooded with saliva, wanting to reject its contents.

"I don't understand," a woman whispered nearby. "How are you still alive?"

The voice caught my attention, and I put my spoon down. I turned to find a group of three of the culled huddled together by the fire, observing me like I was some sort of spectacle. I didn't know who had spoken.

All three of them stood at once and advanced toward me cautiously.

"I'm sorry, what?" I looked them over. They appeared equally frightened and in awe.

It was the blonde one who spoke first.

"What's your name?"

"Mavis."

"I'm Lily. That's Aeva, and he's Brenn."

The blonde one—Lily—had wide, feverish eyes. Aeva's hair was brunette and wiry, and Brenn's shoulders looked too narrow for the weight he carried.

Lily stuck her hand out to me, and I tentatively shook it. Aeva and Brenn just dipped their heads in acknowledgment.

"Where are you from?" I asked them.

"We're from Lameer," Lily said.

Lameer was just south of Athelney, the capital of Ravaryn.

My father once told me that Athelney could be seen just as clearly at night as it was during the day. He said that it was because they had no need for candles or oil lamps, and that light could be commanded with the flick of a switch. He was always full of stories.

The three of them stared at me curiously, like they wanted to pick apart my brain. I stretched my neck and arms out, trying my best to ignore their intrusive gazes.

"What?" I asked a bit impatiently. My legs twitched under their unsettling scrutiny.

Lily responded, "How do you get away with it?"

"Get away with what?"

"You talk to them with such bravery," Brenn said, half-amazed.

"Or stupidity," quipped Aeva in a monotonous tone. Only her lips moved when she spoke.

"Why aren't you afraid of their retribution?" Lily asked.

"What more can they do to me they haven't already done? They've taken me from my home and everything I've ever known. They want to see me break, but I refuse to cower in front of monsters."

I returned to my bowl of stew and devoured it. In part because I felt the bite of acidity in my stomach from prolonged emptiness, but also because I wanted to send a message that I wasn't in the mood for conversation.

I wasn't a fool. I knew I needed allies, but I didn't need friends.

Acts such as giving Isaac a warm blanket earned me favors. Making small talk only further humanized them, which was dangerous. The more I saw the other culled as actual people with families and homes, the more sympathy I gained for them. I would never admit it aloud, but Rowan was right.

I couldn't get attached. Not to them. Not to anyone.

# CHAPTER 9

*"It is wise to question,*
*for nothing is granted freely."*
- *The Old Book*

We rode until nightfall, taking breaks only for occasional nourishment and allowing the horses to rest. Each time we stopped, I became more and more aware of just how far from home I was.

The wind blew strands of onyx hair over my eyes, casting everything in shadow. When I could see clearly, it was always the grasslands below. They stretched for hundreds of miles. It was simple, yet utterly foreign. I could see how the prairie might feel like home to some, but I was not one of them. I was used to trees, tall and reaching. The prairie was quiet, and I missed the sound of birds and rustling branches.

Even the stars looked different in the Sky. One particularly shone brighter than all the rest. I admired it reverently, wondering if maybe that was Our Lady shining down upon us.

That, maybe, I wasn't as alone as I had originally thought.

Rowan and I rode in silence, neither of us saying a word since our tense confrontation earlier.

I was grateful we didn't talk—he seldom said anything useful. He liked to answer my questions with vague comments or deflect them altogether.

Once we made camp, he vanished. His absence was grating for two reasons: I wanted it and loathed it.

Our journey had just begun, and I was already becoming annoyingly familiar with his presence. We'd spent so long pressed together that I'd grown accustomed to his warmth. Without him, I felt colder.

I despised that fact and tried my best to ignore it.

To no one's surprise, we feasted on stew for dinner. It was squirrel stew again, but this time with fewer vegetables in the stock. I preferred it to rat, so I wasn't entirely complaining. However, one would assume that a team of skilled Veilers could hunt animals other than just rodents.

Perhaps they were just better at killing people.

The Veilers said their prayers before eating, making me think about whether the gods listened to such mundane whispers.

I also wondered why the gods would allow such cruelty to be carried out in their name. They were supposed to protect the balance of life, but the scales felt rather tilted. How closely did they watch us? When would they intervene? I knew gods liked to meddle, but they also liked to sit back and watch.

The silence of the gods felt heartless. As if all we endured was torture. Judgment was supposed to come after death—life was the test.

But what kind of test was this cruel?

Maybe the gods didn't have souls like mortals did. Perhaps that was why they stood above humanity—by existing beneath it.

I sounded like a heretic. Grandmother Alma would be so disappointed.

The night air thickened, full of whispers and unease. Fires crackled low, and though I stared into the flames until my eyes stung, sleep would not come easily.

Not because I was afraid—though maybe I should have been—but because something was wrong.

I felt it in my bones.

When I finally lay back, I didn't fall asleep. Not really.

It felt more like being pulled downward into a waiting void.

# CHAPTER 10

*"Pray to the gods—they are your protectors.*
*But do not expect them to save you from your own doing."*
*- The Old Book*

"Elias, stop! My mother will be angry if you ruin another one of my gowns!"

"It's just mud, Mavis. It washes off. Don't be such a baby." Elias poked me with the stick, grinning like the pest he was.

Elias was Kaven's friend for reasons I never understood. He was a year older, red-haired, smug, and about as pleasant as ticks in summer.

"She said stop," Kaven cut in, shoving him back.

I looked down at the mud streaking my dress. It was one of my favorites that my father had gotten me during his travels. It was made from pure Athelnean silk, spun from caterpillars only found on the island of Reliss.

"You destroyed it!"

"Now it matches your face," Elias snorted.

I lunged, shoving him into the muck, and snatched the stick from his hand. I began smacking him with it as he cowered beneath me.

"Mavis, stop!" Kaven grabbed my hand and held me back from further hitting Elias. "You can't beat him with a stick—even if he deserves it."

Elias frowned at Kaven and opened his mouth to speak.

"Watch me," I growled, and Elias flinched. But I didn't hit him again.

Though the sight of Elias dripping in mud made me smile, I dropped the stick with a scream of frustration. Elias wobbled to his feet, sniffling and wiping the moisture from his eyes. Then, he stomped off scowling, his pride as dirty as his clothes.

"He won't forget that," Kaven warned.

"Good. Next time, I'll go for the eyes." I curled my fingers like claws.

Kaven laughed, the sound light and boyish. "You're violent, you know that?"

"Only to those who deserve it," I huffed.

"He was wrong, though."

"About what?"

"You're beautiful."

Heat flushed my face. I knew the way he looked at me, though I wasn't sure I could return it. "Thank you," was all I said.

Kaven sighed. "I'd better catch Elias before he tattles. Otherwise, Grandmother Alma will quote *The Old Book* at us all night."

We both laughed at that, but the sound died in my throat when I looked up at the Sky. Dread pricked at me when its aura changed. What was once a clear and vibrant summer blue had become partly cloudy and washed with a green tint.

The back of my head buzzed, and I dropped my gaze to the Ground. As I rubbed my humming skull to ease the sensation, I heard a voice speaking to me. The soothing voice sounded as though it was whispering directly into my ear. I could almost feel the heated breeze hit my skin. The words were quiet and serious.

It said *Look, be quick.*

Confusion coiled within me.

My breath hitched at the sound of its impatient tone. I forced myself to avert my attention back to the Sky, because something deep within me I didn't quite understand was being lured to look. I studied the clouds through squinted eyes.

The eerie hue also had a distinct scent that settled on my skin. One I couldn't quite place at first, but then I remembered the first time I went hunting with my father. When his arrow pierced the doe in the neck, we hurried over to the creature.

The animal was lying on the Ground with its watery eyes still open and its breathing shallow. My father was quick to end its suffering, cursing under his breath for missing the kill shot. But I'll never forget those few moments before the doe died. It knew its time had come, and the odor it gave off was that of encroaching death. It was the same stench I smelled in the air now.

The green tint of the Sky slowly faded. The clouds quickly shifted to smother the sun, blanketing the land with darkness. I looked over toward where Kaven and Elias had been standing, but they were gone.

It was only me in the shadowy field.

Unease crept up my spine as another familiar scent wafted over me. It consumed every sense until it burned, and I couldn't focus on anything other than its dominating presence.

Sandalwood.

Then it hit me—this wasn't a dream at all. It was a memory, but altered. Panic surged within me as I was overcome with a sense of clarity.

I needed to wake up.

I needed to warn *him*.

# CHAPTER 11

*"Life ends. Death is eternal."*
*- The Old Book*

I argued with the Veiler guarding the outside of my tent for several minutes. He was being extremely frustrating. I tried to explain just how important the situation was, but he kept repeating that "no one disturbs the commander."

Once he put his hands on me to guide me back into the tent, I slammed my knee into his groin and watched him wince.

I needed to find Rowan's tent.

I made my guess based on location, assuming that the tent in the center of the camp would be the commander's. I prayed I was right.

I entered the central tent and immediately made a note of how spacious it was. It was slightly smaller than the tent that the culled shared, but it was considerably less cramped.

I saw Rowan spread out underneath a large fur blanket, with his head resting on a pillow. Rowan shifted out from underneath the blanket and stood.

I raised my gaze to his face—his bare, unmasked face—and my breath hitched.

It somehow felt indecent to glance at his face when it was so naked. It seemed too intimate, nothing I should have borne witness to—but I couldn't look away.

The oil lamp flickered in the corner and shone brightly enough that I could take in his unrestricted features for the first time. He scratched the hair along his jaw and then brushed his brunette waves behind his ears.

My eyes trailed his sharp jaw, and then up over his high cheekbones until they locked with his. Rowan's eyes were a striking light brown that complemented his strong, dark brow. I'd seen his eyes before through the narrow slits of the mask he wore, but seeing them unobstructed made my throat tighten.

"To what do I owe the intrusion at this hour?" Rowan rasped just as the other Veiler entered his tent.

"I apologize, sir, but she insisted. When I tried to redirect her back into her tent, she attacked me. I didn't harm her—just as you requested—but she got past me." The Veiler flustered, trying to pivot me toward the entrance.

I twisted out of his weak hold and turned back toward Rowan, who watched with one brow raised curiously.

"I must speak with you. It's about the safety of the camp." I struggled to get my words out as the Veiler began tugging me away again.

"Let her speak," Rowan said with a wave of his hand, making the other Veiler halt his movement. "If it's truly about the safety of our camp, then it's imperative I'm made aware."

I rolled my shoulders back and straightened my posture.

"Something or someone is coming, and there will be death," I said.

Rowan huffed a laugh.

"That's vague. You know this, how?"

"I saw it in my dream—"

"A dream?" Interrupted the Veiler. "You stormed into the commander's tent in the middle of the night because of a nightmare?" He turned to Rowan. "I'm sorry for the intrusion, sir. I will escort her back—"

"It was a vision!" I barked out, pleading for them to hear me.

If they didn't listen, then we would all be dead.

"Why should I believe you?" Rowan said as he walked toward me. My body tensed as he drew closer.

"I've had them before. I know what they are."

"I understand that's what *you* believe, but I asked why *I* should believe you?"

"Because I have nothing to gain from lying to you."

We stared at each other briefly, but in those few moments, I felt like the air had been sucked out of me. Every muscle went stiff, and my hands clenched the hem of my tunic.

"Lorena!" Rowan yelled out. A few moments later, a tall, stocky woman with short brown hair entered the tent. "Send our scouts out."

"Yes, sir," she said and swiftly departed.

"Get her back to her tent," Rowan commanded.

"Will do, sir."

I fought against the Veiler's hold, but he grabbed me by the back of my shirt. I let out a yelp as I was dragged back to the tent. He quickly unfastened the tent and threw me inside.

"If you're smart, you'll stay put." The Veiler tied the tent shut once more.

I needed to get back to Rowan. I needed to make sure he believed me.

All the culled were awake and actively watching me as I panted in frustration before them.

"What's going on?" Lily asked, wariness coating her voice.

"I have to sneak out. Can you distract the guard while I do that?"

Lily didn't reply. She just stared at me as if I'd lost my mind. Which I might as well have.

I agreed that the idea of protecting Veilers was as ridiculous as it was reckless. But I couldn't shake the feeling that whatever I had seen in my dream was some kind of warning for all of us—the culled included. I didn't believe Rowan had trusted my word, so I desperately needed to get back and convince him.

Sending scouts out wasn't enough. We needed to brace ourselves against the impending danger—whatever it might be.

It was Isaac who broke the silence.

"I'll do it."

Everyone's head turned toward him.

"Thank you," I sighed, chest aching from holding my breath.

"You saved my life. I owe you a debt."

"Alright, then. If you're sure?"

"I'm sure."

I explained the plan, and Isaac gave a quick nod to show he understood.

We took our places at the entrance to the tent. Fear was written all over Isaac's face, but he didn't bend to it. I quietly untied the tent while another culled held it shut. Then, I counted down on my fingers.

Isaac sprinted as fast as he could out of the tent. I watched the Veiler take off after him, and then a moment later, I was soaring in the opposite direction.

I ran until I reached another tent, pressing my back to its side, out of the guard's line of sight. I sank to the Ground and hugged my knees as I gasped for air. The temperature was frigid, but my skin was heated from adrenaline, so I barely felt it.

Once my breathing evened out, I stood and looked around the camp. It was empty. Tents were open and lights were flickering inside, but I saw no movement within them.

"Look who's out here all alone," said a familiar gravelly voice. "Lost, are you?"

I turned my head and met Balor's black eyes. I internally screamed at my body to move—to run—but it didn't budge. Not again. Why did I always freeze?

Balor tilted his head slightly, like a predator sizing up a wounded creature. Amusement flickered in his gaze.

"How's your lip?" I asked, fighting to keep my voice steady.

My insides felt like they were coiling tighter and tighter, but I wanted to appear strong.

A slow grin spread across his face, splitting the already-healing wound. It bled again.

"Hurts like a bitch," he admitted, voice almost playful, "but only when I smile."

"That's unfortunate," I mocked.

He took another step. My fingers curled into fists, and my chest heaved.

"Don't worry," he continued, "the pain will be worth it when I smile down at your dead and bleeding body."

The pit of my stomach turned to ice.

He raised his knife, poised to strike.

This was it—I was going to die.

# CHAPTER 12

*"Hold close to your morality.*
*For when this life is over,*
*kindness or cruelty will find you in either the Realm of Remembrance*
*or the Sea of Sorrow."*
*- The Old Book*

"**D**on't go all quiet on me now, not when we were having so much fun. Please keep talking. It'll make ripping out your tongue even more enjoyable," Balor snickered.

I gripped the fabric of my pants, needing something—anything—to hold on to as adrenaline coursed through my veins once more.

I was stuck somewhere between fight and flight, leaving me paralyzed.

I took a deep breath and pushed my nerves to the pit of my stomach. He wanted me to tremble, to stutter over my words. I refused to give him that satisfaction.

"Normally, I would oblige since you asked so politely, but I'm not feeling up to chatting. Instead of continuing our little song and dance, how about you leave before the commander catches you?"

Balor bellowed out a cruel laugh, and I tensed even more. Panic bubbled up inside me, and the feeling of impending doom was heavy on my chest.

"Look who's begging for the commander to come and protect them," he mocked. "Too bad he's not here to save you this time." His lip, which I had previously split, opened again as he bared his teeth at me.

Balor charged, and my feet uprooted only moments before he struck me.

I ran as fast as I could from the camp and into the chilled darkness. I could hardly see anything, but I felt comforted knowing that Balor was in a similar position. If I could hide for long enough, then maybe he would grow bored and stop pursuing me.

Just when I thought I was getting somewhere, I tripped over a large rock and fell. I tumbled down the hill, scraping my arms. I heard Balor's maniacal laugh in the distance. The sound of his voice grew louder as he drew closer.

I was lying on the Ground, feeling like a crumpled piece of parchment while screaming inside, telling myself to *get up.*

*Get up.*

The words were both mine and someone else's. I felt a flood of energy wash over me as I struggled to stand. It was almost as if I were being picked up. The feeling followed me until I was upright and stable.

"Where are you, you little rat?"

He was very close now.

I ran again, but this time I circled back toward the camp. If I made it back, surely I would be safe. The other Veiled Ones didn't want me dead.

They needed me alive for something.

I saw the lights of the camp coming back into focus—and then I felt myself get yanked back by the hair at the nape of my neck.

The tip of an icy knife caressed my spine.

"Now tell me—how should I kill you?"

He twisted me to face him. The blade traced my cheek, opening a thin line. Blood mingled with the single tear I couldn't stop. Balor leaned in, licking it away. I gagged as his grin widened, tearing his wound even more until blood oozed down his chin.

"Sweet," he murmured. "Sweeter than I imagined. I wonder what the rest of you tastes like. Flesh boiled down—would you make a decent stew?"

He snipped a lock of my hair and shoved it into his pocket, chuckling.

"Or maybe I'll just see what you've got in here." His knife tip pressed against my abdomen, hard enough to sting. "I love the stringy bits."

*Go for the throat.* The voice inside me snapped. *Now.*

I clenched my fist, gathering every scrap of strength, and drove it into his jugular. Balor gagged, stumbling back, clawing for air.

*Grab the knife.*

I lunged, but he was faster. His hand closed around my throat, squeezing until my vision blurred. The knife hilt dug against my ribs, his weight forcing it there. My lungs screamed. I kicked—he twisted, my strike landing on his thigh instead of his groin.

Time was running out.

So I prayed.

I prayed to any deity listening for help. I knew it was a stretch. While the gods enjoyed their reverence, they were not liable for our lives. Their primary purpose, just like every other god in the universe, was to maintain our world's delicate balance.

However, at that moment, I felt like someone had answered.

A shiver ran up my arm, power surging through me. I raised my fist and elbowed his throat. This time, the impact was far more intense than the last. Balor stammered backward, releasing his grip on my neck and dropping the knife. He fell to his knees and wheezed.

Everything was hazy from the loss of oxygen to my brain. I pushed through the dizziness and quickly picked up the knife, wobbling as I found my footing.

When I raised my arm to strike, I memorized the look of fear on Balor's face. It was more satisfying than it should have been. A part of me faltered, knowing that taking a life would follow me forever. But logically, I knew—it was me or him. I moved to plunge the knife into him, but a strong, assertive voice stopped me before I could.

"That's enough," the voice demanded.

I looked over and saw Rowan. He was standing with his arms crossed, observing us like bickering children. He was wearing his mask again and had an emotional wall erected around him.

I was speechless.

Rowan said he would protect me, and yet there he was, stopping me from finishing what Balor started. Had I been a fool for trusting the word of a Veiler? The answer, of course, was yes, but some part of me had been hopeful.

"I think you've made your point," he said, looking at me. "Balor, I trust you've learned your lesson? Because the next time you attack this woman while under direct orders not to, it will cost you more than just your pride."

Balor pushed off the Ground to stand, still clutching at his throat. My pride flickered at the sight of his pain. He deserved worse for his cruelty, but I could settle for matching purple bruises around our necks. The others would learn I wasn't so easily taken down.

"Balor, return to camp."

"Yes, *sir*," Balor grumbled. He stole one last glance at me and curled his lip. I ignored his sneering and looked to Rowan, who was observing Balor sulk with every footstep back to camp.

Once Balor was out of earshot, Rowan faced me.

"Are you alright?" His voice held a slight tremor, which he quickly tried to mask by clearing his throat. But that didn't erase the fact that I'd heard it.

"How much of that did you witness?" I squinted my eyes at him, fruitlessly attempting to gauge his expression in the darkness.

"Most of it," he said flatly.

"And you stood by and just watched?! He could have killed me!" I shrieked into the night, not caring who heard.

"I know, but he didn't."

"You vile, lying, monstrous piece of filth!" I spat at his feet. "So much for not wanting to watch everyone die."

"Death is inevitable sometimes."

"You are so contradictory, and I'm done trying to understand why."

"Maybe you shouldn't try to. Maybe you won't like what you learn if you do."

"I already know that you're a Veiler, and that's about the worst thing that there is."

"Maybe," he shrugged.

"This entire conversation is pointless and not worth my time."

He stepped closer.

"Last time I checked, you were directly disobeying orders. Shouldn't you be in your tent with the others? By the way, smart move having that boy make a run for it as a distraction."

"Not quite smart enough," I muttered. "I got caught."

"What *was* your plan? To run off in the middle of the night without food, water, or a blanket?"

"Is that what you think I was doing?" I crossed my arms and glared at him.

"Is it not?"

"No, it wasn't. I left to find you."

Rowan stared at me for several moments, trying to decipher whether what I told him was the truth. When he found what he was looking for, he started back toward the camp.

"Follow," he clipped.

I hurried after him, rushing to keep up with his quick pace.

"Aren't you going to take my weapon?" I said, clasping the knife tightly at my side.

"How do you expect to fight without one?"

When I didn't reply, he let out a small sigh and stopped to look at me.

"You won it, so keep it."

"Aren't you afraid that I'll use it?"

"I expect you to."

# CHAPTER 13

*"There will always be deceivers among you.*
*Heed not the loudest cry, but the truest whisper."*
*- The Old Book*

When we reached Rowan's tent, a group of Veilers were standing outside, murmuring and glaring. Rowan didn't seem to care or pay any mind to the scornful stares, but I was consumed by them.

I rolled my shoulders back and stood as tall as my height would allow. I wasn't short, but I felt like a mouse standing next to Rowan.

Rowan lifted the tent flap and gestured me inside. Gasps rippled through the crowd. He gave the Veilers a withering glance, and they scurried away.

Once they were gone, he turned to me and asked, "How do your visions work?"

"I'm not entirely sure. They come to me in dreams. Often, they are flashes of images I can't fully decipher. But other times, they're so vivid I don't know if I'm awake or not."

What I didn't say was that I usually ignored my dreams altogether. I didn't want this power. If I could see into the future, that meant I could have possibly prevented some of the darkest times of my life—and I couldn't live with that guilt.

But now was not the time for denial. I did have a gift, and I needed to use it.

"How long have you been having them?"

"About nine years, just shortly after puberty started."

"Can you summon your visions?"

"I've never tried before," I admitted honestly.

He watched me warily.

"Will you try now?"

I nodded.

This wasn't about protecting Veilers. This was about protecting myself and the other culled. If I could save us, I had a duty to do so.

I closed my eyes and attempted to return to my dream. If I could get back to that altered memory and look deeper into the Sky, maybe there was more to see.

The seconds stretched slowly by, and nothing happened.

A dark, empty nothingness was all I could see. A yawn forced its way up my throat just as a shiver coursed down my scalp.

When I opened my eyes to tell Rowan I had failed, I found myself back in that dreamworld field alone.

The sun was fully covered by dark gray clouds that swirled in the Sky. There was a feeling luring me to look deeper into the darkness. And as I dared to look further, I felt all of my focus hone in on the heavens.

I followed the spiral in the atmosphere to its center, where the smallest light flickered. A part of me screamed to look away—to hide—but I knew that if I did, then the information I sought would be lost.

I had to know.

The light grew brighter, and inside it I saw faces.

Even though I couldn't make them out entirely, I knew enough to recognize that they weren't ones I'd seen before. The smell of sandalwood hit me suddenly, and that's when I saw him.

I saw Rowan.

He struck down another with perfect ease. I felt his anger and determination. It was a mix of emotions I knew well.

The voice inside me whispered: *Do not linger long. Stay, and you change what comes.*

I watched the way Rowan fought—how he used his entire body to sway in and out of combat. Despite how violent the scene was, I couldn't help but admire the wonder of it all. Rowan commanded the battlefield.

*Let go. Now.*

I didn't want to let go, but my chest ached, and the smell of blood filled my nostrils. I loosened my grip on the vision, and darkness shrouded the light.

*Open your eyes.*

I felt my eyes roll back into place. When I opened them, Rowan was standing beside me, intensely studying my face.

"What did you see?" His voice was still, careful.

"Enemies."

"How many?"

"Around thirty," I slurred. My dreams were never taxing, but that had been. Perhaps it was because I had gone searching.

All I knew for sure was that my head felt too heavy for my shoulders, like I was teetering just standing still.

A horn blared in the distance, snapping me back into the present. Raised shouts from the camp filtered into the tent.

Rowan's face grew serious, and he gestured for me to follow. Once outside, I rubbed my chilled arms. The breeze had picked up, and it was biting. I could see my breath in the air, misting up into the night Sky.

"What is it?" I asked.

"Rebels."

My breath caught, and my brow rose. Rowan noted my reaction, and his eyes narrowed.

"They are not your heroes."

"Of course you would say that. Their entire purpose is to rid the world of Veilers."

"If only that were the case," he muttered under his breath.

"What do you mean?"

"They aren't well known for their treatment of women. They expect a certain type of *repayment* for their valiant rescue," he mocked. "Willing or not."

I swallowed hard, a wave of nausea hitting me.

"You are to return to your tent. This battle is not for you."

"Let me guess, I'm a liability?"

"Yes, but even more, you are an asset. To hand you over to our enemy—for them to have access to your gift—would be idiotic beyond all reason."

"I'm not just something you can wield! I am *not* a weapon!"

"No, you're more than that. You have been blessed with a godlike power. Used properly, it could turn the tide in war."

Rowan turned away from me and called out to a passing Veiler.

"Lorena, take her back to her tent and keep her there. You make sure she does not leave that tent under any circumstances. I do not care what actions you take to keep her there as long as she stays alive. If I find out she leaves that tent tonight, you better pray to every god in the universe, because none of ours will save you."

"Can you afford to have fewer Veilers fighting?" I quipped, but Rowan ignored me.

"Am I clear?" he asked the Veiler.

"Yes, sir," Lorena said firmly. She grabbed my arm and jerked me away from Rowan.

I started kicking and screaming for her to let me go. I was tired of being dragged around from one corner to the other. Every time it happened, it made me feel weak.

When we got to the culled's tent, the Veiler guarding it unfastened it, and Lorena tossed me inside.

"The commanding officer permitted me to use all methods to keep you in here for the night, so long as you are kept breathing. Do you understand?"

I scowled. The sound of another horn drew my attention.

Followed by distant screams and the clatter of swords.

# CHAPTER 14

*"Once the sails of death have been raised,*
*Anam demands burial in His namesake.*
*All must reunite with the Ground from which they once came*
*as payment for the time they spent above."*
*- The Old Book*

I sat on a rock at the edge of camp, overlooking the side of the hill and the twenty-three fresh piles of tilled dirt that lay atop it.

Five Veilers and over three times the number of Rebels were buried in the Ground. I don't know why I mourned the loss of the fallen Veilers. I still hated them; that fact had not changed, yet I could not deny that I grieved their deaths all the same.

Behind me, the remaining Veilers tore down the tents and packed them away in their satchels. There was no breakfast this morning. My stomach twisted at the emptiness, but I ignored the discomfort. It was something I'd gotten used to doing in my few days on the road.

I pulled out the knife I'd won from Balor, and I ran my finger along the smooth side of it. It was a decent knife, artisan-crafted. The oak hilt reminded me of home, while the blade reminded me just how far away from it I was. I lifted my hand to my cheek and felt the scab that was forming, just another reminder of where I was and who surrounded me.

I clung to the knife as if keeping it near could keep me safe.

Doubt wrapped my mind, and I questioned whether I had done the right thing by warning Rowan. He had watched me fight Balor—watched me struggle to breathe as he strangled me, and did nothing to stop it, even though he swore to protect me from him. Maybe, and the thought was painful, Rowan had been lying about the Rebels as well.

If Rowan lied, then my warning wasn't betrayal—it was just ignorance. I repeated that until I almost believed it. I had enough guilt weighing on my shoulders already. Knowing I might have stolen a fate where the culled could have been freed was too much to bear.

I was too lost in my daydreaming to hear the approaching footsteps behind me. It wasn't until she stood right before me that my attention snapped to her presence.

Renata's hands were on her hips, and she was gritting her teeth at the sight of me. Nothing out of the usual.

"What are you doing with a knife?"

"It's mine." I clutched it to my chest protectively.

"You're a thief. Who did you steal it from?"

I caught myself contorting my face at her sharp accusation. I wouldn't tolerate being called a thief. That allegation was an attack on my character, and I wasn't risking that lie running rampant among the other culled.

"I won it," I sneered.

"Bullshit. You're too weak to win anything."

"I am *more* than capable of fighting," I growled.

Renata stepped toward me, eager to accept the challenge.

I had gotten lucky with Balor. Over the course of the morning, I replayed the previous night trying to figure out how it all happened, and it still made no sense. I should never have gotten the upper hand with him. He was far more skilled than I was in fighting. Perhaps I bested him at hunting, but hand-to-hand combat was out of the question.

Someone or something had interfered.

Renata grew tense and retreated a step. She never lifted her eyes from me. Her hatred was thick and humid, radiating in the air over my skin. If stares could kill, then I would already be dead.

We both would.

A voice that I instantly recognized coughed. "What is going on here?"

"She has a weapon!" Renata exclaimed.

"Indeed, she does. She won it in a match," Rowan articulated.

"With whom?!"

"Balor."

"Yet he still breathes?" She didn't seem convinced.

"It was not to the death. I made sure of that."

"Clearly," she murmured. "Aren't you at all concerned that she will use it against us?"

"You know the rules, Renata. If you win a match, the weapon is yours by right. Even I cannot change our customs."

"They won't allow her to keep it."

Her words piqued my interest. Who were *they*? More Veilers?

"Then I guess she will have to get better at concealing it."

I bristled at the intended jab.

Renata dropped her arms and narrowed her eyes at me.

"You think winning one match makes you a warrior? Balor should've finished the job."

She stormed back into the camp. I hadn't shifted to look at Rowan, but I knew he still stood behind me. I felt his undeniable presence; it was domineering and all-consuming. Rowan stalked forward, footsteps heavy, until he was practically breathing down my neck. I refused to look at him.

"Can you stop trying to get into trouble?" he all but growled at me.

"Why do you suddenly care?"

"Is this about last night? About why I didn't step in sooner?"

"He was *killing* me, and you stood by and did *nothing*!" I whipped my head toward him so fast that it made me slightly dizzy.

"I wouldn't have let him kill you."

"That's hard to believe."

"That's fine," he shrugged.

"Why even let it get that far?" I pressed, irritated with his nonchalance.

I took my survival seriously.

"I wanted to know what you were capable of."

I almost believed the lie.

He had said it so simply, like it was all a harmless experiment.

I was fuming, my nails biting deep into my knees as I squeezed. I turned my gaze back to the hills to contain my rage. My anger had taken on a life of its own ever since my capture from Oak Hollow. I had allowed it to flourish to keep myself strong and motivated. However, I found it much more difficult to control and rein in now.

I took several deep breaths in and out. The breath control helped some, but not as much as I needed it to.

"Go away."

"I know you're frustrated—" He tried to reach for my arm, but I shrank away. He dropped his hand to his side, and I watched him subtly clench his fist. It was a move I'm not sure he realized he made.

"That's an understatement," I muttered under my breath.

"I know you're frustrated, but I would really appreciate it if you stopped getting into situations that require my intervention."

"Last night I didn't need it. I had it covered."

That was a lie. Something miraculous had occurred, and if it hadn't, then I would be dead.

"I know you did." He paused, tone skeptical. "Lorena trapped some rabbits this morning. It's not much, but even the smallest amount of sustenance can mean the difference between life and death. You need to eat, so come."

My stomach must have heard his words, because it chose right then to speak. I reluctantly stood, and he followed me back to the camp.

This wasn't the end of our conversation.

# CHAPTER 15

*"Anam reaps every soul.*
*If one goes missing, He will find it."*
- *The Old Book*

We had been riding for several hours, and all I wanted was to rest.

I had barely slept last night because of the battle.

I was scared to rest while on horseback. There was no rope tethering me anymore, and I didn't want to fall off. That, and the first time I did, I woke up with my head on Rowan's chest. That was not something I wanted to repeat.

"Are you still angry?" Rowan asked since I had been pointedly ignoring him.

"Yes."

He let out a disgruntled sigh.

"If I let you ask me a question, will you speak? I don't enjoy traveling in tense silence."

I contemplated being spiteful, but I did have something I was curious about.

"She calls you by your first name," I said.

"Who?"

"Renata. She calls you Rowan, not by your title or by *sir*."

"That's not a question."

"Why can she do it, but the others can't?"

"Renata has been in the Order much longer than I have. She's earned it."

"How much longer?"

They both seemed to be the same age. A number I still hadn't learned, but would soon ask about.

He didn't immediately answer, and I thought perhaps he was going to evade the answer under the pretense that I only got to ask one question.

But he surprised me.

"She was raised by the Order."

"Her parents were Veilers? That explains why she's so bloodthirsty and ruthless."

Rowan chuckled.

"You and she are very similar in some regards—both fueled by anger."

"Do *not* compare us. I am not volatile like that monster."

"You're definitely no sweet, innocent flower now, are you?"

I changed the subject away from me, because the thought of being compared to a Veiler—especially one as cruel as she—brought out the exact rage he was describing.

"What could *she* have to be angry about?"

I glanced over at her on her silver horse. She didn't have a companion riding with her. She probably would never deign to be saddled with one of the culled.

"It's not as if she had to spend her entire life wondering if her village was going to be culled," I continued. "Or if tomorrow were the day she, her friend—her brother—or someone else she cared about was going to be taken away forever."

There was a tense moment of silence.

"Her story is not mine to share. But maybe she has just as much to resent as you. Many of us do."

Rowan's voice sounded honest and protective. Maybe it wasn't purely platonic between them. It was not my concern either way, so I dropped the thought.

"And you?" I asked.

"I have made peace with my past," he said bluntly, making sure I understood that the topic of his past wasn't a road he wanted to venture down.

"Is that a long past then?" I asked not so subtly.

"If you are trying to ask my age, Mavis, I have seen twenty-five summers."

"Oh."

"Does that surprise you?"

"I mean, I knew you were young, but I didn't know you were *that* young. Should you be a commanding officer when there are others older and more experienced than you?"

"Would you rather Balor be in command?"

"Gods, no!" I choked out, and he chuckled again. If Balor had been the commanding officer, then I would never have left Oak Hollow alive. "I'm just curious how a Veiler rises in the ranks at such an early age. You must be very skilled at killing."

"Something like that," he murmured.

"How did you get the scar on your lip?"

Rowan's body immediately stiffened. I almost felt bad for asking—perhaps it was too much—but I shut that thought down at once. I did not pity Veilers.

"A shaving accident," Rowan said flatly.

"A *shaving* accident?"

That was a lie. It had to be. Though the scar had paled and thinned over time, it was far too prominent to have been an accident.

"You've asked enough," he stated. "It's my turn. Do you know how to fight?"

"Are you asking because most women aren't taught how?"

"I know many women who can fight, and fight well. But you don't come from an area that typically condones such teachings."

"I love my home," I said, crossing my arms over my chest.

"I never said you shouldn't."

"My brother taught me how to wield a knife, and my father took me hunting with a bow. Oak Hollow isn't against teaching women how to fight; there just isn't a need. We mainly hunt with our weaponry, not use it to kill."

"Combat doesn't mean killing. It's about protecting yourself."

For a few long moments, we didn't speak.

"I've visited cities where women hold positions that are just as high, if not higher, than the men. And they can all defend themselves in combat."

"Athelney?" I asked.

"No, in the Free Isles."

My eyes widened. The Free Isles were not welcoming toward the Ravarie, or vice versa. There was some trade between our lands, but they mostly kept to themselves. Why anyone would want to visit the land of the godless pirates was beyond me.

"You've been to the Free Isles?"

"Many years ago, during my travels."

"I always wanted to explore the continent," I murmured thoughtlessly.

"Why didn't you?"

"Because I had responsibilities, I couldn't just abandon them. Not everyone can leave their life behind to gallivant across the world."

"Then I'll ask again: why did you offer yourself up instead of that girl?"

"I made a promise to keep her safe."

"You want to know what I think?"

"No." I didn't. I had a feeling I wouldn't like it.

"I think you wanted out, away from your responsibilities. You saw an opportunity, and you took it."

"You know *nothing* about me," I snarled.

My temper was rising again. He had a way of doing that to me.

"I've grown quite familiar with you these past few days."

"If you knew anything about me, you'd know that I would do anything for those I love."

"I don't doubt that."

"I had the chance to leave before. I didn't take it."

Kaven's pleading eyes flashed in my mind. The memory stung.

"Oh? Was it with that boy from before?" he mocked.

"His name is Kaven." I corrected.

"And was he your lover?"

"That's certainly none of your business."

"So no, then."

"I didn't say that."

"Whatever you two were, I got the impression you didn't agree on it."

I knew he was riling me up intentionally; I just didn't understand why. I should have stopped replying, but I didn't.

"He was—is—my friend."

"I see." He hummed to himself quietly. I hated the sound of it—the sound of arrogance.

"And you and Renata?" I snapped. After the words spilled, I silently kicked myself for asking. Especially since I had decidedly chosen not to.

"What of us?" he asked with a hint of amusement.

"Is she your lover?"

"Why would you think that?"

"You're protective of her."

"At one time, I wanted her to be. But we were both young and had yet to discover ourselves."

My reply caught in my throat as the acrid stench of smoke reached my nose. Ahead, a thin column of black curled into the Sky. The closer we drew, the heavier it became. Then I saw it—orange tongues of fire consuming what was left of an encampment.

Bodies lay scattered across the scorched Ground. Some were in Veiler black, and some wore the plain tunics of the culled.

"Riders—water! Put it out now!" Rowan ordered. His voice was steel, sharp and commanding. In seconds, several Veilers leapt from their horses toward the scene.

I watched as the Veilers threw water onto the roaring flames and stomped on the embers. The fire hissed and spat as they worked.

The heat stung my eyes, forcing tears I didn't want to shed.

A small hand peeked out from beneath a fallen tarp.

My stomach dropped when the wind blew it aside, revealing the vacant eyes of a girl no older than fifteen. Gone.

The thought was unbearable.

When the worst of it was under control, I found my voice.

"What happened?"

There was a moment of silence before Rowan finally replied.

"Rebels."

# CHAPTER 16

*"The most atrocious acts are those made in vain against life.*
*Those who commit such crimes condemn themselves to the Sea of Sorrow.*
*May the salt burn."*
*- The Old Book*

Two weeks on horseback had made my thighs so sore and chafed that my walking turned wobbly. The skin there was almost rubbed raw from the near-constant friction with the saddle. The pain was dull and persistent, which made it especially aggravating.

Unfortunately, in the past couple of weeks, I had also grown uncomfortably familiar with the scent of horse and sweat. I kept hoping that I would become desensitized to it, but it never happened.

We stopped only once in those two weeks to bathe. I felt like I was removing a century's worth of dirt and grime from my body when we did. The coat of filth was heavy on my skin, and my clothes were rancid.

Rowan had commanded that the caravan stop just north of the village, Oar's Rest, for the evening. We bathed in the River Rael, which flowed down from the Sacred Mountains to the Gulf of the Gods.

Even though the water was extremely cold, I relished the opportunity to be clean. The stench of travel was thick and suffocating in the air. I wondered if the Veilers were immune to it, considering they showed no aversion to the permeating odor. Meanwhile, the rest of us were practically choking on it.

There wasn't any outright privacy while bathing in the river alongside everyone else, but there was an unspoken rule to focus on oneself instead of peering about. However, at one point, I caught Rowan watching me. When I saw him staring, he immediately moved his gaze elsewhere, and I swore a flash of pink flared in his cheeks. He had seen nothing explicitly indecent, but he saw enough that it raised the hairs on my arms.

That was a week ago, and now I had returned to smelling and looking putrid once again. I guess I was lucky that there were no mirrors for me to see just how vacant and disheveled I truly appeared.

Winter was closing in, and I worried just how far we still had left to journey. The temperature had dropped low enough that our breath lingered in the air. The nights were icy, and I found myself in my tent, clutching hard onto my wool blanket to preserve as much heat as possible. My bones still rattled, but at least I could feel and move my toes. A few days back, a boy named Reston had three of his toes go black. One Veiler had to cut them off. All I could do was sit on the opposite side of the camp and try to ignore his shrill screams.

I thanked the gods again for the shoes.

We had traveled to the edge of the Great North, where very few leaves remained on the trees, and mountains spanned the entire northern horizon. The Sacred Mountains stretched up toward the heavens like glorious monuments to both Anam and Aeta, closing the gap between Ground and Sky. The snowy peaks made me shiver, thinking of just how far north we had truly ventured.

The Great North was the common name for the barren tundra that stretched from the Sacred Mountains to the northeastern edge of the continent. It was a frigid place filled with apex predators that rivaled humans in their ruthlessness. Out there, we were not the only ones to be feared.

The Sky was growing dark, and the stars were twinkling into existence. The view of the stoic mountains mixed with the starry night was a vision to behold. The entire atmosphere was scattered with brilliant constellations that shone clear as day. I looked for the star from before that had shone brighter than all the rest, but it was no longer there.

In the far distance, at the base of the mountains, I saw torches flickering. My stomach dropped in realization.

It was a village.

I knew exactly what the Veilers did when they entered villages. If I had to witness another Culling, I didn't think I could sit idly by as people were ripped from their homes and subjected to what I had been through. I reached for the knife in my pocket.

"Easy," Rowan breathed into my ear. I stiffened at the light contact. "You won't be needing that here."

I tentatively pulled my hand back and flattened my palm against my leg. It was a warning, but it wasn't threatening.

The Veilers rode into the village as if they were welcome. And maybe they were, because as the villagers left their homes, they seemed curious, not afraid. I soon realized that the villagers weren't looking at the Veilers at all. They were looking at us, the culled.

"Where are we?" I asked Rowan.

"Summit's Ridge. It's an outpost for the Order."

"That explains why people aren't running in fear."

Rowan snorted.

Our horse slowed as we entered, coming to a complete stop when a woman stepped out in the middle of the road. She was dressed all in black, like a Veiler, and was blocking our passage. However, unlike the Veilers, she wore no mask. Rowan quickly dismounted, leaving me atop our horse. The rest of the Veilers and culled remained seated, watching intently.

The woman was petite, with straight midnight hair that fell to her chin. Her skin was warm beige with swirls of red ink tattooed on both her hands. Her dark brown almond eyes flicked up to me and narrowed in careful assessment.

It was Rowan who broke the silence first.

"Lieutenant."

His voice seemed strained, but his back was turned toward me, so I couldn't make out his expression.

"Commander," the woman said, turning to him and giving a small bow of respect. "We have been expecting you."

Her accent caught my attention. It had been a long time since I'd last heard it. The accent was native to Northwestern Ethorians. I found it interesting that she was a soldier for the Ravaryn Crown, the very kingdom her people supposedly despised.

My eyes traced the intricate red tattoos on her hands, which swirled up and underneath her long-sleeved tunic. The markings were a tribute to her Northwestern ancestry, ones I'd only ever seen etched in faded history books. They were incredibly rare, and those who bore such ancient markings were loyal warriors.

"We would have arrived earlier, but unfortunately, we ran into a band of Rebels on the way. We lost five of our own."

"I assume they lost more?"

"Yes." It wasn't an enthusiastic response, but it wasn't somber.

"I'm sorry for those you lost. However, I'm glad to see that you are not one of them."

"As am I."

The woman's stone-cold demeanor warmed, and a bright smile appeared. Rowan stepped toward her with his arms spread out, and the two of them met in an embrace. He towered over the woman and bent down even further to whisper something in her ear. She let out a hoarse laugh, patting him on his arm and then stepping away. The woman then turned to the rest of us on horseback.

"Welcome to Summit's Ridge. Baths are awaiting you all." I almost sobbed in relief. "I know that must sound like euphoria compared to what you've grown accustomed to in the past few weeks. Please wash up before dinner. All of you reek." She looked at Rowan and gave him a disapproving scrunch of her nose.

He laughed in response.

It wasn't just a snide chuckle like what he offered me. It was a rich laugh, and the sound made my pulse skip a beat.

Rowan walked back to our horse and mounted behind me in the saddle. We started forward, and the rest of the Veilers followed.

Veilers, followed by the culled, dismounted outside a large cabin. Rowan, without so much as a glance in my direction, wordlessly followed the tattooed woman and a few other Veilers across the outpost. I watched them until they entered another cabin. Then, I fixed my attention back on the Veiler gesturing us inside.

The large room threatened to swallow me whole. Especially as the culled filtered in. I watched as they all looked just as lost as I was. The culled stood in silence, patiently awaiting orders from the Veiler.

There were fourteen cots lined in two rows, stacked with another bed on top, and equipped with a ladder for climbing. The room was fit for twenty-eight people to sleep. Some beds looked to be in use, with linens pulled back and a few personal items scattered on top. My heart plummeted at the sight of a worn stuffed animal on top of one bed.

The Veiler who showed us the cabin was speaking, but the words he spoke were muffled in my ear. The only thing I heard was something about there being one chamber pot to share among ourselves.

No plumbing. Wonderful.

He distributed pairs of clean linens to each of us. While I itched to get out of my filthy borrowed clothes, my body wouldn't move. All I could do was sit and stare blankly at the floor, clutching onto the clothes like a lifeline.

The harsh reality of the situation was finally setting in, and fear had its talons in my back. I felt as though I was going through the motions of being alive when, in reality, something in me had died long ago.

The past few weeks of travel had been so exhausting that I barely had any time to grieve being away from home. And now that I was in this place—so very far from the comforting smell of oak—I felt empty and afraid.

Sleeping on the cold Ground, Rebels, Balor, Renata, and even bantering with Rowan, had all felt like a fever dream. None of it had been real.

But now, the truth of that weighted reality was crushing down on me, forcing me to accept all that had happened and might happen.

I was alone.

# CHAPTER 17

*"Not all prayers need to be spoken.
There is reverence in silence."*
*- The Old Book*

By the time I pulled myself together and made my way to the communal bathing chamber, there was no one else there. The others had already washed and dressed. We were less guarded at the outpost. Fewer eyes were constantly watching. Probably because we were over a hundred miles from any other civilization, and the grounds were crawling with Veilers.

Any attempt to flee would be foolish.

The bathing chamber was large with two medium basins. I peeled off my dirty garments and dropped them onto the floor. I took slow steps into the slightly murky reservoir, descending into its lukewarm water. At least there was still some heat remaining, despite the others absorbing the majority. The hot springs linked to these baths were a blessing.

I let out a disgusting moan I hoped no one outside heard, and then I sank deeper into the water. Layers of oil and dirt pooled around me as I washed my skin with what little soap was left behind. I dipped my head briefly, savoring the feel of warmth against my more sensitive skin. When my head emerged from underneath and I moved to wipe the water from my eyes, I was startled by a loud pounding on the chamber door.

"You have five minutes to get dressed!" someone shouted from the other side of the door.

"Well, that's just great," I murmured to myself. It seemed I would not be granted time to decompress like I had hoped for.

I spent what little time I had scrubbing myself down. Once I rinsed, I rose from the pool and toweled myself off as quickly as I could. I tugged the white long-sleeved shirt I had been given over my damp skin, and then I laced myself into the black pants.

I was grateful for the laces because my pants were slightly too large and slumped at my hips. I rolled up the ends that gathered at my feet. Then I put on my shoes and donned my overcoat just as the chamber door opened and an unfamiliar Veiler appeared.

"Times up. Let's go," he commanded.

I hurried out of the bathing chamber. The wind slammed into me, and I shuddered. My hair was still wet, and I muttered a curse under my breath for not spending longer drying it.

We entered another vast cabin that had three tables, large enough to seat twenty people each, maybe more. I saw Rowan sitting at the center of a table, a sea of Veilers in black surrounding him. There were a few Veilers I recognized from our journey, as well as the tattooed woman from earlier. They were conversing over plates of solid food, not stew.

I noted potatoes, chicken, and string beans. My stomach panged at the delicious vision. After so many bowls of rodent stew, the sight of an actual meal had me salivating.

There were more culled seated at the tables. I counted the ten from our journey, not including myself, as well as sixteen others. The culled murmured among themselves, but there was no fervor, no sense of companionship.

They were just as alone and weary as I was.

Renata brushed past me, paying me no mind. She didn't even bother to glare. She walked up behind the tattooed woman and rested her hand on her shoulder. The woman sprang up from the table and met Renata in an embrace. I figured they were close friends—until their lips met. The kiss wasn't long, but it had enough emotion in it to cause my chest to flutter at the sight.

It was rare for Veilers to have partners because their commitment to their position came first. A Veiler's top priority was their oath of servitude. Rowan had mentioned that Renata's parents were *both* Veilers, even though two Veilers having a child together was nearly unheard of.

Veilers weren't celibate. They visited village brothels often. So it made sense that Veilers would have children. However, no child ever claimed their Veiler lineage. To do so would be worse than being a bastard itself.

It was strange to see. Not because they were two women, but because I could sense the passion in their kiss, as if they loved each other. That was the strange part, because I never would have thought that a cold-hearted Veiler could be capable of such a feeling.

My attention diverted to Rowan, who was looking at me as if he were trying to read my thoughts. I ignored his questioning stare and walked toward the buffet of food. The hunger pains only grew in intensity as a plate was piled high with food for me. I took the offered plate and silverware and found myself a spot at a table.

I didn't notice the glances at first.

If it weren't for the swift departure of the few around me as I sat down, I wouldn't have noticed anything amiss at all. I looked around at the scowls I received. It was odd because it wasn't just the culled I had traveled with who were grimacing. It was the others who had arrived earlier than us as well. The ones I had never met.

I blocked them all out and ignored the unsettling feeling of sour stares. I focused on taking a fork and consuming my first bite of food that wasn't mush in weeks.

I ended up eating far too much.

After eating so little for so long, my stomach had shrunk. I was all too eager to consume every bite of food on my plate. Now my stomach ached, swollen and tight. I was one moment away from keeling over.

I slowly climbed under the sheets of my cot, careful not to move too quickly for fear of losing my dinner. The sheets were rough, but warm. I wasn't expecting luxury by any means, but the fabric was close in kin to sandpaper. I was still grateful for the warmth they provided. It was better than just a wool blanket and the cold, hard Ground.

I was near sleep when I was met with an assault on my senses. Someone dumped a cup of cold water on my face. I pinched my eyes shut and coughed out what little water I had inhaled. Then they opened again, and I stared at the four individuals who stood around my bed. I could feel the heat of their hateful glares even in the cool darkness.

"You lying *bitch*," someone cursed with a lethally calm voice. I realized who it was after a few seconds had passed, and I had become alert.

Lily.

"What is wrong with you?!"

"What is wrong with us? *Us*? *You* are the traitor! What is wrong with *you*?!" Lily spat in my face, and I flinched.

"What are you talking about?" My thoughts raced, trying to figure out what I'd done.

It wasn't Lily who spoke next, but Isaac.

Isaac's voice cracked as he shouted, "You lied to us! You lied to *me*! I didn't receive a slap on the wrist for helping you escape that night, more like a *fist*."

"Isaac..." I said, emotion choking my throat at the sound of his raw voice. "I don't know what—"

"They were coming to save us. And they would have, had you not warned the Veilers," Aeva interrupted.

"We know, Mavis. We know the Rebels came for us that night. The night you begged us to help you—the night we trusted you and then you betrayed us!" Lily raged.

"We could have been home by now! We could have been in our own beds, with our families, safe!"

Those words were laced with fury, but they didn't come from Lily, Isaac, or Aeva. That voice was familiar in a way that reminded me of home. I rubbed my eyes and squinted again at the figure that had spoken. It was too dark to make out any of his facial features, but I knew.

It was Oliver.

"It's not what you think, I swear! The Rebels are not who you think them to be. We were no safer with them than we are with the Veilers!"

Oliver, the boy whom I sat next to by the fire just weeks ago and begged not to break, now stood by my bed with so much hatred directed at me. It cracked something inside me.

"Is that what *Rowan* told you?" Lily questioned. My mouth opened, but no words came out. "You don't think we haven't noticed you siding with the enemy?"

"It's not what you think! I hate him just as much as I hate any Veiler!"

"You're on a first-name basis," Aeva said bluntly. She was right, too. Gods, it looked like I had forsaken them in favor of the Veilers.

My brows raised at the accusation. "I promise nothing is going on there!"

"Your promise means nothing to us! It's just empty words and pretty lies." Oliver fumed, and I could hear the tears in his voice. It wrecked me.

"This is how it's going to work," Lily said. "You're on your own from now on. Aeva suspects we are going to have to brave those mountains soon, and I've heard that the path is *very* narrow. It's getting colder, and the wind is picking up. One slip is all it would take, and not even *Rowan* could save you from tumbling down the mountainside. Watch your back, Mavis. You condemned us to this fate, and now we condemn you. *May the salt burn.*" Her icy words sent a shiver down my spine, and I clutched onto my covers in response.

The four of them walked away as I remained still, barely breathing, reeling from the encounter. No doubt they had told every single one of the culled about my so-called betrayal, and that's why I received such nasty looks at dinner. They truly thought that I was working with the Veilers, and now I was a target.

My eyes did not close for the rest of the night.

# CHAPTER 18

*"Trust no one but your king and your gods."*
*- Article 3, Section 1, of the Veiled Compendium*

The second night in Summit's Ridge was worse than the first. The floorboards creaked with every whisper of wind, and I lay rigid on the cot, eyes fixed on the ceiling like it held the answers.

Sleep never came—not with Lily a few feet away, breathing steadily, plotting.

They'd threatened me once. If they tried again, I'd have to act. Gods help me, I'd already pictured it—the weight of my blade, the warmth of blood—but I wasn't sure if I could strike first.

Telling Rowan had crossed my mind more than once, but that would only feed the culled's whispers. No, this was my mess. There was no dignity in cowardice, no safety in begging mercy from wolves.

So I lay awake, counting breaths and imagining exits. By dawn, I had none.

We left at first light, traveling in the groups we had arrived in.

Once we reached Lowry's Pass, a rocky path that ascended and snaked through the mountains, Rowan warned everyone that we could not ride our horses until the trail plateaued. He said it would take about a day to reach the caves that cut through the core of the mountain range.

Rowan looked back at me as I trailed behind him, lifting his brow in a questioning glance. He could tell something was on my mind, but it was none of his business. He had gotten rather comfortable asking personal questions in the past few weeks, and it was my fault for letting him.

He was my captor, not my confidant.

I may have been able to walk untethered, but I still went where I was commanded to go. My leash was invisible, but still present.

Rowan subtly took my wrist and pulled me closer to him and our horse, leaning in to speak.

"You've been sending daggers at me all day with those eyes. What have I done this time?"

I tugged my wrist out of his hold and stepped away from him. "Do I need another reason to hate you?"

"I will not apologize for doing my sworn duty."

I was about to retort when I tripped over a rock that had been kicked under my feet, nearly causing me to tumble over the edge. I watched as loose rocks cascaded down the mountainside. An image of my body among them filtered into my head, and my breathing became ragged. Rowan had caught me by my elbow and reeled me back against his chest. My eyes were still focused on the edge when he brought his hand to my face and turned it toward him.

"Can you look where you're going?" His words were curt, but his touch was oddly gentle.

He scrunched his nose and examined me for any injuries.

"Sorry," I said breathlessly.

He released me and inhaled sharply.

"Just... watch your step." His voice was stern, but raspier than normal. He resumed guiding the horse up the road, and I tentatively followed. A crisp clearing of someone's throat had me turning my head backward.

It was Aeva.

"Oops," she said with a devilish grin.

When we reached the plateau, the colors of the setting sun painted the Sky. I looked out over the vast landscape, and my breath caught at both its beauty and the height. Rowan had given the command for us to make camp at the pass' large, cavernous entrance. My eyes could see little inside because of its midnight interior that burrowed deep.

I understood that going through the mountains was quicker than going over, but I did not entirely trust the stability of a cave that had been carved out over a century ago. The stuffy scent of musk wafted through the air. I knew it would only grow thicker the deeper we ventured.

Rowan and the other Veilers began setting up camp while the culled took their blankets and claimed a spot further in. Torches were lit and lined up against the rock. A few Veilers set off into the tunnel, clapping their hands loudly and letting out shouts to scare away any predators lurking in the shadows. I peered back into the darkness of the mountain, unsure of what I would see, but I was met with nothing but stale air.

One Veiler, Yan, was building a small fire within the cave. He was a large, burly man with a long black beard and a hairline that started mid-scalp. Despite his sheer size and power, he didn't radiate the same dangerous energy that the others did. He had a calmness that made me feel steadier.

I walked over to Yan and sat close by while he struck two pieces of stone together. I watched silently as sparks kindled the fire before us. There was no one in our immediate area, and my curiosity beckoned me. I'd rarely spoken to any Veilers other than Rowan, except for my occasional spat with Renata and the few times Balor attempted to attack me.

"Why are you here?" Either my voice or bluntness startled him, because he jolted back slightly, brows half-raised as he faced me.

"What?" His voice was ragged, almost like he was out of practice.

"Why are you a Veiler? You hardly seem like the type."

I understood why the Veilers would want him. His sheer strength and stature could make anyone cower at the sight of him alone. However, his gentle nature opposed that visual persona.

There was always a twinge of sadness clouding him. I saw him smile only once, and he never laughed when the others joked.

Yan gave me a small, knowing nod of his head. His next words were soft as he returned his gaze to the glowing embers.

"My son passed away five years ago." His words were a brutal truth I wasn't prepared to hear. His being a Veiler meant he was not innocent, but I couldn't help feeling empathetic toward him. Even if only because we carried a similar pain.

"What was his name?"

Yan didn't answer right away, and it made me wonder if he had to search the deepest reaches of his mind for the answer, if he pushed it back far enough so as not to be haunted by it every day. Or perhaps it was the exact opposite. Maybe the name was always on the tip of his tongue, trying to escape, but the release of it was worse than keeping it at bay.

"Arlo." His jaw clenched as he peeled off his coat, pulling up his long sleeve to reveal the name tattooed in delicate script along his forearm. He let me stare at it for a few moments before covering it once more.

"That's a beautiful name."

"He was a beautiful boy." The silence was icy, even in the presence of heat licking at our skin from the fire.

"I lost my brother and father many years ago," I said just as softly, and Yan flicked his eyes back to mine. His honesty made me want to impart some of my own, which I seldom acknowledged. "I understand the control that grief can have over a person. I did many things that I regret in the wake of losing them, all in attempts to curb the pain. Yet it never really goes away."

"I don't regret joining the Order." His words were more bitter than they had been seconds prior.

"Why?"

My confusion must have been clear on my face, because Yan let out a small sigh.

"Arlo was our miracle child, blessed to us by Netali herself. He had his mother's eyes but... but he had my face." I watched his chest shudder as he took in a deep breath and closed his eyes. "Every time she looked at me, it reminded her of him." His eyes opened, and great sorrow flickered in the reflecting flames. "Being in the Order keeps me away while still allowing me to make sure she remains provided for. When my service is done, I pray I will return home to a wife who can look upon my face once more."

"But Veilers can serve for years, sometimes decades, before they are pardoned. You might be an old man by the time you return home. How do you know she will wait for you?"

Yan rolled his shoulders back and stiffened his neck. I thought that perhaps my line of questioning had gone too far. However, it didn't stop him from replying.

He looked to the dimming light on the horizon, and his throat bobbed.

"I don't."

"Why risk it then?"

"Love."

That was all he said before he suddenly stood and walked away.

I continued to sit on the stone floor, listening to the crackling firewood. What Yan had said struck a nerve deep within me. My mind stirred in the silence that followed until all distant conversations faded away.

My thoughts were littered with flashes of a large, calloused hand, firmly holding my own. The sound of my father's boisterous laugh rang in my ears. His blue eyes were as pale as mine, and his smile was the warmest sight that sent pangs to my chest. After all these years, I still felt the space created by his absence. I spent most of my past grieving the loss of my brother, too embittered to mourn my father.

Tears slipped, burning my cheeks. I quickly wiped them away and stood, glancing around to see if anyone was watching. There were too many people, and I needed to get away before I made a fool of myself and had a breakdown for everyone to see. Thankfully, no one seemed to notice when I quietly disappeared outside the cave.

I ventured just far enough away from the entrance to feel both security and solitude. On the way out, I bit my lip so hard to keep myself from sobbing that I drew blood. The altitude made it harder for me to catch my breath as the world spun around me. I sank to the Ground and anchored my knees tightly to my chest, dropping my head between my legs. I let the thick mountain air settle in my lungs while I tried and failed to take purposeful deep breaths.

Once my breathing evened out, I leaned my head back against the hard stone of the mountain and tried to imagine absorbing its grounding power. It was working until a gust of wind hit my face, making me shudder and my teeth chatter.

"All alone?" A dark voice purred.

My eyes snapped open, and my muscles seized. The silhouette before me was none other than the shadow that had been haunting my nightmares for the past few weeks.

*Balor.*

# CHAPTER 19

*"A sword taken is a sword earned.*
*Bear your steel with pride."*
*- Article 4, Section 2, of the Veiled Compendium*

Balor twirled one of his beloved daggers, picking at the underside of his nails like this was a game. There were no threats present in his eyes, just a wicked promise of death—my death.

"One would think you'd learned your lesson about being alone in the dark. Dangerous creatures lurk there."

I stumbled to my feet and carefully stepped backward. He let out a cruel laugh that twisted my insides. I could practically smell my fear—and so could he, judging by his widening grin. That damn split lip had healed, leaving behind a faint line of pink skin.

"I dare you to scream. I *want* you to call out for help so that they can see how pathetic you truly are."

I wanted to do what he said. But I couldn't. I would not die today, not like this.

"I won our fight. Remember that," I taunted. I just needed time to think.

Maybe someone would recognize my absence and come searching, but I wasn't that optimistic about it. We were far enough away from the cavern that he could still lunge and strike me down before another arrived.

Balor's grin immediately dropped, and his left eye twitched. He took a step closer to me, and I nearly stopped breathing altogether.

"I made an error. One I shall now remedy."

"What was the mistake? Underestimating me?"

I drifted my hand toward my pocket. If I grabbed the knife I kept there, then I could defend myself. Hopefully.

"The mistake was taking too long to play with my prey. I got too excited and gave you the upper hand."

"If you kill me, Rowan will—"

"Rowan," Balor snorted, "has been far too distracted of late. You may have fooled them all into thinking that you are divinely chosen, but I know better. A pathetic waste like you could never be chosen."

My hand inched closer to my pocket.

"I have been looking forward to our rematch," he said, eyes falling to my hand just as it slipped into my pocket.

Then he smiled once more—I'd been caught.

Balor lunged at me, and I barely sidestepped his attack. I heard the scraping of his blade on stone. I pulled the knife out of my pocket and clutched it tightly. He saw the weapon and sneered at me. He clearly remembered how it had come into my possession, and that fueled his hatred even more.

He lunged again—and I dropped to the Ground, barely missing his attack. I was getting slower and more out of breath.

"Do you really think that little blade will save you? Go on—show me your courage," he growled.

The whistle of steel cut the air before I even turned—Balor's dagger missed my ribs by inches.

"Come on! Fight me!"

Once Balor pivoted to strike me, I grabbed a handful of dirt from the trail and threw it at his eyes. He cursed as I temporarily blinded his vision. His boot caught on something—small, gnarled, and buried under the dirt. A root. He stumbled, still half-blind.

He pitched forward, off-balance, rubbing at his eyes.

In that second, I reacted. I didn't plan. I didn't aim.

I stabbed.

The knife drove into his side—not deep, not clean—but it hit.

He howled and swung wildly, still not able to see clearly, slicing my forearm.

He took another step back, but this time his foot missed the ledge.

His bloodshot eyes widened.

"No—"

Balor flailed, trying to grab the edge—but there was nothing to hold. He tumbled backward into the abyss.

I stood there for several seconds, blood dripping down my arm, processing the haunting look of a man on the brink of death. A death that I had called forth. I dropped to my knees, and my limbs shook violently.

"Are you hurt?" The voice pierced the ringing in my ears. I turned to the source, only to find Renata carefully assessing me from several paces away. I bent over and hurled up everything I'd eaten that day. "You're going into shock. Put your head between your legs."

I bent over and did as she bade me. I heaved, but nothing more came up. Renata came closer and took a piece of cloth and bound it around my wounded arm.

He had sliced me good.

"Why?" The word was broken, but it was all I could muster.

"No one was there my first time, and I wish someone had been. It makes the burden a bit more bearable—to share that with someone."

"Don't... don't tell *him. Please.*"

"He'll have to know about Balor, but everything that happened after will stay here—it won't follow us."

"Thank you." I sputtered a sigh of relief.

"Control your emotions, otherwise everyone will know everything."

Renata sauntered off, leaving me panting and gripping my legs with bruising strength. When I could muster the energy to move, I tentatively lifted the knife from the Ground and stared at all the blood. I could look nowhere else. The blood was everywhere.

It stained the blade, the Ground, and my shaking hands.

# CHAPTER 20

*"Death is a shadow that follows everyone and haunts some."*
*- The Old Book*

The blood wouldn't wash out. No matter how hard I scrubbed, it lingered.

Four days had passed since Balor's death. Four days of sleepless nights, seeing the haunting look on his face as he realized his death was imminent. A death caused by my hands.

Logically, I understood it had been his life or mine. While I was glad to still be breathing, I couldn't shake the feeling that I had sullied my soul.

I worried about the day I met Anam. I wondered if he would see me for what I was: a soul fit for eternal drowning.

I knew I had sent Balor there, but I prayed I had not condemned myself as well.

How was I supposed to get justice for my family if I could barely function after killing one of them in self-defense? Balor was vile and cruel, but his death still kept me awake at night. I think a part of me believed I would take down the Veilers through dismantling their very system of governance, not bloodshed. That I would find a weakness in their armor and expose it.

From what I gathered by listening to the dispersed chatter surrounding me, we were only about a week away from our final destination. Even though no one stated exactly where or what our final destination was, everyone was weary enough from travel to relax at the prospect of our journey ending.

Rowan had kept his distance during the past four days. He knew what had become of Balor, everyone did, but he never pushed for any details on the matter. I wasn't sure if Renata had gone against her word and told him just how much Balor's death had affected me, or if it was just that apparent.

Either way, he left me to my suffering in peace.

It was supper, and everyone lined up around the new fire that Yan had built. The standard bone-carved bowls were handed out, and stew was ladled in. I kept myself seated several paces away from the fire; I didn't want to be that close to the others. I'd also lost my appetite over the last few days. While I knew it was weakening me, I didn't have the inner strength to fight its pull.

I watched the other culled eat their meals and chatter among themselves. They didn't care that I had taken down a Veiler. To them, I was still a traitor, and I wasn't sure there was anything I could do to change that.

Footsteps fell behind me. Fire-lit red hair shimmered in my peripheral vision, and I already knew what awaited me. I pulled my knees closer to my chest to prepare for the onslaught of her judgment.

"Starving yourself won't bring him back, nor should you want it to."

I glared at her in silent reply. I had expected her to scorn me for being weak, but I didn't suspect her to speak ill of one of her own. She rolled her eyes at my suspicion.

"He's dead. You killed him. If you ask me, the world is all the better for it. Stop weakening yourself further just because you lack a spine and suffer from an overactive moral compass."

There it was—the belittlement.

"What even is the difference between you and me?" I whispered.

"I'm not a sack of bones keen on further drying myself out like jerky. I'm not a pretentious—"

Growing frustrated, I growled.

"That's not what I meant, and you know it." I twisted back toward the crackling embers, ready to forget our conversation entirely.

"If you are referring to my aptitude at killing, it is rather spectacular, especially given I've only ever used it twice."

I darted my gaze toward her once more. It was a reaction that she surely had predicted, going by her smug expression.

"Despite the clothes I wear and the title I carry, I'm not interested in adding more tallies to an already too-long list. After Balor fell, I told you it was a burden to be responsible for even one death, self-defense or naught. That was not pity. That was me telling you I understood the weight."

I wiped away the tear threatening to fall as she continued.

"There are people here with a ledger of souls that even Anam would be jealous of, but there are also those of us who do not savor the thought of turning into such cruel creatures of death and destruction. Every Veiled One's story for donning the black is different, much like every culled one's story is. So that is the true difference between you and me. I acknowledge the gray, whereas all you see is black and white."

She made a point of gesturing to our different clothes for emphasis.

"I'm going to tell you what I once told Rowan: Lies are easy to believe; the truth is brutal. So sit, starve, sulk. Whatever choice you make is exactly that—your choice. Don't expect pity. Not from me. Not from anyone."

"You think this is easy for me?" My voice cracked like brittle bone.

"No. But that doesn't mean you get to brood like a child all day. Get up, eat, and then decide that you're going to get past this."

With that last thought, she left to join the others queuing for supper.

Her words kindled the dimmest spark, but it was something—a light in my darkness.

# CHAPTER 21

*"What you choose to remember holds power—even long after the moment has passed."*
*- The Old Book*

A sharp kick to my ribs tore me out of sleep.

I cracked my eyes and found that Rowan was hovering over me with his arms crossed, glowering.

He roused me with his boot. Not a gentle nudge, but a soldier's command.

"What are you doing?" I groaned and attempted to close my eyes again.

Rowan kicked again, but harder, sending shocks through my side.

"*What*?" I spat, sitting up on my elbows and looking around the cavern. The others were still asleep and nestled under their blankets.

"I have given you space, but my patience has run out. You are going to get up, and then we are going to go for a walk."

I rolled my eyes and sank back into my blankets. The action earned me another swift kick, but this time to my thigh. I winced at the sharp pain.

"That'll bruise!" I growled while imagining sticking pins in his eye sockets. Rowan saw the glimmer of animosity in my stare, and his lips twitched.

"Anger. Good. We can work with that. Now, get up."

I reluctantly got to my feet. Rowan's arms were still crossed as he tapped his fingers on his forearm impatiently. I scowled at him as he gestured for me to walk.

We meandered for several minutes in silence. Though the silence wasn't awkward, I could still feel the lurking tension between us. I knew an uncomfortable conversation was on the horizon, and that Rowan would not allow me to evade it any longer. He put the lantern on the floor and looked at me expectantly.

"I don't know what you want from me." I huffed, rubbing one arm with the other.

"I want you to stop letting yourself decay right before my very eyes."

"I'm not sure why you've suddenly grown interested in my well-being, captor."

"Will you give that shit a rest?" He sounded genuinely exasperated. "For such a bright woman, you can be so incredibly daft sometimes. Once we reach the Crown of Ethoria, I will have no say in what becomes of you. I will have no power to protect you there. Everything that happens will be out of my control."

Every whisper I'd ever heard about The Crown rushed back to me like a flood. A place no one returned from. A place meant to be forgotten.

"Our destination is the Crown of Ethoria?" My jaw dropped.

"I suppose that would be all you heard," he grumbled.

I ignored that comment as well, not wanting to touch on anything emotionally related to him. Instead, I thought about the landmark.

The waves that crashed onto the three peninsulas, which jutted out like a crown, were said to be hundreds of feet high, coating the land in thick sheets of ice. The coastal storms that brewed there were notorious for being the most lethal in all of Ethoria. Even the wild beasts of the tundra didn't dare venture that far north.

While the Great North was uninhabitable, the Crown of Ethoria was inescapable. I had heard whispers of a secret prison located there, but the concept seemed too far-fetched to have any merit.

I understood the appeal of extreme isolation, but the journey itself to reach the continent's northeastern peaks was so perilous that the prisoners would likely already be dead upon arrival. That made it useless for anything other than a death march.

Was that what was happening to the culled? Surely not. They needed us for something, not to kill us outright.

"What will happen to us all when we get there?" I asked as my mind continued to race with infinite possibilities. None of which ended with my returning home.

Rowan sighed and closed his eyes briefly.

"I can't speak about it. I took an oath."

He seemed oddly conflicted about that.

"Of course you can't." I scoffed, looking at anything but him in the dimly lit cavern.

"This is not the conversation I wanted to have with you."

"No, you want to ridicule me for not being a monster like you."

His posture stiffened, and his eyes narrowed.

"You're right, Mavis, I am a monster. I have killed, both in and out of service, and I do not carry an ounce of remorse for those I have sent to an early grave. They do not deserve it."

I glowered, but he continued.

"Guilt does not erase sin; it only amplifies it. So why should I bask in sorrow, letting it slowly eat away at my sanity until the day I become as hollow as the corpses I've buried? You may hold the opinion that I deserve death for all that I have done, and perhaps you are right. However, life is sacred, and I refuse to be a coward who doesn't embrace it."

His gaze pierced mine, and his expression softened. There was a plea for understanding and acceptance there. So I offered him a single, gut-wrenching truth.

"I didn't want to kill him. He was wretched and tried to kill me first, but despite that, I didn't want to end his life. Even after the first time he cornered me, when you stopped me from striking him, I'm not sure I could have done it. Death is final; there is no returning from it. Who am I to be someone's reaper?"

"That's commendable. However, others will look to use your bleeding heart against you. I cannot say much about where we are going until we arrive, but I can say this: the weak die. I don't just mean the physically weak, though they perish quickly as well."

I swallowed hard and gave Rowan a timid nod.

Throughout our journey, Rowan and I developed an unspoken truce.

However, the more passionate Rowan was when he spoke and made me see things from his point of view, the more I humanized him and the others. Which was dangerous. We were natural enemies and nothing more.

It was the way it had to be.

Rowan reached out to touch my arm, but I shrugged away. A flicker of hurt flashed in his eyes before it was quickly swept away, and he dropped his arm just as fast. His mask of indifference returned, and he started back toward the camp.

I couldn't forget that he was the enemy.

Even if I wasn't so sure anymore.

# CHAPTER 22

*"Balance is what life craves, and without it, everything will perish.*
*Even the gods have their limitations."*
*- The Old Book*

The first breath of tundra air cut like glass. As glad as I was to see the sun again, the blistering wind outside the caves jolted my senses.

It was the bitter season, and we were in the Great North. The landscape was white with snow, and the temperature was well below freezing. Rowan said that traveling in winter was safer because most of the beasts inhabiting this part of the region were hibernating. He said it was a matter of choosing the lesser evil, and I wasn't sure I agreed with him on which was which.

He merely asked, "Would you rather lose a toe or your life?"

I'd kept Rowan's accidental revelation about our final destination a secret. The other culled still despised me, and I was not looking forward to sharing a tent with them once more. We had slept in the open while journeying throughout the underpass, so there were no opportunities for the culled to harm me without being caught. Now there would be.

I spent the first night in the tent rubbing the hilt of my knife repeatedly and keeping my eyes open, watching the others warily as they slept. I hadn't dared to close my eyes for longer than a second.

Lily had given me a knowing smirk. The others huddled close together for warmth, but since I didn't have that option, I silently shook and gripped my blankets tight the entire night.

The next morning, I kept nodding off while riding. I was just as terrified to sleep while riding with Rowan as I was in the communal tent. Both fears had their reasons, of course.

"Are you going to tell me why you are swaying with such force that my arms can barely keep you upright?" His voice brought me back to reality, and I blinked twice to clear my vision.

"I didn't sleep well," I murmured, barely avoiding slurring my speech. I was beyond exhausted.

"And why is that?" Rowan pressed.

I shrugged.

Rowan grunted—apparently, he didn't appreciate having the gesture turned on him.

"Answer the question, Mavis," he demanded.

"There may have been some miscommunication between me and the other culled, and now they hate me."

"What kind of miscommunication?"

"The kind where they think I betrayed them."

Tense silence followed—but only for a few moments.

"*What*?" Rowan snapped, but I didn't reply. A few more seconds passed, long enough for Rowan to understand what had occurred. "They heard about what happened with the Rebels, didn't they? *Fuck.*" He took one hand off the reins and ran it through his hair. Then, instead of taking the reins again, he gripped my hip. "Have they threatened you?"

"It's not important."

"It damn well is important if you aren't getting any sleep because you are too busy staying alert to protect yourself. You should have told me this as soon as the issue arose. How long have they been threatening you?"

"Since Summit's Ridge," I whispered, and felt his grip on my hip tighten. I didn't think he was conscious of the action. "I don't need you to step in. That will only confirm their suspicions. I can handle this on my own."

Rowan forced out a humorless chuckle.

"Like you've been handling it over the past week? No, this has gone too far."

"You can't tell them to stand down, or it will confirm that I've sided with the Veilers."

"I won't. However, you will sleep in my tent until we reach our destination. It's where you will be safest."

"That's even *worse!* They already think I'm bedding you. Sleeping in your tent all but confirms it!"

"There is nowhere else for you to sleep, not one that I trust. I cannot vouch for every Veiled One here. I cannot trust that they will not... *take advantage* of the temporary sleeping arrangements." The insinuation made my stomach roll. "Besides, you just have to make it to the end of our journey. After that, anyone who attacks you will forfeit their life."

The only reason I held back from complaining more about the situation was what I heard reflected in his voice—fear. There was a lot of anger, so the fear was almost undetectable. Except I had heard it, and I knew it was on my behalf that he was afraid.

Later, when I entered Rowan's tent, my eyes immediately found him lounging shirtless atop his bedroll. He was mask-less again, and I still wasn't used to the sight of it. I thought the cold was brutal—until I felt the heat of Rowan's gaze when it met mine.

Rowan gestured with his head to the blankets in the corner, already laid out.

I lay down, but my eyes refused to shut. My interactions with some of the culled from dinner played in my head. Specifically, when Aeva *accidentally* bumped into me and made me spill half my food. The others just laughed.

When I knelt to pick up what I could, someone muttered, "Veiler whore." I stood and walked away, no longer having an appetite. I decided it was best I head off to bed early. Gods knew I needed the extra rest.

Rowan's sleep-ridden voice broke through my train of thought.

"Do you want me to put the light out?"

I did actually. I didn't need to see him so exposed. It wasn't because I was modest. He only had his shirt off—but that was enough to notice certain attributes I had no business seeing, let alone appreciating. Veilers had muscles. It was a laborious job. However, reciting that fact didn't make how much I enjoyed the image of them disappear.

"It isn't too bright. I'll be fine," I said instead.

Rowan shrugged and went back to reading.

My body was splayed out on the blanket, but it refused to settle. Despite the frigid temperature outside, I was overheating. Time felt like it was stretching on forever. The silence was deafening, and it was eating at my sanity.

So I broke it.

"Why did you become a Veiler?" I asked Rowan. I had been wondering about it for a while now, considering he never acted quite how I expected a Veiler to. He certainly was no Balor.

"I didn't have a choice."

He had said something similar before, but it only made me more curious.

"Why didn't you have a choice?"

There was a long moment of hesitation. Long enough that I thought he was going to ignore the question altogether. I would have if I had been in his shoes. None of this was my business, and it only further gave away bits of his identity, which could later be used against him if I escaped. He didn't seem troubled by that, though, because he answered.

"I angered my parents, and this was their version of punishment." His honesty carried the sting of lingering pain. I almost felt sorry for him—almost.

"Why not just run away instead?"

"They would have found me no matter where I went, so I didn't see the point."

"Are your parents important people?"

"They used to be."

I heard Rowan shuffle, so I turned to face him. I watched as he leaned over and blew out the candle in the lantern, encasing the room in darkness.

And in that darkness, I realized something that terrified me.

I was starting to see *him*.

# CHAPTER 23

*"To show respect, you wear black and forgo all past identities.*
*Until the day you shed the black, you are a sentry, a servant of the Ethorian gods and*
*the Ravaryn Kingdom."*
*- Article 1, Section 2, of the Veiled Compendium*

I could trace each rib through my skin, and my hip bone was sharper, pressing painfully against the saddle as we rode. I had always been thin, but never this skeletal. Though traveling with the Veilers had given me muscle and calluses, my body fat had reduced to unhealthy levels.

Rowan kept me tightly anchored to his chest with his arms wrapped securely around my abdomen. Without his arms around me, I'd have been blown away.

The so-called Great North was nothing but a pathetic, bitter wasteland. We had been traveling for half a week in the barren lands, and I could confidently say that there was nothing *great* that far north. We were surrounded by snow, ice, and the constant screeching of the wind.

I was a summer child being forced to endure blisters from the cold, chattering teeth, and chapped lips.

I asked Rowan how the horses could survive such severe temperatures, and he said that they were bred for it. How any creature could be bred for this weather was beyond me.

We spent the first few days in the tundra enduring harsh winds that bit and clawed at our freezing bodies. Despite Rowan covering us with two thick bear hides, my bones still rattled. However, that was nothing compared to the storm that settled upon us on the fifth day.

On the fifth day, we could barely see through the blizzard that plagued us.

I heard a piercing cry coming from one of the nearby horses trudging through the snow. Several muffled screams followed shortly after. I couldn't see through the haze of white, so I nudged Rowan in question. My tongue was too dry and cracked to speak much.

"That would be the frostbite," he grumbled.

"It hurts that much?"

"No, that's the sound of it being removed."

I squeezed my eyes together, attempting to push the agonizing imagery out of my head. Then I covered my ears to ignore the strangled, blood-curdling cries. I tried not to think about who it was. They probably wanted me dead.

I squinted, trying my best to peer through the thick flurries, and in the distance I saw something odd. Something that did not belong in this landscape.

As we advanced toward the strange spherical structure, I noticed that the two lights that had originally caught my eye were posted on either side of a wide door—at least I assumed it was a door.

The building's architecture was like none I had ever seen before. It was made completely of smooth silver metal. It was also rather small. I thought we could all fit, but there wouldn't be much room for movement.

We approached the metal complex, and Rowan slipped off the saddle. He trudged through the snow, making his way to the front of the building. Rowan then pressed a large red button on the door, and it lit up instantly.

Upon closer look, the button and the two sconces on the side of the door appeared to be of the same make. The material seemed familiar to me. It looked like the precious material my father brought back home once—*plastic*. And the light they illuminated was not normal candlelight.

My inspection was disrupted by a loud buzzing sound that rang out. The door pulled apart, revealing sharp, serrated edges that reminded me much of metal teeth. The image of getting squished between them made me automatically stiffen.

When Rowan let out a loud whistle, all the horses rushed into the building. The inside was extremely bright, so bright it burned. Panels of light were plastered to the ceiling. They were just like the sun, but unnatural. I hated them.

The inside was just one room with a grated floor that I couldn't see anything below, only darkness. Rowan stalked over to a small, rectangular box on the wall that featured an array of numbered buttons. Then, he pressed a sequence of numbers, and within seconds, I felt the floor move.

I panicked, clutching onto the horse. Several of the culled let out minor screams and yelps, which made me feel justified in my fear. I'd never experienced a world-shake, but I'd read about them. It wasn't until I heard the amused chuckle of a Veiler that I noticed the world wasn't shaking—we were sinking.

The entire metal platform beneath us rumbled as it descended. The walls stayed still, but the Ground dropped as if we were being lowered into it.

Rowan came over and stroked our horse, subtly moving his hand to pinch my knee. I buried my face in the horse's mane, putting it level with Rowan's.

"Hey, it's alright," he whispered in my ear.

"What's happening?" My voice quivered.

"It's just an elevator."

"What's an *elevator*?"

"A contraption that transports people to different levels of a building. The facility has three levels, but only one of them is above Ground. The upper level only serves as an entry point to the lower ones."

"So, no stairs?" I swallowed back the bit of bile that had crept up my throat.

"There are stairs in other parts, but those aren't used nearly as much. Elevators are the most common form of transportation here. Though the others are much smaller than this one. This elevator is the biggest because it has to carry many people and animals. It's also the only one that can reach the surface."

The elevator stopped when it landed at what I assumed was the bottom. The wide steel doors opened once more, and I was met with the sight of pristine white walls and reflective tile floors. A woman was standing just outside, sporting a wide smile and shoulders hunched to her ears. She was dressed in a matte baby blue pantsuit, and her brunette hair was pulled back tightly into a high ponytail.

She unclasped her hands, and her mouth opened before she started speaking.

"Hello everyone, my name is Corsica Marwood! I am very excited to get to know everyone in the coming weeks. In the meantime, I'd like to welcome you to our facility! We take great pride in the research that we conduct here and are endlessly thankful for all of our wonderful program participants!"

Her chirpy voice made my head ache.

"If you will please follow me," she continued, "I would like to take you to your quarters and give you all a chance to wash up before meeting the most important person at the facility—my father!"

Most of the Veilers broke off to lead the horses somewhere else, but a few Veilers, including Renata and Rowan, remained with the culled. Those of us who remained followed Corsica down a hallway filled with even more panels of fire-less light.

These lights did not allow for any shadows, which meant there would be no hiding here.

Corsica's black heels clicked and clanked on the floor as she charismatically preached the importance of the facility's research. Coincidentally, she never once mentioned *what* that research was or *how* the research was conducted. She did, however, refer to us all as participants in "the project."

It meant that whatever research they were doing here included us somehow, and that fact made me extremely apprehensive.

We reached our "wing," as Corsica had called it, which was just a large oval room that seemed like the sterile version of what was supposed to be a gathering space. It looked like a waiting room, with generic decor and too-firm seating. There was another rectangular box hanging high on the wall, but this one was much larger, and it was flashing various moving images. Attached to the main area were five smaller hallways that branched off in different directions.

"Each of you has been assigned a room and corresponding roommate for the duration of your stay here," Corsica said with all her teeth showing. I knew she was trying to come across as someone familiar and friendly, but I could see the predator she truly was.

"And exactly how long is our stay?" One of the culled spoke up. Everyone looked at her and then back at Corsica expectantly. We were all wondering the same thing.

"That depends entirely on your performance in the program. Know that if you succeed in the program, both you and your family will be richly compensated.

Not to mention the glory and admiration you will receive from the royal family itself!" There were a few subtle gasps, but the rest of us remained suspicious. It was far too vague and promising to be true.

"How does one 'succeed' in the program?" A boy no older than eighteen asked.

"That, my dear boy, is an excellent question. One that my father, the head chairperson of the GRC in charge of running the program, is more qualified to answer. I will send the sentries to collect you from your rooms in half an hour. Please use that time judiciously to dress and acclimate yourselves. See you all soon!" She waved, fluttering her fingers down into her palm, and strolled away.

I followed one of the Veiler's directions to go to my room. Said directions included a guttural "C-7" and a finger pointing to the hallway labeled C. I muttered a sarcastic "thank you" and tottered down the hallway, disoriented.

Rowan had left, just as he warned. Yet it still stung.

I found my room. It was nothing grand, just two twin beds, several feet apart. The bedspread was much like everything else in the complex—brilliant white. One bed had sheets slightly ruffled and pulled back.

There was one abstract piece of art hanging on the wall, featuring some shades of red and orange. But that was it as far as the diversity of the facility's color palette was concerned.

Across the beds were two sets of dresser drawers and a large circular mirror between them. Attached to the room was a small bathroom with a toilet and a lone showerhead. There was no bathroom door or curtain.

How wonderful.

I looked through the dresser that was directly across from the unused twin bed, assuming it was meant for me. There were three drawers: the first had several pairs of underwear, and two corsets. The second had four dresses with shades of white, red, blue, and green. The third drawer had two pairs of black flats.

I didn't wear dresses. Ever. They reminded me too much of my father.

The thought of wearing a dress for the first time in years in *this* place—for *these* people—made my skin itch. I wasn't an object that they got to dress up and parade about.

Despite my anger, I needed to play along enough to bide my time. I was finally here, the place with answers about Willam. Through clenched teeth, I selected the blue dress and black flats. I placed them on top of the dresser and made my way to the shower.

I needed to scrub my skin off. It smelled that strongly.

We had plumbing in Oak Hollow, but nothing this fancy. The water was always lukewarm, and the toilets had cranks instead of petite metal levers. Given the climate, I thought the water would be cold as ice, but it was surprisingly warm. There was a selection of ornate floral soaps on the counter that made me frown.

They were trying to make us comfortable, and nothing good came from letting down one's guard.

It made me even more cautious.

# CHAPTER 24

*"A kingdom without faith has no moral direction.*
*If we put our faith in scripture, we are saved."*
*- Article 4, Section 7, of the Veiled Compendium*

A knock at the chamber door startled me.

"Ms. Ashbone?" a voice called, muffled by the door. "I'm Karina, your designated sentry. I'll be escorting you to the dining hall."

I opened it to find a tall woman in all black. No mask, but she didn't need one. Her posture, her clipped politeness—it all screamed Veiler. Or "sentry," as they called themselves here. It was almost funny, the effort they went to in renaming things, as if language could change what they really were.

Karina corralled a group of us into the hall. We moved like sheep, tired and quiet, until the doors to the dining hall swung open—and I halted mid-step.

The room was massive. Higher ceilings than Summit's Ridge. Longer tables. Fifteen, at least six already filled. Culled and Veilers alike sat side by side, eating from trays topped with actual food—meat, greens, cheese, fruit. My stomach gave a traitorous growl.

I took my place in the line, watching as trays were handed through a square cutout in the wall. When it was my turn, the warmth of the bread in my hands almost brought tears to my eyes.

I chose a half-filled table far from everyone else and ate slowly, savoring every bite.

The silence didn't last long.

A deep voice boomed from the front of the room.

I looked up to the dais and found the speaker: a man in an amber tunic, hair the color of slate. He bore the Ravaryn Seal, pinned above his heart—two ravens perched upon a willow branch.

His smile was the same as Corsica's, just stretched wider.

"Good evening and welcome to our facility," he announced, voice rolling like thunder. "My name is Marcum Marwood, head chairperson of the Guild for Religious Conservation. I oversee the program here."

He paused, sweeping the room with his gaze. It lingered on faces like a weight, searching for cracks.

"I know the journey here was difficult..."

I scoffed, loud enough to earn a few glances.

"...but I hope you find comfort in knowing that you are now safe. You will be taken care of here."

*Safe.*

As if being dragged here against our will had been mercy.

"You are free to roam the facility as you please when your presence is not required for program activities."

His tone was casual, almost warm—too warm.

And then, the illusion cracked.

"I'm sure many of you are wondering why you were chosen," Marcum said.

His eyes glinted like glass as he grinned.

"You may be familiar with a certain passage from *The Old Book*... a passage some call 'the prophecy.'"

I stopped chewing.

Every culled one within earshot went still.

"We believe this prophecy is not allegory, but instruction," he continued, voice dropping lower. Softer. More dangerous. "A divine formula. And you—each of you—are a part of it."

I gripped my tray harder.

"True ascension," he said, his hands spreading like wings, "can only be achieved by a pure soul. But we believe purification is possible—of the body, the blood, and the spirit. Through science, discipline, and faith."

The bread in my mouth turned to ash.

Lies. It was all lies, and people were dead because of it.

"There are only two rules," Marcum said, raising a single finger. "Rule one: participate in all mandatory project testing."

He paused, letting the word *mandatory* sink in

He lifted a second finger. "Two: Harm none, except in self-defense."

His voice brightened, almost cheerful now.

"If you cannot abide by these rules, then you will face certain consequences."

The way he said *consequences* sent a shiver crawling up my spine.

"You are, of course, free to leave. The doors are not locked." His eyes flicked toward the entrance. "Be warned that they do not reopen. And the cold here can be quite formidable."

The silence that followed was louder than his voice.

Finally, he clapped his hands together once, sharp enough to make a few people flinch.

"I think that is enough information for one night. I will see you all at breakfast, where I will speak a bit more about routine. Until then, rest easy, and welcome to The Ascension Project."

The Veilers burst into applause.

The culled did not.

My head spun with questions I didn't want to ask.

How many had died in the name of this *project*?

What happened if I failed? Where did I go?

I felt a hand on my arm and jumped. The familiar calluses gave him away immediately, and my nerves settled slightly.

Rowan's grip was tight with tension. He had also forgone his mask.

"Make it to breakfast," he said, low and clipped.

He let go and walked off before I could ask what he meant.

I sat there motionless as crowds of people moved past and around me. I was frozen and reeling from all I had learned, and all that I still did not understand.

For the first time since Oak Hollow, I wasn't sure what would become of me.

# CHAPTER 25

*"Sentries take no spouses.*
*Your attention belongs to your kingdom and your gods.*
*Bearing children is dishonorable."*
*- Article 2, Section 1, of the Veiled Compendium*

### The Facility - Day 2

I was being watched.

I opened my eyes and saw a young girl sitting on the bed next to mine. She didn't make a move to hurt me, so that was good.

Dressed in only my underthings, I pulled the blanket up a little higher before I spoke.

"Who are you?"

"I'm your roommate."

My shoulders relaxed. Not a threat.

"What's your name?" I asked the girl. She sat with her legs crossed on her bed, twiddling her fingers on the end of one of her tight, brassy braids.

The girl hesitated before speaking barely above a whisper. "Talia."

"How old are you, Talia?"

"Thirteen."

My throat constricted. I knew she was young. It was evident from her innocent appearance. But hearing it still made my chest squeeze. She was too young to be here.

"Well, Talia, I'm Mavis. It's nice to meet you."

She tilted her head, examining me. "You're the one they call a traitor."

"Well, don't believe everything you hear," I said, sitting up a little straighter.

"I don't," she said firmly but sweetly.

Talia gave me a tentative smile before standing and heading for the door.

My stomach rumbled. "Is it time for breakfast?"

Something I couldn't name quickly flashed in her eyes. I waited for her to explain, to say what she was thinking, but she only nodded and walked away.

The interaction had been slightly awkward, but at least she didn't seem to harbor any resentment toward me like the other culled. That was promising.

Rowan had told me to "make it to breakfast," whatever that meant.

While he was still a Veiler, meaning I implicitly couldn't trust him, I could begrudgingly admit that he cared to some extent about what happened to me. I wasn't sure what his motives were, but it didn't entirely matter. If he was interested in keeping me alive, that was enough for now.

I made my way to the dining hall, got my breakfast, and seated myself toward the back of the room. I ate in silence, impatiently waiting for the man from the night before to reappear and explain exactly what was going on.

I tapped my foot so fast that the table slightly shook from the force of it, earning me a few side glances from the culled around me. Dread was slowly eating at me as I tried to piece together Rowan's warning.

Something was going to happen. I just didn't know what.

Marcum Marwood finally made his appearance half an hour later, a wide grin plastered on his face. It was a facade.

Marcum took the stage and tapped what I heard others refer to as a *microphone*.

"Good morning, participants. I hope you all slept well. It is with a heavy heart that I announce the death of two program participants: Mina Summers and Dorian McFinney. They attempted to flee in the night, and as previously stated, the doors to the outside are not locked. Their frozen bodies were recovered this morning and returned to the Ground as Anam demands it." There was a long moment of silence before Marcum continued. "Anyway, I have a few notes from our head chef here concerning dietary needs..."

His voice trailed off, the room lurched, and it felt as though the walls were closing in on me. I could no longer hear anything other than the alarm ringing in my ears. Just two people who had tried to escape, two lives lost, now reduced to nothing more than a cautionary tale.

Realization dawned on me, and my breath hitched. *That* was what Rowan meant by needing to "make it to breakfast." He wanted me to hear the death roll.

He wanted me to understand just how much danger I was in.

I searched the crowd of Veiled Ones for Rowan's face. They had all stopped wearing masks, probably figuring that their identities were now safe. If we tried to run, we were as dead as Mina and Dorian.

Eventually, I spotted Rowan. He was leaning against the wall, arms crossed, eyes locked on me. When he tilted his head toward the dais, I understood. Look at Marcum.

"I would like to speak briefly about the creation of The Ascension Program..."

Here it came.

"One hundred fifteen years ago, the Ravarie King, Acaelar Bloodborne, had a prophetic dream the night before his coronation..."

I felt the beginnings of a headache blooming behind my eyes.

"He dreamt of salvation—of a mortal ascending into everlasting life. In his vision, the act of ascension was both disintegration and formation... the becoming of pure energy."

A beat of silence passed before he added, "He also foresaw the Stone Plague. The Great Prairie Fire."

A murmur rippled through the crowd. I wasn't the only one trying to make sense of this.

Someone shouted, "It's unnatural!" and several voices agreed in hushed affirmation.

Marcum held up a hand, unbothered. "This building was erected with materials sourced from natural land. This building is not naturally occurring, but does that mean it is *unnatural*? You are currently being warmed by an artificial heating source. Is your comfort and safety so *unnatural*?" he asked coolly. "I challenge you to question any preconceived notions you may have traveled here with. Learn for yourself what the truth is."

When I looked back at Rowan, he was staring at Marcum with a strange, almost wounded expression. Not quite anger. Not quite fear. Something quieter and more personal.

"I'm sure many of you have heard the prophecy," Marcum continued, "but for those unfamiliar, I'll read it aloud now."

He didn't need to. I already knew it. We all did.

"*Death is not the only end. Ascend from ruin and rejoice in being made anew. One must both choose and be chosen. For hidden in flesh and accessed through spirit, a pure soul may find its light at last.*"

The words felt heavier. Less like hope. More like a threat.

Marcum's voice grew smoother, almost reverent. "From Acaelar's vision, we discovered the path to ascension is simple: purification of body, blood, and spirit. That is why this program exists."

I swallowed the bile rising in my throat. If it were so simple, how come they had yet to achieve it?

"As participants, you'll undergo regular blood draws, immunizations, and spiritual evaluations. We have two types of sessions: truth and faith sessions. Truth sessions will target trauma and promote acceptance, cleansing the soul. While faith sessions aim to bring you closer to the divine."

No one moved. No one breathed.

"You are part of something greater than just yourself. You should feel honored."

Then, as if the sermon hadn't ended in the shadow of two dead bodies, "Please report to the infirmary for your initial screenings. After that, the day is yours. I'll see you all tomorrow morning."

Marcum stepped down. The room shifted in eerie unison—chairs scraped, feet shuffled. No one spoke. No one looked at one another.

Not even the Veilers. They stood as if nothing had happened.

Only one stayed still.

Rowan.

His eyes found mine again—steady, unreadable. Arms still crossed. But tension coiled beneath his stillness like a snake in waiting.

I tore my gaze away, heart thudding. My stomach churned. Whether from fear, nausea, or the knowledge that I'd be next on the chopping block—I couldn't tell.

I pushed my tray forward, appetite gone.

And then a hand grabbed my wrist.

I stiffened, my body tensing on instinct, but when I turned, I was met with a pair of wide, anxious brown eyes. Talia. She hadn't said a word to me since we had met that morning, but now her small fingers trembled against my skin.

"We must leave," she whispered. "They're watching."

I looked around. She was right.

The ones stationed at the doors started herding the culled toward the hallway, directing us like livestock. I didn't hesitate. I pried my hand from Talia's grasp and stood, walking with measured steps toward the corridor. There was no reason to resist. There was nowhere to run.

The walk to the infirmary felt longer than it should have, the hallways stretching endlessly under the harsh glow of the overhead lights. I let my feet move forward, step after step, but my mind remained stuck on the prophecy, on the so-called purification process, on the uncertainty of the future.

We waited in a long line for our turn to enter the infirmary. I attempted to enter with Talia, but I was stopped by a Veiler—or sentry—posted at the door. It was a one-at-a-time situation. I gave Talia a reassuring smile and a brief nod before she went in first.

I waited for about five minutes before it was my turn.

Once I entered, I was immediately hit with the suffocating stench of bleach. The sterile room was too pristine, too barren. It had fancy equipment that I had never seen in the Oak Hollow infirmary. There were two physicians in white lab coats gesturing for me to sit in a reclined chair.

The male physician stood holding a chart, while the woman sat in a chair opposite mine and smiled at me.

"What's your full name?" She asked while putting on gloves.

"Mavis Emmaline Ashbone."

The man scribbled the information down on his chart. The woman picked up a thin needle and tube from a tray on top of the side table.

"It is nice to meet you, Mavis. My name is Dr. Sinters, and this is Dr. Holcrum. Today, we will just be taking a few blood samples to analyze. We want to see how healthy you are right now and what we might need to work on." She cleaned my arm with a wet wipe that smelled of alcohol. "We will also give you a vitamin booster shot today," she said as I felt the sting of the needle going in, "because we know participants arrive rather malnourished."

Dizziness threatened to overwhelm me. I had never been good with needles.

A few more seconds, which felt like minutes, passed by before the needle was finally removed and a bandage placed over the entry site. Dr. Sinters placed the four vials of blood she had taken on the side table and grabbed another, much larger, needle.

"You may notice a heavier appetite. That is one effect of the booster. We need you to gain more weight to strengthen your body's resilience."

Without warning, she stabbed into the same arm with the new needle. I flinched back, but she had already administered the dose. She stuck another bandage over the fresh wound, which was truly a wound since it bled. Dr. Holcrum then walked over to a device and used his fingers to input information onto its surface. A few moments later, there was a beeping noise, and he returned holding a bracelet, which he then handed to Dr. Sinters.

"This is your identification bracelet. Your name and information have been recorded in our database. Now, each time you visit, we can scan your bracelet, and all your previous results will appear for us to view. Please do not remove it."

"Do you keep a log of all past participants?" Hope fluttered in my chest.

"Not here in the infirmary, but there should be a record in the facility's library. You are free to go, Ms. Ashbone. I will see you in exactly one week. If you forget, someone will remind you."

That last line was phrased in a neutral tone, but I understood it for the threat it was. If I didn't show up, then I would get dragged back.

I made my way back to my room and stopped in the doorway. On my bed were new articles of clothing. Tunics and pants. I sorted through the new clothing, wondering who knew I hated wearing dresses.

That was an odd coincidence. Or was it? Did they look into my past?

I got undressed until all I wore was my underthings, and then I slipped under the bed's warm blanket.

Tomorrow, I planned to go to the library. But tonight? Tonight I'd sleep knowing they already had a piece of me—and wondering what parts they'd take next.

# CHAPTER 26

*"Self-sacrifice is either the most altruistic or selfish act that one can partake in.
The soul chooses which, so make your intention clear."*
*- The Old Book*

**The Facility - Day 3**

T he moment I stepped out of the dining hall, I headed down the corridor that led to the library. As I rounded one corner, a hand latched onto my arm and yanked me sideways. I stumbled into a darkened room, and the door clicked closed behind me. My eyes quickly adapted to the darkness, and I whipped my head toward my kidnapper.

I exhaled sharply and forced my shoulders to relax.

Renata.

"Is this the part where you finally kill me?" I muttered, half-taunt, half-truth.

We weren't friends, not by any stretch of the imagination. But I didn't truly think that she wanted me dead.

Renata scoffed, arms crossed over her chest. "Don't be ridiculous. You know what this is about."

I blinked, momentarily thrown. "I can assure you I don't."

She didn't hesitate.

"You're a seer."

The words landed like a slap—sharp, undeniable, and dangerous. She didn't phrase it as a question—she said it as fact, one with no room for argument. My throat tightened. I had never dared to say the word aloud.

"I don't know what you're talking about," I lied. Poorly.

Renata's lips curled, unimpressed. "Stop playing coy. Rowan told me every-thing. I know about the visions."

My pulse spiked, and my anger renewed. My nails bit into my palms as I ground my teeth together. I was going to cut him the next time I saw him. *Slowly.* The knife I won—*my* knife—was tucked away in my top dresser drawer, where I kept it safe from prying eyes. I wasn't foolish enough to carry it on me. Not in a place like this.

"For goddess' sake, I'm not going to tell anyone," Renata said, exasperation lacing her voice. "I'm only here because I want to make sure *you* don't either."

I narrowed my eyes. "Why do you care?"

Renata exhaled sharply, then tilted her head, watching me the way a predator watches prey just before deciding if it's worth the effort. "You're not quite the leech I pegged you for upon our first encounter."

"How lovely," I mocked.

"The moment I saw your blood get swallowed by the Ground, I knew you were different. Do you know how many times I've seen that happen?"

I hesitated. "No."

"*Once.* You."

A cold weight settled on my chest. "What do you mean?"

Renata's expression remained unreadable, but there was something in the way her jaw tensed, like she was considering how much to say.

"I thought it suspicious that someone supposedly blessed by Our Lady would find themselves in such a predicament." She studied me, gaze calculating. "But I saw the evidence of your blessing right before my own eyes. I couldn't dispute it—nor could I turn you away. We had to take you."

"*Had* to?" I echoed.

"The whole thing felt like a ruse—a setup." Her voice was edged, sharp as steel. "I watched as you wormed your way closer to our commanding officer, and I thought—this girl is a threat. I truly believed you were infiltrating our ranks to stab us in the back." She let the words settle, let them sink in before she added, "Until I saw Balor's blood on your hands."

My breath caught at the memory.

"That's when I learned," she said, voice almost bored, "that you don't have nearly as much fight in you as some people seem to think."

Anger crawled up my spine once more. My muscles went taut, heat burning behind my ribs.

I bit out, "Yeah? Well, I saved your life with the rebels."

"Maybe," she said carelessly.

"Is there a point in this conversation?" I snapped.

Her expression darkened.

"Yes." She stepped closer until I could see the shadows flickering in her green eyes. "Do you know how rare you are? There hasn't been a known seer in Ravaryn for over a hundred years, not since the Prophet King himself. You must tell no one about your abilities. If the Guild learns what you can do, they will strap you to every monitor and bleed you dry in search of how to recreate you."

My breath stilled.

I swallowed, forcing down the rising panic. "Since when do you care about what happens to me?"

Renata scoffed, but there was something else in her expression.

"It's not in my best interest for you to die yet."

She stepped back, the tension between us unraveling into something murky and indecipherable. Then she turned, striding toward the door. Before she stepped out, she tossed one last look over her shoulder.

"So live."

Then, she was gone.

I exhaled shakily, my pulse still thrumming in my ears. For a moment, I stood in the darkness, letting the silence settle over me. A heavy unease settled deep in me, mixing with the lingering frustration and confusion from our encounter. I swallowed the rising bile down. Then, with no other choice, I left the room, carrying her warning with me.

Before I could fully gather myself and head toward the library as planned, a voice sharply cut through the haze of my thoughts, drawing my immediate attention.

"Ms. Ashbone."

"Y-yes." I stuttered. I never stuttered. I turned to find the sentry Karina standing a few paces away.

"It is time for your first truth session. Please follow me." With that, she took off in the opposite direction from the library.

There went my plans again. I reluctantly followed.

Karina led me into a room with light brighter and whiter than any I'd ever encountered before. It felt like staring into the sun, and my eyes had a hard time adjusting to the harshness. There were two white leather armchairs facing each other. In one of them sat a middle-aged woman, looking at me with a smile that didn't quite meet her eyes.

The woman had tight black curls that sat atop her head, and her dark skin radiated in contrast to the room's atmosphere. She was sitting with one leg crossed over the other and a notepad in her lap.

With a voice like velvet, she greeted me.

"Hello, Mavis, my name is Adina. It's wonderful to meet you. Would you like to have a seat?" She gestured to the other chair.

I took hesitant steps toward the seat. Once I sat, I tried to settle myself, but every angle felt uncomfortable. It had nothing to do with the quality of the chair, and everything to do with the prodding gaze I felt boring into me. She was already attempting to psychoanalyze before the session had truly even started.

This was going to be a challenge.

I met Adina's prying eyes just as a sharp sting registered at the back of my neck. I whirled around to see Karina stepping away, holding a thick syringe. A needle she had just plunged into the base of my skull.

"It's a biodegradable transmitter," Adina said casually, bringing my attention back to her as I rubbed circles around the injection site. "It will dissolve naturally within a day. Actually, it's a rather fascinating invention if you ask me. It attaches itself to the base of the cranium and can sense the physical changes that occur when lies are told. When a lie is detected, it emits an electric shock. Nothing too powerful to do any permanent damage, but I have heard reports from participants that it left them feeling dazed for a few days."

She leaned forward.

"My advice? Tell the truth."

It was a threat disguised as a friendly warning.

Turning to the side, she grabbed the steaming mug off her desk. She sipped the beverage and hummed before placing it back down.

"I should warn you," she said, pulling out a little rectangular box from a drawer. "This remote can trigger the transmitter manually, should you choose not to answer at all." She placed the remote on the desk. "I want you to achieve inner peace, Mavis, but sometimes the journey comes with a little pain. Don't fight me, and I'll ensure you make it through this as pain-free as possible. Are you able to do that?"

"I don't have a choice, do I?"

Adina smiled, false sympathy waxed on.

"Let's begin with your family. Who is waiting for you back at home?"

I reflexively tensed, and Adina saw. A glimmer of interest shone as her pupils slightly dilated.

"Tell me about them. It's a sore topic for you, which means it's a great place for us to start."

"I have a brother, and I live with my mother."

"Is your father out of the picture?"

"He's dead," I said curtly.

"Oh, that's unfortunate. How did he die?"

I swallowed hard, turning my face to the side. The answer was never easy to verbalize, not without remembering the image all over again. I was holding onto my composure the best I could, but the cracks were there. A shock pulsed from the back of my head forward. It was twice the strength of any headache I'd ever experienced.

I clutched onto the sides of my head and whimpered. I was just about to scream when it faded. It had only lasted a few seconds at most, but it had been agonizing. My brain felt rattled, and I had a bit of difficulty refocusing my eyes upon Adina.

She was holding the remote, and not an ounce of remorse shone on her face.

"How did he die?" she repeated.

"He ended his own life."

I rubbed my temples, trying to clear the fog that clouded me and wipe away the residual pain.

"Did you find his body?"

"No, my mother did." I paused and looked at the floor, seeing my reflection peering back. When I glanced upward, I saw Adina moving her hand toward the remote.

"I saw him, though," the words spewed out. "My mother refused to remove his body for three days after his death. On the third day, several townspeople came and took his body."

"My condolences for your loss, and the depth of tragedy it surely brought to your family. The lack of a father figure during such pivotal developmental years can be detrimental, especially when the death is traumatic. Did having your brother there with you during all of this help?"

"My brother was taken in the Culling of our village a year before our father passed."

"I apologize for the misunderstanding." She furrowed her brow briefly before smoothing it out once more. "You spoke of him as if he were still with us."

"I have hope that he is."

"Hmm." Adina looked down and scribbled something on her notepad before looking up once more. "What about your mother? How did she handle the loss of both your brother and father?"

"It broke her."

"Did it break *you*, Mavis?"

"What?"

"Did the loss of both your brother and father, and the inadequacy of your mother's ability to parent you through such important and difficult times, break you?"

The harshness of her words hit like a slap to the face. They were blunt and apathetic.

"I'm fine."

Pain laced through my head once more, but this time, I did scream. I fell out of the chair and landed on my knees, cradling my head.

"Now we both know that's not true. Tell me, do you feel guilty?"

The pain slowly increased until tears were streaming down my cheeks involuntarily.

The voice in my head yelled, *Don't give in! Fight!*

But I couldn't do it. I couldn't handle a second more of the pain, and so I cried out.

"I could have stopped it!"

Adina scooted to the front of her chair and cocked her head. I had one hand on the back of my neck and the other gripping my knees to my chest.

"What could you have stopped, Mavis?" She pressed.

"My father's death," I whispered, shattered by the truth behind those words.

"Why do you think that?"

*Stop!*

I opened my mouth to spill all my secrets. Every damnable one. I was going to tell her about the visions. All because I couldn't handle the agony anymore. It felt like my head was going to implode.

A timer rang, and the pressure receded.

"Well, unfortunately for us, that is all the time we have today. I will see you again sometime next week. You'll be summoned to this same room. It was a pleasure meeting you."

I stood shakily from the floor, feeling every muscle in my body trembling in protest. I closed my eyes tightly, attempting to clear the dizziness trying to take over. Each step toward the door was like trudging through thick mud, heavy and unsteady.

I reached out to brace myself against the wall, fingers gripping the cold, unyielding surface as the room tilted and swayed around me. I fought to take a deep breath, but even breathing felt difficult, like the air had turned syrupy.

As I stepped out into the hallway, the change in the lighting intensified the ache in my head, deepening the shadows creeping along the edges of my vision. I trembled, warm sweat coating me like grease.

I couldn't keep my breath under control. Was this what they called a panic attack?

It felt like a heart attack.

I barely registered the figure standing before me until familiar, concerned light brown eyes pierced through the encroaching haze. Rowan's expression shifted rapidly from mild curiosity to alarm as he took in my pallid complexion and trembling form.

"Mavis?" he called, his voice sounding muffled and distant.

I opened my mouth to respond, but no sound emerged. Darkness pooled at the corners of my sight, blotting out Rowan's worried face piece by piece. My knees suddenly gave way beneath me, my strength evaporating completely as gravity pulled me downward.

Strong, warm arms swiftly encircled me, halting my fall just inches before I hit the floor. The scent of sandalwood enveloped me, comfortable and soothing. It cut through the overwhelming sensations. My head rested heavily against Rowan's chest, feeling his steady pulse beneath me.

Finally safe, I sank into the welcoming darkness.

# CHAPTER 27

*"A child is considered a part of its mother's body, not its own entity, until birth.*
*When a sentry takes their oath, they promise their body to service.*
*Therefore, any child present in the womb when a sentry's vow is taken is held to that*
*same oath."*
*- Addendum to Article 2, Section 1, of the Veiled Compendium*

I came to while still in Rowan's embrace, which was surprisingly comforting, as he held my limp body.

"I'll take it from here, Karina. You're dismissed."

"Yes, commander." Karina bowed her head and departed.

"Can you stand?" Rowan asked me with a softer voice than the one he had used to address Karina.

"I think so."

I wobbled to my feet, with Rowan holding my arm to balance my weight.

Once standing, I turned to him, and the memories of my truth session came flooding back. Tears welled up in my eyes, and I didn't have the energy to keep them at bay any longer. They started flowing freely down my cheeks in streams. I heard a choked sob, and to my abject horror, I realized it had come from me.

Rowan gently but firmly grabbed my arm and led me down the corridor. I didn't care where we were going—just that my tears would stay quiet.

We approached a door without a handle, unlike most of the doors I had seen in the facility. Next to the door was another device with numbers on it. Rowan let go of my arm and pressed a sequence of four numbers on the device, ones he didn't think to shield from me, and the metal door slid open. Rowan gestured for me to enter the room, and in my distraught state, I didn't even think to question the request.

Upon entering the room, I took in the layout. It was like mine and Talia's, although there were slight differences. Rowan had a much larger bed than we did, and he had one of those square moving picture screens they called a *television* hanging on his wall.

I turned my body to face Rowan. He was looking at me expectantly.

"Is this your bedchamber?"

"These are my quarters, yes." He then gestured to the bed. "Sit."

I was reluctant to move until he sat in an armchair opposite the bed. I moved to sit, watching Rowan as he placed his hands on his knees and squeezed tight. He was nervous about something. Was it because I was in his room?

"What happened?" he asked.

"She asked about my family. That's not exactly my favorite topic to discuss." I folded my arms and looked away, pretending to examine the white walls that I was far too familiar with.

"Did you tell her about your gift?"

"No," I said, hearing Rowan let out a sigh of relief. "But in truth, I'm not sure how long I could have held out." I glanced back at Rowan and saw his face harden. Now he was angry. With who? It was unclear. His mood swings were unpredictable sometimes.

"You can't tell anyone," he said firmly.

I didn't care much for his tone.

"I know that. I'm not a fool," I quipped. "You didn't need to send the redhead to tell me what I already know."

"Renata came to see you?"

"Don't act like you didn't send her to scare me." I rolled my eyes at his pathetic play of confusion.

"Telling anyone is too risky. It could mean that the Guild finds out. Marcum is a sly, manipulative coward. If he catches wind, all of his attention will turn to you. You don't want that."

"Strange of you to condescend one of your own people."

"Marcum is *not* one of my people. He's the farthest thing from one of mine." He gripped his knees even harder until the whites of his knuckles showed, and then he released his hold when he saw me staring.

"How am I supposed to lie with that gods-damned transmitter in my head?"

"You can't unless you want to experience searing pain." I flinched at the memory. "You don't lie. Instead, you evade certain facts. The transmitter can only detect deceit, not omitted truths. Be vague as possible and learn to manipulate the conversation. Remember that they are the hound chasing a scent, but it's you who has control of where that scent leads."

"I felt like I was going to implode from the agony."

The honesty of that statement hurt. I had experienced nothing so painful in all my years. It felt like lightning striking every nerve, lighting up my spine.

"The sessions make you confront your deepest fears and insecurities. They want you to hurt. It's just another way they sort out the weak."

And the weak *die*. That's what he had said before.

"How long do I have to do the truth sessions for?"

"Until Adina feels that you've conquered whatever past that haunts you."

"What would she know of the past that haunts me?"

"It shows. When you aren't so focused on keeping your guard up and replying with snarky comments, I can see it. You're just as traumatized as the rest of us."

"As traumatized as Veilers?" My condescending tone couldn't be hidden.

"You know, not all Veiled Ones crave bloodshed, but all are required to act as if we do."

"Well, some of you do it *really* well," I mocked.

"Balor was not a soldier of merit. Balor took the black to abuse his authority over others. Unfortunately, that is something that happens when certain people gain power. They become obsessed with wielding it and bending others to their will." He took a deep breath. "I'm not sorry he's dead, but I am sorry you're the one who killed him. His reign of torment should have ended long before he ever came in contact with you."

"I'm fine."

"I saw you struggle to rinse your hands of his death, even long after the blood had cleared."

"I just... don't want to be so vulnerable again. He almost killed me several times, the others want me dead, and I'm just so tired of relying on luck to protect me. What happens when my luck runs out?"

I rubbed my arms slowly. Exhaustion was beating down on me.

"Perhaps I can help you feel you have a bit more control over your fate."

I scoffed. "No one can control their own fate."

"Being able to protect oneself is a way we can exert control in our lives. I can teach you to fight in hand-to-hand combat."

"You would do that for me?" I scrunched up my nose. "Why? I'm your enemy."

"Although I've always been your enemy, you've never been mine, Mavis."

The stretch of silence in the room seemed never-ending. Pin-pricks raced up my arms and throat as I tried to swallow. I wasn't sure how much of it was because of the truth session, and how much of it was stirred by Rowan's quiet confession.

One thing was for sure—the lines between us had blurred beyond comprehension. Enough that I couldn't even be disgruntled about sitting on his bed. Rowan made me forget about our titles and the color of our clothing. The importance of our distinction was skewed. And I didn't know what that meant anymore.

Rowan cleared his throat and continued.

"There's an old gym here. No one uses it since the newer one was built a few years back. It's on the base level, at the end of the third corridor on the right. We can meet there once a week. We have to be discreet, though, you understand?"

"I know."

"Good." Rowan stood from his chair.

"Rowan, what's going to happen to me?"

The vulnerability of my question startled him, as it did me. A few moments passed before he replied, a foreign gentleness coating his words.

"I'm not entirely sure. Once the blood transfusions start, people *change*. Some become more aggressive, and others become more reclusive."

"What about the faith and truth sessions?"

"The faith sessions are a ploy; they just want to test you and see if you will blindly believe everything they say. But the truth sessions—those shatter your mind. They want to rebuild you themselves. They call it *enlightenment*."

"Great," I murmured. It seemed it was only going to get much worse.

"The transfusions, though—those are different. They don't just want to alter you mentally; they want to physically change you, too. By modifying you on a molecular level, they believe they can strengthen you, make you more durable. They say the goal is to genetically *improve* you and rid you of all disease markers."

Disgust churned in my stomach. I swallowed back the nausea and spewed my frustration instead.

"How are you able to sit back and watch these horrors unfold? How can you do nothing?"

"I help when and where I can. I reckon that there are more eyes on me than there are on you," he imparted. I opened my mouth to ask further, but he continued. "Let's get you back to your bedroom before anyone notices your whereabouts."

I followed Rowan to his door. He opened it and stuck his head out, scanning the hallway for any signs of others. Once he determined the coast was clear, he looked back at me and nodded.

His expression was back to being the guarded mask I knew so well, but also the one that made me the most uneasy. While his closed-off demeanor was what he showcased most often, I had grown accustomed to the relaxed conversation and small smirks he reserved for me. To see him barricade himself behind an emotional wall made me bristle at the unintended offense. Honestly, it wasn't my place to be offended at all, but I couldn't deny that a small part of me was disappointed.

He escorted me back to my room and hesitated at the entrance. A part of me wanted him to stay. Another part wanted to shove him through the door and bolt it shut. Instead, I let the silence press between us like a held breath, until he slipped away without a word.

Our interaction had been weighted, and I forced myself to push it to the back of my mind to dissect later. There was no sign of Talia in our bedroom. She had picked up craft-making in the recreation room. She even brought back a few bracelets and clay figurines that she had sculpted and painted. They were currently decorating the top of her dresser.

I staggered over to my bed and let myself unceremoniously collapse onto it. I felt the tension in my muscles relax ever so slightly as I allowed my body to deflate and sink into the mattress.

The day had been draining physically and mentally. I closed my eyes and felt the residual sting from the truth sessions buzz throughout my bloodstream. The pounding pain in my temple had ceased, replaced by a faint echo of all that I had endured.

Eventually I surrendered to sleep, quietly hoping that I could escape into the dreams I once thought too illusory.

# CHAPTER 28

*"When the soul sleeps, the truth wakes."*
*- The Old Book*

Laughter spilled through the hallway like sunlight. Mine and his—the kind of laughter that left your cheeks aching and your stomach sore.

"Willam!" I called, breathless, pressing my back to the wall as I peeked around the corner. "I'm going to find you!"

The floorboards creaked beneath my bare feet as I tiptoed down the narrow corridor of our mother's house. The smell of old wood and lavender soap hung in the air—the scent of home.

Hide and seek. Our favorite game. He was always better at it than I was, even when I swore I'd beat him this time.

I darted into our bedroom first, flinging the quilts aside to check under the beds. Nothing. I yanked open the closet door, clothes brushing against my arms as I shoved them aside. Empty.

"Ugh!" I groaned, stomping my foot. "This isn't fair, Willam! Where are you?"

Silence. Then—his voice.

"I'm here."

It sounded close, but not too close. It was almost as if it had curled around the walls and whispered just for me.

"Come find me."

I gritted my teeth and marched back into the hallway, determined. My gaze swept the old wallpaper, the framed sketches Mother hung with pride. Everything looked the same as always—until it didn't.

At the far end of the hallway, there was a door I'd never seen before.

Rounded at the top, its wood was dark, weathered, and the handle was a smooth iron latch.

My feet faltered, toes curling into the floor as I froze.

That door didn't belong here.

Not in my home.

"Willam?" I whispered, voice trembling.

"I'm here."

It was the same voice—gentle, teasing. But now it seemed to hum from beyond that door, wafting like smoke under the crack.

Each step I took was heavy, as if the air had thickened around me. The boards groaned louder, stretching long, drawn-out creaks that made the hair rise on my arms.

I reached the door. My fingers hovered over the latch, slick with sweat.

"Willam?" I tried again, barely a breath this time.

"I'm here."

The sound sent a shiver racing down my spine. Not fear exactly—something else. Something that beckoned me to go forward.

I curled my fingers around the latch and pushed it down. The door gave a low groan as it opened, just a sliver, and in that sliver—darkness. Thick and endless.

I leaned forward, shaking, my breath shallow—

And woke with a gasp.

The ceiling loomed above me, unfamiliar and dim. My hands flew to my face, damp with cold sweat. My nightshirt clung to my skin like I'd run for miles.

"Mavis?"

I flinched, jerking toward the voice. Talia sat on the edge of my bed, her small frame haloed in the soft glow of the wall lamp. Her wide eyes searched mine, concern etched in every line of her face.

"You okay?" she asked gently.

I dragged in a breath, forcing the tremor from my voice. "Yeah. Just... had a weird dream."

Her head tilted, brassy hair slipping over her shoulder.

"My mother used to say dreams carry messages."

Messages. The word crawled under my skin.

"Messages from whom?"

"From the beyond."

"Like... the gods?"

"Sometimes," she said, furrowing her brow. "The night my grandfather died, I dreamed he came to my bed. He held my hand and told me he loved me. When I woke up and learned that he had passed, Mama told me he had come to say goodbye."

Unease coiled tight in my stomach. I didn't want to think about it. Not now. Not when the echo of Willam's voice still lingered in my ears.

Nothing good came of visions. I learned that long ago.

If that dream was even one to start with.

I swung my legs over the side of the bed, needing movement, needing anything but stillness. "Come on," I said, forcing a thin smile. "Let's go get breakfast."

# CHAPTER 29

*"Do not blame others for the comfort you take in blindness.*
*It is your choice to remain in the dark when a torch has been lit."*
*- The Old Book*

### The Facility - Day 4

"**G**ood morning, participants! I hope you all have been faring well these past few days. I know it all must be quite an adjustment. Today, each of you will be summoned to the infirmary for some routine medical treatment..."

Marcum droned on about various other "activities" occurring in the facility, like this were all some sort of vacation. Like I was supposed to be having fun rather than fixated on my survival.

I already had my agenda for the day. I was finally going to find the library.

I discarded my breakfast tray and exited the dining hall with a reinvigorated sense of determination.

The corridor was brisker than usual. Or perhaps it was only my frail state. I was quick to shiver nowadays. Trailing my fingers along the wall as I walked, I felt the surface smooth under my skin. I tried to remember which turn led to the library—the third corridor on the left, or was it the second?

It all looked the same.

The facility was a massive labyrinth of corridors that looped around, and around, until you didn't know where you were anymore. I counted doors to know where I was, with the main elevator that reached the surface being the starting point.

The approaching sound of footsteps made me slow. Voices, soft but unmistakable, drifted from around the corner. I exhaled sharply, bracing myself.

Serene appeared first. The moment she saw me, she cast her gaze downward. Then, she folded her arms across her chest, and hunched her shoulders like she could disappear into herself. Lily was right behind, chin lifted, looking more annoyed than upset.

I kept my pace steady, even as my body grew stiff. Maybe I could avoid the interaction altogether. Doubtful—but I was going to try.

"Hey, traitor," Lily said casually as I passed by her. I stopped and pivoted on my heels.

Serene's gaze flicked up—just once, a flash of wide, uncertain eyes—before it dropped back to the floor again. Her fingers fidgeted absently with the edge of her sleeve.

Lily sneered. I ignored her pathetic attempt to rile me and focused on Serene. Although she despised me at the moment, I still viewed us as having a sort of kinship. We knew the same woods and the same people. Surely that had to mean something.

"Are you alright?" I asked Serene, my voice softened.

For a second—a heartbeat, no more—she met my eyes again. And in that flicker, I saw the crack: guilt, maybe. Regret. But then she looked down again, her voice soft. "We're fine."

I forced a tight smile. "Good."

"We'd be better without a traitor roaming the halls among us," Lily chimed.

I ignored the comment because it wasn't worth an argument. Nothing good would come from it. I strode past them, resuming my search for the library. I didn't have the energy for petty confrontations.

From behind me, Lily's voice—barely audible—carried just one word.

"Soon."

I found the library after a few too many right turns. It matched the rest of the facility well—just another stale, colorless, all-too-bright room. Even the books lacked color.

I'd never seen so many books untouched by mold or dirt. They didn't smell weathered—they smelled like nothing.

I wandered around the first large room, uncertain where to even begin. There seemed to be more rooms attached by open archways, scaling down like nesting dolls as you continued through them. Before I could venture farther, a cough sounded behind me. An older man watched with stern eyes. He was holding an open paperback book in his hands and examining me like an insect. Like I was nothing more than a nuisance.

"Are you looking for something?" His voice was rough, almost as if a bit of mucus was permanently stuck at the back of his throat.

I rolled my shoulders back. "I was told you keep a record of all program participants. May I see it?"

The man raised one eyebrow and gave me a strange look. Without a word, he turned and walked off. He was several paces away when he finally spoke.

"Well, are you going to follow?"

I hurried after him as we wove through the library stacks until we finally reached a small glass cabinet. The librarian took off the chain that had been dangling around his neck. He sifted through the few keys there until he found the one he was looking for. After unlocking the cabinet, he pulled out a large bound book with serrated paper edges.

"Do *not* bend the pages. If I find any damage done to this book, I will have you transcribe the entire thing," he threatened. He continued to murmur to himself as he left. "They always interrupt the good part."

I flipped to the most recently filled page, running my finger across the list of names until I found my own.

*Mavis Emmaline Ashbone. 20.*

I went back ten pages. Each page represented one year. Each year was a list of names Anam had collected. Well, I still held hope that perhaps not all had been reaped.

When I found the year Willam was taken, I scanned the page thoroughly. And then again. And again. I skimmed it, lips moving soundlessly over every name—until I heard myself whisper his. *Willam.* As if saying it would summon him from the paper.

But his name was nowhere to be seen.

My mind raced with over a hundred possibilities. Maybe this was a list of the deceased? But that made little sense. My name was listed. Or perhaps he used a false name? More probable, yet still unlikely.

I closed the record and rushed to the librarian, who didn't bother to look up from his book.

"Excuse me, but your book is wrong."

The man snorted, "My book is not *wrong.*"

"It's missing a name."

He sighed in utter exasperation and closed his book to meet my unsteady gaze.

"Every name recorded in that book belonged to someone who completed intake upon arrival. Whoever you're looking for never set foot in this facility."

My world tilted, and my stomach hollowed out. I gripped the edge of the desk, the cool metal biting into my palms as the room seemed to lurch sideways. How could he not have made it? He was strong, much stronger than I was.

This was supposed to give me answers, not tear the Ground out from under me.

I stumbled out of the library; the corridors stretching ahead in dizzying lines. My legs moved on instinct, but my mind stayed behind—somewhere between the cracked spine of that record book and the space where Willam's name should have been.

I hugged my arms to my chest, pressing my fingertips into my elbows until it hurt, trying to think. None of this made sense. None of it added up.

A sharp voice broke through the fog.

"Mavis Ashbone."

I turned, blinking hard as Karina approached from the end of the hallway, boots clicking briskly on the white, panelled tile. Her expression was unreadable, but her hands were gloved and her pace carried a quiet urgency.

"You're required in the infirmary," she said, as if she were telling me the weather. "Come with me."

I opened my mouth to ask why, to protest, to tell her I needed a minute, just one—but the words stuck somewhere behind the tight knot in my throat. Instead, I nodded stiffly and fell into step beside her.

We walked in silence, the hallways narrowing, the air turning sharper and bitterer the deeper we went. A shiver shot up my spine, making me shudder. Rubbing my arms, I studied how fragile they appeared underneath the thin fabric of my tunic sleeves, and how each step seemed to echo louder than it should.

Karina led me through a set of heavy double doors, the smell of antiseptic biting at my nose. The infirmary was pale and spotless, filled with gleaming metal trays and rows of glass vials that caught the sterile light. A healer I didn't recognize stood waiting, her hands folded neatly, her eyes already on me.

"Lie down, please," the healer murmured.

"Where are Dr. Sinters and Holcrum?"

"They focus on analysis. I oversee the physical testing."

My gut clenched.

I exhaled slowly, trembling, forcing my legs to climb onto the narrow cot.

The cot's frigid surface pressed against my back as I settled, arms folded stiffly over my chest. The healer approached without a word; her face partially masked, eyes sharp and assessing.

I stared at the ceiling—white, segmented panels, each humming faintly with light.

"Left arm, please," the healer murmured.

I unfurled my arm, swallowing hard as a tourniquet tightened around my biceps. My pulse jumped. The healer's hands were quick, efficient—swab of cold antiseptic, glint of a needle, a sharp pinch, then a slow, spreading ache.

A slender tube snaked to a strange machine beside me. Inside, the liquid glowed faintly—not the dark red I'd expected, but something pale, shimmering, almost white. My stomach turned.

"What is that?" my voice rasped.

"Purified blood," she said without looking at me. "Synthesized from your own cellular template. Please remain still."

"Is that going in me?" I swallowed hard.

"Yes, but first I have to draw some of your blood out. We don't want you to clot, causing a stroke."

Once a pint had been drawn, I felt the second needle enter. First, I felt a coolness at the bend of my elbow, then a slow wave of tingling traveled up my arm, into my shoulder, creeping toward my chest. My teeth chattered faintly. I bit down hard to stop it.

Across the room, a monitor blinked and whirred, displaying numbers I didn't understand. I wanted to lift my head, to watch the healer's face for any flicker of concern, but I felt heavy, not pinned, just sinking.

A soft, chemical smell filled my nose—sharp, metallic, laced with something sweet and sickening. My tongue tasted faintly of copper.

"Breathe normally," the healer said, adjusting a dial on the machine. "It's normal to experience lightheadedness, chills, or a metallic taste."

Normal. I almost laughed.

Nothing about this felt normal.

If this was what it meant to be purified, I wasn't sure how much of myself would be left by the end.

# CHAPTER 30

*"Faith does not exist without hope."*
*- The Old Book*

Karina had to physically escort me back to my quarters because I could barely walk and had lost consciousness twice during the transfusion. It wounded my ego a little, but I didn't have the energy to fight both the dizziness and her. So, I begrudgingly accepted the arm around my waist.

I lay on my back in bed, my breathing shallow. My entire body was so sore that I felt like I'd gotten kicked by a horse. I was also unbelievably cold. Tremors wracked me. My body had refused to stop shaking since the moment the second needle came out of my arm.

A nearly silent knock sounded at my door, and an all-too-familiar figure opened it and walked in.

*Rowan.*

My pulse sped up at the sight of him.

The light from the hallway framed Rowan's figure for a moment before the door clicked softly shut behind him. His boots barely made a sound against the floor as he crossed the room, his expression unusually tense.

"You look awful," he murmured, crouching beside the bed. His eyes swept over me, quietly assessing the damage.

"Thanks," I rasped. My voice was hoarse, my throat dry and raw.

"I was coming to get you for training, but it seems you're indisposed at the moment."

The corners of his mouth tightened.

I tried to lift my head, but the movement sent a sharp ache down my spine. Wincing, I let it fall back against the pillow.

"I think you're right."

Rowan's brow lifted momentarily before dropping and furrowing. He reached out, his fingers brushing lightly against my hand where it peeked from underneath the blanket. His touch was warm, and I fought the urge to curl into it.

"The chills and soreness are common after the transfusions. It's your body adjusting. It'll pass."

I rolled my eyes. "That's reassuring."

Rowan's thumb brushed over the inside of my wrist absently, almost as if he didn't realize he was doing it. "I've seen many go through this. You'll be fine. You're stronger than most." His words sounded reassuring, but I wasn't sure that they were meant for *me*.

A small wave of vulnerability washed over me.

"I'm not sure I feel very strong right now. Just look at how fragile I've become."

His hand stilled, fingers curling briefly into a loose fist before he pulled back. "Strength isn't just fists and swords."

I closed my eyes briefly and exhaled through the tightness in my chest. I was trying my best to stay angry—though my fire had dimmed, stay determined—though my will had wavered, and stay alive—though my body was breaking. When I opened them again, Rowan was still there, still watching, still not leaving.

"Rest," he whispered. "I'll check on you tomorrow, and if you're in better sorts, then we'll start your training."

As he rose, his hand skimmed the edge of the blanket, almost like he didn't want to leave. It was the smallest, most unthinking gesture. But the weight of it stayed with me even after the door closed quietly behind him, even after the room fell back into bitter silence.

Sleep claimed me in fragments, shallow and uncertain. When I finally stirred again, someone was nudging my shoulder.

I expected to see Rowan again, but it was Talia standing before my bed. Her brows knitted as she studied me.

I shifted to face her, shaking. I was far too cold.

"Is everything alright?" I slurred.

I still felt incredibly weak from the transfusion.

"What's it like?" She asked.

"What?"

"The transfusion."

I moved to sit on the bed. My body screamed at me, and it took every bit of strength I had to pull myself up.

I didn't know what to tell her. On one hand, I could tell her the truth, but I didn't want to scare her. She needed to be prepared, but not terrified.

I patted the mattress beside me, and Talia sat.

"I'm sore, but I'll live."

"I don't like needles," she said, moving her thumb to her mouth and biting the nail.

"I don't either, but they're quick about it. I promise."

Talia nodded, dropping her hand to her side.

"Have you had the faith sessions yet?" she asked.

"No, what are they like?"

If they were anything like the truth sessions, I'm not sure I could make it through them.

"Not bad. Dr. Holcrum just talked about our relationship to the gods. Stuff like that."

"I thought he worked with Dr. Sinters in the infirmary?"

"He does, but he leads the faith sessions too."

I stiffened.

"Is he anything like Adina?" I asked breathlessly, betraying my fear.

"No, she scares me."

"She scares me, too," I admitted.

"Dr. Holcrum is just odd, and he smells weird."

My body relaxed, and I laughed. Talia tentatively joined in. My lungs began burning, and I coughed. Talia put her hand on my back and gently patted, like she wanted to help but didn't know how.

After a few seconds, the coughing fit stopped. My lungs felt scratched, and my throat raw.

"Mavis?" Talia whispered.

"Yeah?"

"Do you think we'll make it out of here alive?"

There was a breath of silence. The heaviness of the question sat on my chest.

"I hope so," I said.

But I knew hope wasn't enough. If I wanted to make it out alive, I'd have to do more than hope—I'd have to fight.

# CHAPTER 31

*"Sentries are tasked with protecting the realm from threats both foreign and domestic.*
*Duty knows no kin to lawlessness."*
*- Article 3, Section 5, of the Veiled Compendium*

**The Facility - Day 6**

"This is where we're doing this?" I asked, voice flat.

Rowan didn't even glance back at me as he walked toward the center of the gymnasium.

"It's private," he replied.

When Rowan first appeared at my door this morning and told me to "put on something you can bleed in," I had half a mind to slam the door in his face. Instead, I followed him.

He led me to the base floor, down a maze of concrete halls that reeked of metal and rust. It was nothing like the main level. The lights flickered as we passed, their buzzing like a chorus of dying flies. I was skeptical that we could go somewhere without watchful eyes.

The gym looked like it had been abandoned for decades. The air was thick with mildew and old sweat. One of the ceiling panels was cracked and drooping. The floor mats were torn and uneven, crackling underfoot like dried leaves.

"Why is it so humid down here?" I asked, wiping sweat from my temple already.

"The boiler room's on the other side of that wall." He gestured lazily. "Turns this place into a sauna. Perfect for training."

"It's creepy."

"It works. That's what matters."

I scoffed as Rowan tossed me a set of knuckle wraps that I barely caught. I didn't know what to do with them, so I just watched him tighten his and repeated what he did.

I squared up opposite him on the mat, mimicking his stance. It felt awkward, stiff—like I was wearing someone else's body. In contrast, he resembled a predator toying with its prey.

"Don't go easy on me," I warned. If I were pitied, I would never advance.

Rowan smirked. "First, let's just see what you know."

I launched forward—too fast, too wild, and entirely off balance. Rowan side-stepped, anticipating the strike before I even moved, and my fist sliced through empty air.

"Try again," he said smoothly.

I turned and struck again—this time with more focus—but he ducked, spun, and ended up behind me before I could blink. My elbow came up, hoping to catch him on the turn, but all I hit was the ghost of where he'd been.

"You're dancing," he said. "Not fighting."

I gritted my teeth and tried again. Another miss. And another. He wasn't even breaking a sweat.

I charged, this time with a growl of frustration, aiming a low kick at his side. He caught my ankle midair.

"Better," he murmured, before shoving me back. I stumbled, nearly falling, but caught myself.

"You're infuriating."

"You're predictable."

I straightened, jaw clenched. "Is this how you treat all your students?"

"You're not a student," Rowan replied, expression unreadable. "You're trying to survive. That's different."

I looked at him then, really looked—at the ease of his movements, the sharpness in his eyes, the way he held himself like nothing could ever strike him down.

"You could kill me right now if you wanted," I stated. It wasn't a question, but he answered it anyway.

"Yes."

That single word rang louder than any blow.

Then he added, quieter: "But I won't."

Something lodged in my throat.

"Again," he said, stepping back and opening his stance. "And this time, stop hesitating."

I exhaled through my nose, shaking out my hands. My muscles ached from clenching, but I couldn't seem to stop. The sweat at my hairline wasn't just from the heat.

I lunged again. This time I didn't think—I just moved, letting my instincts take over. But Rowan was already moving before I did. He knocked my wrist aside, stepped in close, and swept my leg out from under me.

I hit the mat with a loud thud, all the air fleeing my lungs.

He hovered above, not gloating, not mocking—just... observing. "You think too much," he said simply, offering a hand.

I smacked it away and climbed to my feet on my own.

"Great," he said dryly. "She has pride."

I gritted my teeth. "She also has a powerful desire to punch you in the face."

His lip quirked just barely. "Then by all means, stop showing your movements before you've made them."

I squared up again, hands raised, breath steady. I moved—quick jab, pivot, feint to the left. He blocked with ease, but I saw the flicker of approval in his eyes.

Then he came at me.

He threw his fist at me slower, yet I barely ducked in time. If it had been real, my nose would've been shattered. The next hit came low, toward my ribs, and I twisted just in time to avoid the full brunt. Still, it knocked the wind out of me.

Rowan didn't stop. He stepped into my space, crowding me. His arm hooked around mine, trapping it.

"You keep moving backward," he said. "That's not defense. That's retreating."

His breath was warm against my temple, his voice low—too calm for someone who'd just disarmed me.

"You're faster than you think," he added. "But you don't trust yourself. You hold back. That'll get you killed."

I jerked my arm free with a snarl and shoved at his chest. He barely moved.

"Again," he said, not unkindly. "Use the anger."

I stepped back, breathing hard. Sweat clung to my spine. My limbs trembled—not from exertion, but from restraint. From the sharp, twisting cocktail of humiliation, heat, and something dangerously close to attraction.

I moved again—this time with less technique and more desperation. I aimed a punch at his side and followed with a knee.

Rowan blocked both, but I saw it. A half-second. A shift in his stance. I had surprised him.

That flicker of satisfaction lit something within me.

"Better," he said again, but this time, there was something new in his voice. Something akin to pride.

We stood there, both breathing hard, close enough that my next step would put me against his chest. Neither of us moved.

Then Rowan stepped away, and I let out a breath I didn't know I had been holding. "You're learning. We meet here every week, an hour after dinner. Don't be late."

With that, Rowan exited the gym, and I stood there panting with my hands on my knees. This was going to be challenging, in more ways than one, but I prayed it was worth it.

# CHAPTER 32

*"The gods reward obedience.*
*As a servant, you are to breathe their words and execute their will.*
*That is doctrine."*
*- Article 4, Section 4, of the Veiled Compendium*

**The Facility - Day 7**

My thumb tapped anxiously against the polished cover of the book I clutched. It was a copy of *A Brief History of the Ravaryn Crown*, borrowed from the library. It felt wise to brush up on my enemy.

I was slowly but surely making my way through the connecting rooms of the library. It was expansive, almost as if they had a copy of every book published. I'd found a shadowy alcove in the library, and I was planning to disappear into it until someone came to drag me out again.

"Maaavis!" a syrupy voice sang behind me.

My spine stiffened, and I turned slowly.

Corsica stood in the middle of the hallway, arms folded behind her back like she was posing for a portrait. Her glossy hair was swept into an elaborate braid, and she was wearing the brightest shade of coral lipstick I'd ever seen in my life.

"You've been skipping the group activities," she said with a tilt of her head. "You know we track attendance, right?"

"I didn't realize they were mandatory," I said flatly, already bracing myself for the inevitable lecture.

"Oh, they're not." She smiled wide enough to show nearly all her teeth. "But they are... encouraged. Socialization is important."

The lilt in her voice made it almost seem as if she cared, but I recognized it for the controlling ruse it was.

"I don't get along well with others."

Corsica giggled, high and musical. "No, no. I think you have the *opposite* issue, sweetheart."

I blinked. "Excuse me?"

She didn't elaborate. She just smiled wider, like we were sharing some inside joke I hadn't been told.

"I host music night every Thursday," she said brightly, as if that eerie moment hadn't happened at all. "Rec room. Eight o'clock," she tapped her watch. "It's always a delight. You should come."

"I'll think about it," I said quickly, already angling my body away from her.

Corsica's eyes lingered a moment too long. Then, with a wink and a spin of her heel, she vanished down the corridor like she'd never been there at all.

I stood there in the silence, hand tightening around the book.

What did she mean by that?

I saw Karina out of the corner of my eye and turned toward her before she had the chance to speak.

"Where are we going now?"

I wasn't ready for another truth session or transfusion. The idea of going through that torture again made my palms sweat and muscles tense.

"It's time for your first faith session."

My stomach knotted. Not another truth session, thank the gods—despite that, I couldn't stop the prickle in my palms or the way my pulse hammered like a drum. Faith sessions sounded harmless. A little talking, maybe some empty philosophy. But the truth sessions had sounded harmless too—and they'd scraped me raw.

Karina didn't offer comfort. She just walked, silent as always, through hollow halls that echoed with each step. I trailed after her, questions chewing holes in my tongue. Finally, I said, "You're always escorting me around, but I never see you leave like the others. Don't you ever wish you could go home?"

She stopped. Turned just enough that I caught the flicker in her eyes before the mask snapped back on.

"This is home."

Then she pushed open a door with her hand and looked at me expectantly. I got the message.

I took a deep breath and entered the room.

I'd expected a small, quiet room. Instead, a dozen chairs formed a loose semi-circle, half-filled with the other culled. Their heads turned as one when I stepped inside. The air shifted—thick, sharp with unspoken judgment.

"Find a seat," a man's voice said.

Dr. Holcrum stood at the front. I'd seen him before, when I first met Dr. Sinters. His watery hazel eyes locked on me now, bright with something that wasn't quite warmth.

I slid into the chair farthest from the others, leaving a single empty seat as a buffer.

Holcrum clasped his hands and scanned the crowd of us.

"Welcome. For those who don't know me, I assist Dr. Sinters from time to time, but my primary position within the program is lead faith counselor."

He let his gaze sweep over us slowly, like an angler deciding which hook to cast first.

"Questions before we begin?"

The boy to my left raised his hand. "Why do we have to do both truth and faith sessions?"

Holcrum's eyes gleamed. "Ah, good question. Truth sessions are individual. They strip away what holds you back—your lies, your illusions. Faith sessions..." He splayed his hands. "Faith sessions are about the soul. Ascension is impossible if the spirit isn't open to receive it."

He paused, grin sharpening.

"Shall we begin?"

Silence.

"Good," he said, stepping closer. "When you think of divinity, what comes to mind?" He pointed suddenly at an unsuspecting boy in the crowd. "You. Answer."

"Um... the gods?"

"Most assume divinity belongs only to the gods. But did you know mortals carry divinity too?"

Low whispers rippled through the circle. Holcrum grinned wider.

"Mortals are shaped from both the Ground and Our Lady herself. Half deity. That spark is buried deep inside—but with the right key, we can unlock it."

"How do we unlock it?" someone asked.

"By lowering your defenses and embracing your connection to the universe." His tone was soft, coaxing, like honey over glass.

I almost rolled my eyes. If it were that easy, everyone would have done it already.

"Not our connection to the gods?" someone asked.

"Yes—and no. Connection with the universe is the end goal, but the key to unlocking it is through communion with the gods." Holcrum clapped once, sharp as a knife. "I want you all to try something. Hum."

I snorted before I could stop myself. Quickly masked it with a cough, but too late—his gaze pinned me like an insect.

"Is something funny?" His voice was calm. Too calm.

I straightened in my chair. "I just... don't see how humming is supposed to make us divine."

He walked toward me slowly, each step deliberate, until the air between us felt charged.

"The vibration teaches frequency," he said. "Divinity is a frequency. Energy within us. But if you're too inadequate to produce even the smallest vibration..." His smile didn't reach his eyes this time. "...then perhaps my time is wasted on you."

Low whispers and snickers from the other culled surrounded me.

"Leave."

My breath hitched. "Don't I have to be here?"

"Not if I don't want you here." His voice cracked like a whip. "And I don't. So leave."

I rose hesitantly, aware that it could be a test. Every muscle was stiff as I made my way to the doorway. But he never stopped me.

When I finally glanced back, Holcrum didn't look at me. He just flicked his wrist, dismissive, as if I were a gnat.

So I left.

# CHAPTER 33

*"Lies are the seed of rot; from rot comes ruin,*
*and ruin claims all."*
*- The Old Book*

### The Facility - Week 2

T he library was quiet, and as usual, it was just me and the librarian. I could tell that he was growing accustomed to having someone else in his library, because his eyes were less watchful each time I visited.

But I wasn't there to browse today. I was hunting. I searched every participation log, roster, and mission record I could get my hands on—but none of them had a whisper of Willam. It was as if he had never existed. Like someone had erased him from the world.

I was growing weary in my search. Every day I lost a piece of hope. And truthfully, I didn't know how much longer I could keep looking.

The librarian sat at his front desk, slumped back in his chair, reading. I watched him for a moment, waiting for a flicker of awareness, a sign he'd noticed me. Nothing.

Good.

I had a feeling that the information surrounding the culled was tucked away, hidden in one of the back rooms I had yet to enter. I had made it through nearly every room, but one remained.

As I made my way deeper through the rooms of towering shelves, I noticed that the pristine covers began to age. Some books looked to be nearly completely disintegrated, their spines coming undone, words almost illegible.

That's when I saw it.

My breath hitched, and my feet planted, unmovable.

It was the door from my dream.

The exact one, with the rounded top and the old metal latch. It was tucked away next to ancient territorial maps and left slightly ajar. Just enough for a whisper of shadow to seep out.

It felt like fate.

I wanted to turn around. The eeriness of it all gnawed at me. But curiosity clawed at my ribs. Something was pulling me toward that door, and I didn't know what I feared more.

The pull itself, or what I was being pulled toward.

My chest tightened as I slipped through the gap.

The air changed the moment I stepped inside—colder, heavier, like I'd crossed an invisible threshold. The room was small, crowded with narrow shelves and stacks of books too brittle to touch. But the centerpiece was impossible to miss.

It was another glass showcase.

Inside, resting like a relic in a tomb, was a book bound in cracked leather and frayed cloth. Its spine was faded, lettering ghosted by time.

I crouched, pressing my face close to the glass. Dust veiled the surface, but through the grime, I could just make out the letters burned into the cover:

**Acaelar Bloodborne**

The name hit me like a stone.

Acaelar, the Prophet King. His prophecies were the reason the Ascension Project was created. He'd lived more than a hundred years ago, but his legacy still rippled through the kingdom like a curse.

And here his name was, locked away like a secret.

I reached out without thinking, fingertips brushing the cold glass.

That's when it happened.

A shiver shot down my spine, sharp and startling. It wasn't the draft—I knew the bite of cold air, and this wasn't it. It was something else.

The fine hairs on my arms lifted as if stirred by a breath that wasn't there. And for a moment, I felt it—warmth on my shoulder. Familiar. Comforting.

Willam.

The thought rooted itself so fast I didn't question it. The tome would have the answers I sought. I knew it as sure as I knew the woods of Oak Hollow.

Blood roared in my ears.

I didn't know what secrets an old king carried that could matter to me now—but every part of me knew I needed them. I needed to crack open the book and bleed its pages dry.

I curled my hand into a fist and stepped back, eyes locked on the case.

The lock glared at me.

For a fleeting, stupid second, I considered smashing the glass. My fingers even curled into fists, prepared for action. But the sound... the fallout...

No, I needed a cleaner way.

I slipped out of the room. As I walked backward, silently closing the door, I felt myself walk into something hard. I quickly swung around and came face-to-face with the librarian. His eyes were wide, and his expression sharp with suspicion.

"What are you doing?" he growled.

He barged right past me, pushing me out of the way, and studied the latch. Then he muttered, "How is this open?"

He looked at me, leaned in, and demanded, "How did you open this door?"

"It was already open."

"Impossible." He yanked the chain from beneath his collar, chiming the collection of keys hanging there. "Only I can unlock it."

He squinted his eyes, trying to decipher whether I was a liar. When he couldn't find what he was looking for, his brow furrowed, and he resumed examining the latch.

"Leave."

I stood there for one long, dangerous moment, staring at the door.

I needed that book.

"Now!" his voice cut through the air.

I forced my feet to obey, retreating one reluctant step after another. But the further I moved, the heavier my legs felt.

Whatever was in that room—it wasn't just important. It was forbidden. Dangerous enough to lock away.

And deep in my bones, I knew the truth. My answers were sealed in that book.

All I needed to figure out was how to get the key.

# CHAPTER 34

*"Connection mends the soul, whereas division threatens its ruin."*
*- The Old Book*

### The Facility - Week 3

It was Thursday, eight o'clock, in the rec room. I wanted to leave.

Every fiber of my being screamed at me to leave. My ears ached listening to a seventeen-year-old boy screech the lyrics to a popular folk song. His constant voice cracks had me gripping the edge of the table. The frequency was just too sharp, slicing through any attempt I made to block it out.

I was only here to get Corsica Marwood off my trail.

Ever since she cornered me, inquiring why I had yet to attend any organized social events, she had been showing up wherever I was—after transfusions, truth sessions, even meals. Always chirpy. Always asking when she could expect me at an activity night.

I was worried her lurking about would lead her to uncover things she shouldn't know about. Like my sparring lessons with Rowan, or my plot to break into the library.

So now here I was, being slowly tortured, just to prove I was "making an effort."

I stared at the chipped surface of the table and tried to pretend I wasn't spiraling. The noise was too much, and my fingers were trembling. I wanted nothing more than to leave, but I felt her eyes on me even now.

A chair scraped beside me.

My breath hitched as I glanced up, expecting the worst—Corsica. My presence was my participation. If they made me sing, I would croak.

My shoulders relaxed when I realized it wasn't Corsica, but Talia.

She sat down wordlessly, balancing a tray with a cup of cider and a small slice of crumb cake she didn't touch. She didn't look at me, didn't smile, didn't make a sound.

Just... sat there.

I blinked, unsure what to make of it. Normally she had a light in her that drew others in. Now, it was shrouded.

"Is everything okay?"

"Truth session," she whispered.

I immediately understood. My throat constricted, and I tentatively put my hand on her shoulder. She wasn't alone in her pain, and if the only comfort she could take from me was solidarity, then I would give it.

The boy on stage attempted a falsetto note that murdered something inside me. I winced visibly. Out of the corner of my eye, I saw Talia's lips twitch. Not quite a smile, but it was something.

The two of us sat in silence, watching the scene unfold around us. The culled seemed more alive than they had in weeks. A part of me wondered if they had moved past feeling betrayed, but I didn't think so. They still avoided sitting by me at meals, and none ever spoke to me of their own volition. I also hadn't missed that they scarcely interacted with Talia, no doubt punishment for her kindness toward me.

Though she lacked her usual optimism, Talia's presence anchored me. It was quiet and steady. And oddly enough, it helped.

She slid her plate of untouched cake toward me, then folded her hands in her lap and resumed her silent listening.

I didn't say thank you. I felt as if the moment was too raw for words. But I broke off a piece of the cake and ate it anyway.

A shadow fell across the table, and Talia stiffened.

"Ms. Ashbone," Karina's voice called out, causing me to squeeze my eyes shut. She was only ever around for one thing.

When I met her gaze, her expression was stone-cold, emotionless. She was a perfect soldier.

"You're needed for a faith session."

My stomach sank. "It's late."

She didn't blink, continuing to stare expectantly.

Looking at Talia, she was still stiff and staring ahead blankly. I was hesitant to leave her in such a state, but it seemed I had no choice. I never did anymore.

With a reluctant sigh, I stood and followed Karina out of the room. The music dulled behind us, swallowed by sterile halls and the faint echo of our footsteps.

When we reached our destination, Karina opened the door, and inside was a semicircle of chairs—empty. Only Dr. Holcrum stood inside with his arms crossed, as if he'd been waiting long for my arrival.

I turned to Karina. "Am I the first one here?"

But she was already walking away.

"Come in," Dr. Holcrum announced. His voice was silk over steel. "Sit."

I stepped inside, and the door whispered shut behind me. I found my seat, taking a cautious look around the room. It felt cavernous in its stillness.

"You're the only one attending tonight," he said.

The words sent a chill up my spine, raising the hair on my nape.

Holcrum dragged a chair across the tiled floor with a long, scraping groan, positioning it in front of mine. Then he sat, folding his hands over one knee. We were eye to eye.

"Do you believe in the gods, Ms. Ashbone?"

"Yes," I said without hesitation.

His mouth curved. Not a smile, but something questioning.

"Liar."

I gripped the metal legs of the chair hard.

"I'm not lying."

I may not have been a fanatic, but I was no heretic.

"Then why," he asked slowly, "do you reject the scripture?"

"I don't reject it," I snapped. "I just don't support its being used as a tool of control."

His eyes gleamed. "It was written by Our Lady herself. That makes it doctrine. Every verse is sacred, including the one you renounce."

"It doesn't mean what you think it does."

Dr. Holcrum tilted his head, curious. "Then tell me. What does it mean?"

I swallowed hard as memories of Grandmother Alma's lessons flickered through my head.

"I was taught that peace is achieved by having a connection with the gods. And through that connection, you are saved from *true* death."

His expression softened, almost thoughtfully.

"Ah, true death. When one is erased—body, soul, and spirit. A fate worse than the Sea of Sorrow, is it not?"

I nodded, skeptical of his acceptance.

Death was everyone's end, the ultimate act of life. However, I learned that there were two types: physical death and true death.

When people physically died, their memory lived on, and their spirit crossed the veil into either the Realm of Remembrance or the Sea of Sorrow. Whereas true death was reserved for the worst souls, those considered unworthy of any afterlife. Souls deemed unfit even for the pain of eternal drowning were erased, stolen from common thought as if they'd never existed at all.

"I'm surprised that you're familiar with its concept. It can be a dark subject to learn, so many don't teach it. But ignorance doesn't make things go away, does it?"

"No," I admitted. "It doesn't."

Dr. Holcrum leaned back, steepling his fingers. "What do you think will happen when you die?"

"I'll meet Anam." It was a fact.

"But where do you think you'll go?"

I rubbed my arm mindlessly. I hated this question because I hated its answer. Instead of telling Dr. Holcrum what I hoped for, I told him the truth.

"I don't know."

He looked at me so intensely my skin itched. After several moments of tense silence, he spoke.

"You don't need faith sessions."

"Then... why am I here?"

"I'm required to see you twice before I can make my recommendation."

My pulse stuttered. "So this was some kind of test?"

He stood, brushing the wrinkles from his pant leg. "Not exactly. You don't need faith sessions because the connection you lack..." He paused, as if savoring the weight of his next words. "...isn't one I can teach you. It's one you'll have to find yourself."

His gaze didn't waver. It pinned me, sharp as glass, until my chest tightened. Then, with a flick of his hand toward the door:

"Go."

I stood on unsteady legs, confusion coiling like smoke in my lungs. His words clung to me as I walked, sticky, impossible to shake.

"And Ms. Ashbone?"

The sound of my name froze me mid-step. I turned.

Dr. Holcrum's expression was unreadable. His voice, quiet enough to make me lean in, carried like a promise.

"Keep searching for what you're really looking for. I think you'll be surprised by what you find."

His gaze held mine for one unbearable second longer. Then he turned away, as if I were already gone.

# CHAPTER 35

*"Anam keeps the names of all souls from their first breath to their last.*
*They belong to Him, and He always comes to collect."*
*- The Old Book*

**The Facility - Week 4**

Oliver's name spread like a sickness across the dining hall. By the time it reached me, I already felt ill.

*"Who died?"*

*"Oliver."*

*"That boy from Oak Hollow?"*

*"Yeah, they found his body this morning."*

*"What happened?"*

*"Suicide. That's what I overheard a Veiler say."*

*"Or that's what they want you to think."*

*"Maybe, I just know they found him this morning."*

*"I heard the truth sessions were hard on him."*

*"He was a sweet kid. Wrong person from Oak Hollow to go if you ask me."*

I felt the eyes shift onto me, but I refused to meet them. Gripping the sides of my tray hard, my knuckles whitened briefly before I released the pressure. There were too many spectators, and I refused to give them a show. I needed to leave. Now.

I stood abruptly, my chair scraping against the floor through the low hum of whispers. Every eye in the dining hall felt like it was burning holes in my skin. They wanted to see me falter, see me break. But I wouldn't give them the satisfaction.

I stormed out, the tray still clutched in my hands, until I found the nearest bin and slammed it inside. The clang echoed in the corridor.

The air felt too thin. Too bright. Too loud. I could barely breathe it; it was choking me.

I didn't hear Rowan's footsteps until he spoke.

"Mavis—" he said as if approaching a wounded animal.

"Don't," I snapped, whirling on him like a struck match. "Don't follow me. Don't say my name like you understand. Just—" My voice cracked, but I didn't let it stop me. "Give me space!"

I stormed off, but Rowan, of course, followed suit and blocked my path.

"You need the exact opposite."

"Gods," I cursed. "I hate it when people tell me what I need." I tried to push past him, but he moved with me, unshaken.

"You're boiling over," he said evenly. "Nothing gets better by running off to sit in silence and stew."

I spun on him again, fists clenched at my sides. "You think you know what's best for me? You know nothing about me!"

He stared at me for a long, unreadable moment. "Then show me."

"What?" I paused.

"Fight it out," he said simply. "Let the anger burn through you."

I let out a humorless laugh. "You don't want that. It's not safe to spar right now."

His eyes narrowed slightly, and a flicker of challenge danced across his face. "Challenge accepted."

By the time we reached the old gym, I was already rolling my sleeves up past my elbows. I didn't bother asking for wraps. I didn't want protection.

Rowan stepped onto the mat without a word. The growl of the boiler next door made the floor vibrate faintly beneath my feet. Sweat already clung to the back of my neck, but this time it wasn't just from the heat.

"Ready?" he asked, his voice low but steady.

"No," I said. "But I'm doing it anyway."

I swung at him before he could open his mouth again.

He ducked. Of course, he did.

I came at him again, harder this time—fist, elbow, knee. He deflected all of it as if I were swatting flies. But I didn't stop. I couldn't stop. Rage and grief pumped through my limbs like fire, and I let it blaze.

Rowan blocked my fist, redirected my kick, twisted out of reach like smoke in the air.

"Don't pity me," I growled.

"I'm not."

"Then stand still and let me hit you!"

"I'm not going to *let* you do anything," he said. "Earn it."

I screamed—no words, just sound—and lunged again.

This time, I went right and swept low. He moved to counter, but I shifted faster, fueled by nothing but fury and spit. My fist collided with his ribs, hard. I heard the grunt before I even registered the contact.

Rowan stumbled back half a step, one hand pressing briefly to his side.

My breathing heaved in the thick air, and I stared at him, stunned.

He looked up at me, eyes sharp but not angry. "You're getting stronger."

"Why?" I asked quietly, the question falling from my lips before I could stop it. "Why are you doing this? Why help me?"

Rowan straightened slowly. The usual wall behind his eyes seemed thinner now, like something in him had shifted.

"There was someone," he said, voice rougher than before. "A long time ago."

He didn't look at me when he spoke. He looked at the cracked floor like it held a memory.

"Someone who needed help. I failed, and they lost their life."

He paused. Swallowed.

"And now I see them sometimes. In dreams. In reflections. In the faces of people." His jaw clenched. "It doesn't go away. That guilt."

I said nothing. My throat was too tight to allow it. His pain was one I knew all too well. That kind of gnawing grief that's never sated.

"So now I'm helping you," Rowan continued, softer. "It doesn't undo what happened. I'll regret it for the rest of my life. But this—" he gestured to me. "Training you, keeping you alive... It's something."

I stared at him, chest aching. There was something unspoken beneath his words. Something jagged and heavy and buried so deep it had probably never seen the light.

The silence between us pulsed.

My knuckles were bruised, my ribs ached, and my throat felt like it might close—but some tiny sliver of me felt... steadier.

"Okay," I said.

"Okay?" he echoed.

I squared my stance again. "Let's go another round."

Rowan's mouth twitched, and he raised his fists.

He nodded, "Again."

# CHAPTER 36

*"Bonds are strong when the cord is pulled taut.*
*Loosen the thread, and the knot unravels.*
*The same is true of people."*
*- The Old Book*

### The Facility - Month 2

I spent the week studying the librarian. In doing so, I learned he preferred romance novels, often mumbled to himself, and was very sensitive to sound. I also discovered that he removed the keys from his neck when seated at his desk and put them on a nearby hook.

I was in my room reading another book about the Bloodborne dynasty. If the tome locked in that case about Acaelar Bloodborne shed light on what happened to Willam, like I hoped it did, then I needed to know as much about him as possible.

I opened the book and stared at the first line of text.

*Blood is thicker than water.*

It was a phrase that my father used to say often. But when he said it, he meant that a family should stick together and look after one another. He preached that family was the most important thing, because in the end, it was all we had left.

But in this book, the phrase was twisted. It used the quote to refer to the strength of the Bloodborne line. I scoffed. It was a family name only passed down to heirs.

They were a mockery of a monarchy, and I held the opinion that it should be abolished. An opinion that could get me hanged for treason if I ever aired it.

I flipped through the pages until I found an illustration of the royal family tree. Starting with the first Bloodborne king, Avalion, I went down. I stopped a few generations down when I reached his descendant, Acaelar.

I skimmed through his biography; most of it was information I already knew. He was the Prophet King and supposedly saved thousands of lives by predicting several natural disasters. What I didn't know was that Acaelar was said to have had a journal, which was lost over fifty years ago.

Was that what was in that glass case? If so, why was I being pulled toward a dusty book that surely had nothing to do with Willam?

I continued reading.

My jaw dropped. The journal was said to have been a collection of his prophecies. Had Acaelar predicted what happened to Willam? It was yet another question I needed answers to.

I went back to examining the family tree. Tracing my finger downward, I ended at the current king, King Albador. It didn't list his heir, but everyone knew what his name was. It had been paraded throughout the kingdom the day he'd been born: Prince Auren.

All I knew about him was that he was very young, and first in line to be crowned King of Ravaryn. If something were to happen to King Albador, then a child would ascend the throne.

The sound of something shattering caught my attention, and I startled back to reality.

My head whipped over to the source of the sound, and there I saw Talia, on her knees, cleaning up one of her clay figurines. It had fallen on the tiled floor and broken. The little figurine, which was once identical to a deep-sea whale, was now cracked into pieces.

I pushed my book aside and got down onto the floor with her, helping her collect all the little fragments that had broken off. I chanced a glance at Talia's down-turned face, and watched a single, quiet tear drop from her cheek to the floor.

"I'm sorry. It was beautiful."

I knew I'd made a vow not to get attached to anyone, but Talia made it hard. She was like a ray of caged sunlight in this underground pit of darkness. I wanted to help her, even if I didn't know how.

"Do you think we can glue it?"

"Maybe. My mama made it for me."

"You didn't make it here?" I asked.

"Not that one."

She shook her head and then rubbed away the moisture on her cheek.

"I have something at home that's similar," I admitted.

Talia looked up at me in response, eyes glistening and curious.

"It was a necklace. I never wear it. I keep it in a dresser drawer back home because I'm too scared to break it." My eyes widened with the realization of what I'd just said. "I'm sure we can fix your whale, though."

"It's alright."

I handed her one of the larger shards I'd picked up, and she took it gently. Even though the item was broken, no doubt beyond repair, she still handled it with care.

"Can I ask you a question?"

"Sure," I shrugged.

"Do you think the gods listen to our prayers?"

I blinked, surprised by the shift in conversation.

"Sometimes," I offered. "I think they're probably too busy to hear every prayer, though. I think only the loud, important ones get through to them."

"I don't think they can hear mine," she confided.

"I don't think they can hear mine either."

I reached my hand over and placed it atop hers. Then, I gently squeezed her hand to let her know she wasn't alone. Even though I knew we both felt the solitude keenly.

"Sometimes," she whispered, "I dream I'm back home, painting." She paused. "Maybe the gods don't hear my prayers because I'm being selfish."

"Praying that you get to go home is not selfish. Having hope is important. It's easy to lose, and hard to regain."

Talia didn't respond. She just looked at the pieces of the whale in her hands like they were sacred, like something worth keeping even if they could never be whole again.

I stayed beside her, cold floor pressing into my knees, and said nothing more. There was nothing else to say.

We were both holding onto things—some shattered, some still hidden in drawers.

And maybe the gods weren't listening.

But we were.

# CHAPTER 37

*"Two hearts beat as one when the Goddess Netali blesses a union.*
*Her blessings are revered and rare."*
*- The Old Book*

I frantically tapped the arm of the chair I was sitting in. I had been sitting in deafening silence for nearly five minutes now, all the while Adina stared at me expectantly. I told her everything she wanted to know: Willam's capture, my father's suicide, and my mother's subsequent mental decline. Yet here we still sat, face to face, locked in an unspoken battle of wills.

I had followed Rowan's guidance: only tell half-truths and lead the conversation where I wanted it to go. The problem was that Adina knew I was hiding something. Probably through some sort of sixth sense she possessed. The woman was persistent to a fault.

"It's been two months, and most of your peers have graduated out of their sessions. Why do you think you haven't?"

"Because you think I have more to say," I replied dryly. "Or perhaps you just really enjoy torture."

Adina chuckled softly.

"Who is Kaven?"

"A childhood friend." Not a lie, but not entirely the truth. Which is exactly why I felt a small buzz at the base of my skull.

"I don't believe you, and neither does your body. You've mentioned him briefly, but never gone into detail. Why?"

"He's not that important." I flinched at the twinge of pain that radiated down my spine. I hated that gods-damned transmitter. I was so close to clawing my skin off until I successfully ripped it out.

"You know what I think?"

"I'm sure you'll tell me," I said with feigned sweetness, lilting my voice.

"I think he means a great deal to you. That somehow he ties into some of your deepest insecurities, and *that* is why you won't talk about him."

I felt sweat gather on the back of my neck and slick my palms. She was going to force it out of me. The last piece of my life I had tried to keep to myself was going to be ripped from me against my will.

The buzzing at the base of my skull intensified, and I opened my mouth to tell her what she wanted to hear. To tell her how much of a coward I was, how everyone I loved left me. A tear streaked down my cheek, partly from the pain and partly from the intensity of the moment.

The timer rang out, and the pain faded. My gaping mouth let out an exasperated sigh of relief, and my body sank into the back of the chair. Adina's left eye twitched several times before the mask of fake-calm plastered itself on her face once more.

"Well, that was rather anticlimactic. Maybe next session you'll be more ready to talk."

She stood from her chair and exited the room swiftly.

I didn't move a muscle, too depleted of all energy to care that I couldn't stand. I closed my eyes and practiced regulating my breathing. My pulse was still elevated, but I could feel the pressure that had built up within me dissipating.

I mindlessly walked down the corridor, watching one foot step past the other. The space in my head where my thoughts usually lived was empty. All the energy needed in formulating them had been drained. It was getting harder and harder to keep my walls up. Especially since the start of the transfusions, my body had gotten much weaker. Thus contributing to my wavering mental fortitude.

At first, I thought the treatments were working. I felt stronger, sharper. Like I was gaining muscle, even power. But that only lasted a few weeks. Now, it felt like I was losing everything I had built—and then some.

I stopped dead in my tracks when that warning chill crept up my spine.

*They're coming.*

It was the voice again.

*Turn around.*

I stared at the reflective floor, at my distorted image peering back at me. I repeated to myself that the voice wasn't real, over and over. Because if it was, what did that mean?

Keeping eye contact with myself, I continued. Once I rounded the corner, I stopped once more. Laughter—maniacal and heady—echoed down the corridor. My eyes squeezed shut upon recognition.

I lifted my head and caught the unwavering stares of Lily, Brenn, Aeva, and Serene. They had formed a barricade with their bodies across the hall, keeping me from passing them.

I watched as Lily dug into her pocket and pulled out a knife. A knife with a familiar handle and blade angle.

"That's my knife," I said through gritted teeth. "You went into my room and stole it."

Lily pretended to examine the blade, stroking her finger against its spine as a taunt. "Did you know that none of the doors to our rooms lock?"

My eyes never left the blade in her hand. My posture grew rigid as an overwhelming icy sensation froze me in place. There were red smudges on parts of the blade and handle.

Bright red.

Lily looked down at the blade, at the fresh blood that had caught my attention, and twitched her lips upward.

"He didn't even fight back. Isaac, that is. Pathetic really." Lily twirled the tip of the knife on her finger.

This wasn't Lily. Lily hated me and wanted me dead. That much was true, but the woman standing before me was a hollow, unfeeling shell. The Lily that I had ventured here with stood up for her fellow culled and viewed herself as their unofficial leader. *That* woman wouldn't have turned on her own.

"Why?"

"It was him or us. Just like it's you or us."

"What are you talking about?"

"It's all a test, Mavis. They want to see who is the strongest among us. I can feel it—whatever they're doing to us—surging throughout my body. I'm brimming with unlimited power. You should consider what we did to Isaac as a mercy. He never would have survived the program."

"It's strictly forbidden to harm others unless in self-defense. It's punishable by death."

"Gods, Mavis, you're so dumb sometimes. It's a test! Everyone cheats on tests. You just have to make sure you don't get caught."

Lily turned to Serene and handed her the knife. Serene glared at me with hatred shining bright.

"It's going to look like you killed Isaac," Lily said. "I mean, it's your blade after all. And after you killed him, you took it really hard, like that time with the Veiler on the mountain. So hard that you took your own life to end the suffering."

I looked at Serene, pleading.

"You don't want to do this. Taking a life taints the soul. It follows you forever."

She was beyond hearing. Her brown eyes had darkened, and all that I could see was hatred. Even her sweet voice sounded sour.

"Oliver is dead because of you. He was weak and unable to withstand the truth sessions. But he wouldn't have had to endure them if you hadn't betrayed us. You are the reason I'm not home in bed right now. You are why I'll never again taste my mother's cooking, hear my father tell a story, or watch my little sister grow up. I'm going to die here, and it's all because of you!"

All rationality had left her. Only anger and hostility remained. She lunged for me as I quickly pivoted and took off running down the corridor.

"Hold her down!" Lily shouted.

I could hear the clatter of shoes scuffing, chasing after me. My breath came in short pants, much weaker than usual, and my heart felt ready to leap from my chest. I focused on my strides, not daring to look back at how close they were. My best chance was to get to a populated area. I would be safe there.

I tripped over my foot and hit the floor hard. I cried out as my knees were nearly crushed by the fall's impact. Cradling my knees to my chest, I looked up to see Brenn smiling down at me.

"Aw, someone tripped." Brenn laughed as Lily, Aeva, and Serene approached.

Brenn kicked me onto my back as Serene advanced toward me. I turned my head to the side and closed my eyes tightly, preparing myself for what I knew was to come. It would all be over soon.

For a moment, my brain refused to understand. A crack like a snapped branch. A thud. A choked gasp that never became a scream. My eyes flew open, and the only person standing was Rowan.

His gaze held a murderous fury, unrelenting. He walked over to me and pulled me up by my arm. I winced at the sharp pain in my knees as I finally found my balance. He gazed at me as I let my eyes drift downward. Not a drop of blood had been spilled, yet four motionless bodies now littered the floor.

I saw Serene's petite, lifeless body and felt crushed by the weight of it. Her distended neck and vacant eyes would haunt me forever. The little girl who once delivered fresh bread every Saturday was gone. Just another innocent casualty in a game of power and delusion.

The overwhelming feeling of despair poured over me, coating me in its intoxicating sensation of hopelessness. More death. It was inescapable, and I was both a fool and a coward for thinking that perhaps I could evade its impact.

One thing had made itself abundantly clear: death was shadowing me closely.

"Can you walk?" Rowan gritted out.

"Barely."

"Good enough."

Rowan dragged me by my arm down the hallway. I didn't ask questions. I didn't fight. All I did was try not to let my legs lose all their support and crumple under my weight.

We eventually reached Rowan's quarters, and he put in his sequence of numbers. He didn't bother to hide it from me again. Then he pulled me inside and pushed me to sit on his bed. I watched silently for several moments as he paced the length of his room. Eventually, he stopped and looked at me with the same fury as before—but this time it was aimed at me.

"What were you thinking?" he exclaimed.

"Excuse me?"

"You closed your eyes, and all but asked them to kill you!"

"They had me on my back, four to one. What would you have had me do?"

"Fight back! Literally anything other than accepting the situation!"

"You told me I would lose my hope. Well, maybe I have."

"Bullshit. Not you. Everyone else, yes, but not you. You're different."

"You seem to think that I possess some sort of divine strength. I hate to be the bearer of bad news, Rowan, but I'm human. I'm not invincible. I break," I said on a choked exhale.

Rowan threw his head back and sighed. Then he walked over toward me and rested his hands on my shoulders.

"Isaac wasn't your fault."

I shrugged my shoulders in classic Rowan fashion.

"It wasn't. It's the transfusions."

I met his eyes, doubtful and wary.

"What do you mean?"

"They are altering your very essence, Mavis. They do it under the guise of strengthening you, but most of the time, they just create monsters. Whatever they're manipulating in your blood makes a portion of people turn psychotic. I've seen it time and time again. That's what happened to them. It wasn't you, or because they feel you betrayed them. They lost their sanity and were bound to hurt someone at some point."

"Is that what's going to happen to me?"

"Do you feel out of control, like you're bursting with unresolved energy?"

"No."

"Then I doubt it. It usually surfaces around this time, and if it hasn't affected you, then it probably won't."

I let out a breath I'd subconsciously held too long.

"I definitely don't feel stronger." I rolled my shoulders back. They were sore from tensing them so much. I paused mid-stretch when a thought occurred to me. "Is that why they only take younger people in the Cullings?"

"They take those aged thirteen to twenty, not only because they are younger and more resilient, but because it's easier to manipulate DNA when the body is already going through so many changes. It makes you—"

"The perfect guinea pigs," I answered for him.

Rowan only nodded.

I let out a humorless chuckle. "I'll be twenty-one in three months. Not that name-days really mean much here."

"I think they do."

"Well, that's uncharacteristically optimistic of you."

I gave him a small smile and then looked at my hands. They were still shaking. I picked at the undersides of my fingernails. Nothing was under them—they were too clean. I hadn't seen the outside world for what felt like years.

"Why are you still attending the truth sessions?" Rowan asked quietly. "Is it because of your gift?"

"No, she doesn't suspect that."

"Well then, what does she think you're hiding?"

"Nothing important." I shifted uncomfortably, and then I stood and started for the door. "I should get going," I said, reaching for the handle.

Rowan quickly grabbed me by the shoulder and twisted me to face him. I was then pressed between him and the door. I felt exposed and trapped.

"What are you hiding?" Rowan all but growled.

"It's none of your business," I hissed, trying to free myself from his hold.

"Everything to do with you is my business."

I bristled at that.

"You want to know what I'm hiding?" I taunted.

"Yes."

I couldn't speak, couldn't run away. So, I did the only thing I could do.

I surged up and kissed him.

# CHAPTER 38

*"The touch of love is tender yet fierce, capable of healing wounds unseen."*
*- The Old Book*

Rowan stiffened the moment my lips touched his, tension radiating from every line of his body. For a breathless second, he didn't move—then something shifted. His muscles relaxed beneath my hands, and he exhaled slowly, surrendering to the kiss with a quiet intensity that stole the breath from my lungs.

His hands came up to cradle my face, thumbs brushing softly across my cheeks. The warmth of his touch seeped into my skin, anchoring me in the moment. I dissolved into it, savoring every heartbeat, every inhale, every second that passed like a slow burn.

Then his hands slipped to my waist, grounding me, exploring. Heat surged through me, sharp and dizzying. My pulse pounded wildly beneath my skin. I pressed in closer, arms winding around his neck, needing to feel every solid inch of him, needing to remember what it was like to want something that wasn't about survival.

And then—he pulled away.

Abruptly. Sharply. Like the air had grown too thin.

His breathing was ragged—his eyes unreadable. Desire still lingered there, but something colder moved behind it: restraint.

"We should stop," he murmured, his voice rough, barely more than a whisper.

I opened my mouth, ready to protest. But the look on his face stopped me. He wasn't just retreating—he was fortifying. Bricking himself behind the invisible wall he so often lived behind. Whatever freedom he'd allowed himself in those brief seconds was now being sealed away again.

I bit back the sting of rejection and nodded silently, trying to slow the thunder in my chest.

Rowan moved to the door, opening it with quiet precision. I followed, knees unsteady, cheeks flushed and burning with unshed emotions. As we stepped into the hallway, he placed a gentle hand on the small of my back. The contact was brief, but it steadied me, soothed some of the unraveling inside me. I leaned into his touch, savoring the closeness that felt so new yet undeniably right.

We rounded a corner just as two Veilers appeared from the opposite direction. Rowan gave them a brief nod—professional, unreadable. The Veilers' eyes flicked to me, then back to Rowan, their expressions indecipherable but undoubtedly curious. I forced my features into neutrality, but my face burned. I had just shared the most electric kiss of my life and now had to pretend it meant nothing.

To them, Rowan was a commanding officer.

To me... I wasn't sure yet. But I knew my sentiments toward him had changed. He was no longer just another Veiler—cold and detached. He had a name, and that name made me to feel things I never thought possible.

When we reached the door to my quarters, Rowan paused. For a moment, we just stood there, the silence heavy between us.

Then he leaned in, brushing his lips gently against my cheek. "Good night, Mavis," he whispered, the warmth of his breath lingering on my skin.

"Good night," I replied, my voice small, and a little dazed.

I stepped inside and closed the door softly behind me. My body sagged against it. My fingers drifted to the spot where his mouth had touched, my lips still tingling from his kiss.

I couldn't stop the grin that tugged at the corners of my mouth.

For the first time in what felt like forever, I felt light. Giddy. Unsettled, but not in the way fear unsettles—it was the way something *new* stirred. My chest fluttered with a sensation I'd only heard about in stories. Butterflies. And gods, they were riotous.

I crossed the room and flopped onto my bed, my chest rising and falling in uneven bursts. I pressed my hand against it, trying to calm the strange ache there.

It was probably just nerves. That had to be it. Rowan had my emotions in an uproar.

But somewhere in the quiet, beneath the buzz of my thoughts, a different question whispered through me: *What if I had never left Oak Hollow?*

I knew my chances of going home were slim, but it wasn't something I had given up on. I mourned the girl I was and the life I could have had. My thoughts briefly flickered to Kaven. I wondered how he was, if he had moved on. I hoped he had.

All I was certain of was that kissing Rowan hadn't been about games or survival. It also hadn't been like kissing Kaven—about forgetting and comfort.

It had been about desire. About choosing to feel something good, just for myself. Perhaps part of the lure was its forbidden nature, or the mysterious air that Rowan had about him, but the main reason was simple: he made me feel *free.*

It was an absurd thought considering he was my captor, yet I had truly never felt so free in my life. Free to be angry, laugh, and cry. Free to be open about my darkness.

A small cough interrupted my thoughts. I turned and spotted Talia, sitting cross-legged on the floor, a paintbrush in one hand, her face wearing the most knowing smile I'd ever seen.

"Oh, gods, how long have you been here?" I asked, startled.

She giggled and gave a dramatic shrug, clearly enjoying my embarrassment.

"I'm sorry," I said. "I didn't know you were in the room."

Talia waved it off, unbothered.

I walked closer, watching as she dipped her brush into yellow paint and continued working on the dresser drawers.

"What are you painting?"

"Flowers," she said simply. "It's almost springtime at home. I miss the flowers."

I watched her strokes—steady, delicate, and precise. Despite everything, she still found beauty in the world.

"They're beautiful, Talia," I whispered.

She looked up at me, and for the first time in days, I saw a small but genuine light in her eyes.

"Thanks," she said softly. Then, after a beat, she added, "You look happy."

I didn't answer right away.

Instead, I watched her work, the image of yellow blossoms blooming across cracked wood reminding me that life could grow in strange places—even in this one.

Even here.

Even in me.

"I am."

# CHAPTER 39

*"There is give and take in everything.*
*All is measured, and all is accounted for."*
*- The Old Book*

I awoke the next morning feeling lighter than I had been in a long time. I padded over to my dresser and grabbed the hairbrush on top. My hair was less brittle now, so I could finally use something other than my fingers to comb through it. As the bristles moved gently through my waves, I paused at the sight of several starkly white strands.

They were white as snow, completely devoid of pigment.

I examined them closely, twisting one strand between my fingers to confirm it was real, anxiety blooming in my stomach. It had to be stress—that was the logical explanation. The journey here had been brutal, a ceaseless torrent of sleepless nights and constant vigilance. I'd witnessed similar changes in Oak Hollow, grief turning hair ghostly pale. That must have been what was happening to me.

Still, I couldn't shake the feeling that something else was shifting beneath my skin. That something deep within me was fundamentally changing.

Finishing my hair, I quickly dressed. As I tugged my pants on, I noticed their tightness around my hips. Turning to the mirror, I ran a hand down my side, tracing a newly formed curve that felt both foreign and familiar. My figure had regained its fullness, the softness now underlain with subtle strength. Even my arms, once thin and birdlike, now revealed faint lines of muscle.

Consistent meals and rigorous training were undeniably changing me. My reflection was healthier, stronger, yet strangely unrecognizable. My stomach wasn't sunken anymore, and my collarbone no longer jutted out like a weapon. Somehow, amidst all the death and dread, my body had rebuilt itself.

I thought it odd that I once stood before myself in the mirror and regarded my body as foreign. It was just a body, a vessel of life. I hadn't needed to be so cynical.

The wear and tear I had experienced since leaving Oak Hollow was evident in more than just my appearance. My aura had changed.

I wasn't entirely sure how to feel about it all. Gratitude mixed uneasily with an unsettling sense of disorientation. I was thankful I was alive, but at what cost?

Some days, a reckless sensation of invincibility crept into my bones—a dangerous illusion I fought to dismiss. Especially after what Rowan had spoken about occurring with some of the other culled. I didn't want what happened to Lily and the others to happen to me. I didn't want to lose my mind, too.

Shaking my head to clear away the troubling thoughts, I moved swiftly toward the dining hall. The room hummed with its typical tension: trays clattering, whispers filled with suspicion, exhaustion threading through every glance. I scanned the crowd carefully, mentally marking each familiar face. Our numbers had dwindled again. A fight the previous week had stolen three lives, and two more were executed. The group, once sixty-strong, was now reduced to forty-two.

My gaze shifted, searching specifically for one face among the many.

But Rowan was nowhere to be found. Not lurking in his usual shadowed corner, not stationed near the entrance. His absence sent a sharp pang through my chest that I couldn't silence. Was he avoiding me because of our kiss last night? Doubt trickled into my mind. He had been rather quiet afterward, but then he had given me a kiss goodnight. I didn't know what to think.

I grabbed a tray and settled alone at an empty table, picking at my food without appetite. Marcum took the podium, his expression a calculated mask of regret as he recited today's death roll. I listened as he read out the names of those who had attempted to take my life yesterday.

"Lily Thorne. Brenn Hollow. Aeva Ridgefield. Serene Windgrove."

Marcum's voice turned cool and clipped. "A reminder to all participants: violence against others is expressly forbidden. The only exception is self-defense, under provable, recorded circumstances. If you cannot abide by this, you will be removed from the program. Permanently."

I didn't look up when Marcum stepped down, nor when the room resumed its quiet rituals of scraping trays and whispered speculation. My appetite was long gone. I just sat there motionless, pushing a lump of something unidentifiable around my plate.

Still no sign of Rowan.

Eventually, the weight of the silence became too much. I rose, abandoned my tray, and slipped out through the side corridor—half-hoping I might run into him, half-hoping I wouldn't.

The hallway outside the dining hall was colder, quieter. I moved instinctively, following the path back toward the east wing, where the facility's lights were more fluorescent. My footsteps slowed as voices echoed ahead—low, familiar, tense.

I stopped just short of the junction.

Rowan was there.

But he wasn't alone.

Marcum stood with him, back half-turned toward me, posture easy but eyes sharp. Rowan slouched against the wall, but there was a stiffness in his jaw that told me this wasn't just small talk.

I stayed just far enough away so I could still listen. Whatever this was—it wasn't meant for my ears.

"What do you want, Marcum?" Rowan asked, his voice edged with barely concealed irritation.

"Now, now," Marcum replied smoothly, "is that any way to speak to me?"

"Just tell me what this is about."

A soft chuckle. "Maybe you aren't the screw-up everyone thinks you are." Then his tone sharpened like a knife. "There's some business I need you to attend to."

"Ask someone else," Rowan clipped.

A pause. The tension snapped tight.

"Watch your tone," Marcum warned. "I only allow so much, Rowan, before I get angry. You remember what I'm like when I'm angry."

Rowan's hands clenched at his sides. I could see the whites of his knuckles from where I stood.

"Yes, sir. I do."

Marcum stepped closer. "Maybe," he said, voice low and cutting, "if you behave, I'll tell your mother and father what a good soldier you've been."

I lingered long after they left, Marcum's words echoing in my ears. By evening, the unease had settled into my bones.

Dinner came and went, and Rowan had all but disappeared. Anxiety twisted in my gut, an emotion I couldn't dismiss as easily this time. I waited afterward, pacing the corridor outside the dining hall, restlessness coiling tighter within me.

I had overheard his tense conversation with Marcum, and I itched to know more.

I decided I needed answers. Quickening my pace, I headed toward the gym. It was time for our weekly sparring session. As I neared the doorway, I felt a flicker of hope that maybe he was already there, waiting for me with his typical stoicism. Instead, Renata stood alone at the center of the training mat, arms crossed, gaze sharp and measuring.

"Where's Rowan?" I asked, hoping that maybe she would impart more information.

"He requested I take over today's session." Her response was crisp, devoid of warmth.

I narrowed my eyes. "Why?" I demanded, unable to disguise my irritation.

"He's a commanding officer. He has responsibilities beyond babysitting you."

I scowled but said nothing.

She gestured to the mat. "Well? Are you coming, or are you just here to whine?"

I stepped forward. "Let's go."

Renata didn't hold back, and I didn't ask her to. I welcomed the way my muscles burned, the way the sweat dripped down my back. It was better than overthinking.

Better than feeling.

"You and that woman from Summit's Ridge know each other well." I tossed out between jabs.

Renata arched her brow. "Her name is Naia, and you and I aren't friends."

"I was just curious. I saw you two kiss—"

"My personal affairs aren't relevant to your training," she interrupted sharply, throwing a punch I barely evaded. "So I'll ask again, did you come here to train or not?"

I rolled aside, catching my breath. "Why are you helping me?"

She straightened and stepped back. "This is professional courtesy. Rowan asked me—that's it."

The strain between us hung heavy with unspoken questions. Against better judgment, I ventured, "So... is he seeing someone?"

Renata froze, her gaze turning brittle as ice.

She stepped back, posture stiff and formal. "Rowan's private life isn't mine to share, and even if it were, I wouldn't."

I stood motionless, embarrassment heating my face.

Renata's tone hardened. "I don't care what you think you feel—whatever you think is going on between you two—abandon it. Now."

My mouth opened. "It's not like—"

"It's pointless and a waste of air to lie to me," she snapped. "I read people for a living. Your entire body betrays you every time he's nearby."

I held her gaze. "It's nothing."

"It's dangerous," she corrected. "Rowan is so far out of your reach, you don't even realize the distance. And even if—*if* he felt something for you, it wouldn't matter."

"Why not?" I asked, my voice quieter than I intended.

Renata leaned in slightly, her smile cutting.

"Because if you knew him—truly knew him—you wouldn't want to be any-where near him." Renata brushed past me. "Come back when you're ready to train."

I didn't know what frightened me more—her words, or the part of me that wondered if she was right.

# CHAPTER 40

*"Under the proclamation of His Majesty, Acaelar Bloodborne, first of his name, a
new sect of soldiers will be instructed with a specific directive.
The Order shall be charged with protecting the sanctity of faith within the realm,
and falls under the direct command of the king."*
*- Article 1, Section 1, of the Veiled Compendium*

E ver since I first saw the tome in the library, it haunted me—slipping into my
dreams and whispering through my thoughts. Its presence lingered in my
mind, and I felt its sharp pull. Perhaps it was King Acaelar himself reaching from
the grave, or the goddess Elspeth urging me toward destiny.

The library doors loomed ahead. My palm hovered over the handle, slick with
sweat despite the coolness of the hall. I drew a breath deep enough to steady me
and ran through the plan again.

The librarian was a creature of habit—rigid, predictable. Even without seeing
him, I could conjure the image: his narrow shoulders hunched like a crow over
some book, listening carefully for any threat to his domain.

Which was why I needed a diversion.

Something that would get his attention and force him to leave his desk—keys
unguarded. But I had to be careful. I couldn't make him suspect my true agenda.

Pushing open the doors, I slipped inside. The scent struck me first—patchouli.
The librarian loved burning incense, and the cloud of it was thick today.

I scanned the area, but no one else was there, per usual.

The librarian sat at his desk near the entrance, nose-deep in a book. His head
did not move when I entered, but his eyes—sharp as a hawk's—tracked me.

"Back again?" His voice was low, brittle with suspicion.

"I am," I said lightly, forcing a smile I didn't feel. "There isn't much else for me to do now, is there?"

"I suppose not." His hand twitched, a flick of his wrist as if dismissing a servant. "Enjoy."

"I will."

The word tasted like a lie.

I drifted deeper into the library, past towering shelves. The silence pressed in, broken only by my labored panting. My trembling fingers grazed the spines of the many forgotten works. All this knowledge, all these secrets, buried under frozen Ground where no one could see. No one could learn.

But only one book mattered right now.

Every nerve screamed caution, but hesitation was a luxury I couldn't afford. I stopped before a tall stack near the back corner and placed both hands on its edge. The plan was simple.

I pushed.

The shelf groaned, swayed, and then toppled. The crash was thunderous, a symphony of cracking wood and tumbling books. Dust exploded into the air in thick, choking plumes.

A shout ripped through the stillness.

"WHAT HAPPENED?!"

The librarian came charging, his face contorted in panic. He dropped to his knees among the fallen texts, fingers trembling as they traced torn bindings and ripped pages. His voice rose, cracking with grief:

"What happened?"

"I'm so sorry!" I stammered. "I tripped—I didn't mean to—"

"Get out." His tone cut like a blade.

"But—"

"I said GET OUT!"

His roar shook the dust from the air.

I backed away, head bowed, feigning shame while my pulse beat wildly like a drum. My eyes flicked to his throat. No chain. Good.

Once I made it to the front entrance, I opened and closed the door, hoping it was enough to fool his ears. I moved quickly then. The keys were hanging on the hook, and I silently grabbed them. They were heavy in my hands. Their weight was both a promise and a prayer.

I didn't linger long. Every moment felt stolen as I ran to the door at the far end of the library, careful to evade the librarian still cataloging the destruction. I sorted through the ring of keys, trying each one in the lock, until I heard the click of the latch.

Slowly, I pushed in.

Inside, the air changed. Stale, untouched, laced with the sweet rot of aging parchment. The only illumination came from a flickering light that turned on when it sensed me. Tomes lined the walls in regimented rows, their spines dull with centuries of secrets. And there in the center, a glass case glimmered faintly in the gloom.

Inside lay the book that had called to me.

My breath hitched as I wrestled with finding the right key to unlock the case. Once I did, I lifted the lid, and the faint scent of old leather and iron ink wafted over me. My fingers brushed the cover—scarred, dark, whispering of hands long deceased. I gently picked it up, and the weight startled me.

I opened it.

The first page greeted me with words etched in a hand both regal and severe: *Journal of His Majesty, Acaelar Bloodborne, first of his name.*

This was it. The lost journal. Not lost, but hidden. Buried away, and hoped to be forgotten.

The first prophecy was eerie and foreboding:

The Old Book *speaks true:*

*Ascend from ruin, and be made anew.*

*I saw a vision of eyes flecked with gold.*

*Tests shall not break them,*

*nor Death condemn them,*

*for both man and god have chosen them.*

But it was the next prophecy that stole the breath from my lungs:

*From bone and ash, one will rise*

*with eyes that pierce death's guise.*

*The Sky shall watch, the Ground shall claim.*

*The kingdom will fall to those once shamed,*
*marking the end of Bloodborne's reign.*

I stared until the words blurred, burning them into memory. Acaelar had foreseen the fall of the monarchy. No wonder this book had vanished into the shadows. It was dangerous.

A sound snapped me out of my trance—a faint scrape beyond the door. Approaching footsteps.

Panic clawed at me. I shut the journal, easing it back into the case. My eyes darted for cover. But there was none. There was only the cold glass and the silent shelves.

The latch rattled.

"Who's in here?" The librarian's voice was low, venomous.

I knelt, heart hammering against the floor, praying my hair concealed me.

The door opened.

"I know someone's here," he hissed. When he spoke next, it sounded as though he were right on top of me. "My keys are missing."

I let out a shaky breath I had been holding. It was over.

I rose slowly, hands lifted.

"You." His eyes blazed with fury as he stalked toward me.

"I just wanted to look," I whispered.

"Do you take me for some fool?" His voice dripped with menace.

"Of course not."

"Did you touch anything?" His eyes were glued to the case, inspecting the journal inside.

"No," I lied, pulse roaring in my ears.

His eyes flicked back to me, expression carved from stone. "You are banned from this library! If I see you in here again, I'll hand you over to Marcum myself. Is that understood?"

The name hit like ice down my spine.

"Yes," I breathed.

"Good. Now leave."

He snatched his keys from my hand, and I ran out the chamber door. I fled the library as quickly as I could, my breath coming in short pants. When I reached the hallway, I leaned against the cool wall. Its temperature licked at the heat of my skin.

The entire plan felt like a waste of time and too large a risk. I didn't know why my dream had suggested the journal held the answers I sought. It had revealed nothing about Willam, but it shifted my perspective.

Marcum and the Guild surely knew about Acaelar's prophecies. So what was their actual goal?

One thing was certain, though: I could tell no one what I read. If Marcum or any other member of the Guild found out, then there was no way I was leaving the facility alive.

# CHAPTER 41

*"Vows made to the gods are allowed while in service of the Order,*
*so long as they do not supersede the directive."*
*- Article 2, Section 4, of the Veiled Compendium*

When I reached the gym to spar, there was still no sign of Rowan. Instead, Naia and Renata were both inside.

They had their hands intertwined and were giggling with one another. It sounded so foreign to hear Renata giggle I didn't believe it at first. But sure enough, she was smiling, laughing, and looking enthralled with Naia.

I stopped so abruptly that my shoes scuffed the floor, drawing their attention.

Naia's demeanor didn't change, but Renata's warming smile dropped, and her usual scowl returned.

Naia cupped Renata's cheeks and kissed her forehead.

"I'll see you later."

Renata nodded.

Naia sauntered toward the exit, brushing past me, and whispering in my ear as she left.

"Don't let her bully you."

I watched Naia exit, stunned at how someone like her could be with Renata.

"Hey," Renata scolded, snapping my attention back in place. "Don't stare."

"I wasn't staring," I said a bit too defensively.

She narrowed her eyes for a moment and then asked, "Are you finally ready to train?"

"Yes."

"About time."

I stepped onto the mat and assumed the fighting position while Renata tied her hair up into a bun.

"Have you ever thought about binding your soul to Naia?"

Both of them seemed to be committed to one another, and since marriage was outlawed between Veilers, it made sense that they would consider the ultimate vow instead. Marriage was paper, easily torn. *Netali's Vow* was irrevocable.

"What was not clear about the phrase: *we are not friends*?"

She threw a punch, and I flinched back, but it still landed.

"I was just curious."

I touched where she'd hit my collarbone. The ache hurt more than usual.

"I thought you came to spar; talking is not sparring."

"Can't I do both?" I quipped.

"No," she kicked at my feet, and I hit the floor, hard. "You're slow today."

When I didn't get up immediately, Renata let out a sigh.

"We both want to make the vow eventually, when we're free."

I looked up, rubbing my sore ankle.

"Doesn't that scare you? The idea of fusing your soul with another? It can never be undone."

"Nothing scares me anymore." She lightly kicked my wounded ankle, and I flinched. "Now, are you done nursing that scratch?"

"Yes," I muttered.

"Good, then get up. Your stance was all wrong. That's why it was so easy to knock you down."

I pushed myself to my feet, ignoring the dull throb spreading up my leg.

I swung at her, but my arm felt like lead, barely rising fast enough to meet her strike. She easily sidestepped, her foot catching my ribs, and I stumbled backward, gasping. My vision swam, the harsh lights above the gym streaking my peripheral.

Renata didn't give me a moment to recover. She lunged again, fists moving too fast for me to track, and I blocked clumsily, the force reverberating up my arms and into my shoulders. My breath came in shallow bursts, each inhale tasting metallic.

"You're holding back," she said, her voice sharp.

Instead of explaining how strange I felt, I nodded stiffly, circling her, trying to look more in control than I was.

The next flurry of strikes forced me backward, sliding across the mat. My knuckles scraped the thin padding, leaving little welts, and the floor smelled faintly of old blood and sweat. My chest heaved, and I felt a strange flutter in my temples—lightheaded, dizzy—but I pushed through, parrying her blows as best I could.

"You're... slow," she said again, breathing evenly, like she hadn't exerted herself at all. "Why?"

I struggled to catch my breath; black spots speckling my vision.

"Honestly, I'm not sure."

"Does Rowan know?"

I deflected. "Where *is* Rowan?"

"If he didn't tell you, then he probably didn't want you to know. Now, answer my question."

"It's nothing. I just feel weaker today, that's all."

Her expression shifted for a second, almost imperceptibly, but I caught it. She was concerned.

"Have you noticed a shift in your mood at all?"

I scoffed, "I'm not going mad."

"So you have talked to Rowan about the effects."

"Yes, I'm aware of them."

Renata crouched over me, studying me. "You're hiding something," she said.

I swallowed.

She may have been helping me train on behalf of Rowan, but she was right; she was not my friend. I still didn't trust her. Telling her I felt weaker than usual today was already a mistake.

She certainly didn't need to know what I had read in the library.

I shook my head, though the world swayed. "Nothing," I muttered, voice hoarse.

She stood upright, letting her gaze drift around the gym, as if she were satisfied I'd failed. Steam hissed from the pipes, wrapping us in a wet, heavy fog. The sound of the boiler was almost deafening now, drowning out everything except the pounding in my chest.

"You can do better than this," she said finally, crouching back into her stance. "Or I'll think you really are broken."

I clenched my fists, forcing myself to rise, to center. My legs wobbled, but I stood, adjusting my guard. Every movement felt sluggish, like wading through water. And yet, the edge of my fear sharpened me.

Renata smiled then, almost approvingly. "There. That's better. Now, fight like someone who wants to survive."

I nodded once, tight-lipped, and lunged—not because I thought I could win, but because I refused to go down without meeting her blow head-on. Pain radiated with every strike, sweat dripped into my eyes, and the air in the gym felt thick enough to choke on, but I kept moving.

Finally, I collapsed from exhaustion. My eyes were sticking together from the sweat, and I struggled to pry them open.

"We're done for the day," Renata said sternly. "Go rest. You need it."

She left, and I stayed there, heaving, heat pressing down like a weight I couldn't lift.

# CHAPTER 42

*"The weight of life is far too heavy a burden to bear alone.*
*It will crush you."*
*- The Old Book*

### The Facility - Month 3

I stood in front of my bedroom mirror, counting the white strands in my hair that had been multiplying like frost creeping across glass. I wasn't as confident that it was purely stress anymore, considering every other culled one's hair was growing just as white. But at least I was doing better than most—like Talia.

Talia sat cross-legged on her bed, absorbed in her own world as she carefully maneuvered splintered bits of wood across the thin mattress. She had pried them off her dresser days ago. Each shard of wood seemed like a tiny actor in a play only she understood. Her eyes, dull and distant, hardly ever acknowledged my presence anymore.

"Talia," I spoke gently, my voice scarcely above a whisper. "You need to eat something."

Her shoulders tensed slightly, but she didn't lift her gaze. The wooden splinters continued their silent dance.

"You can't keep avoiding meals," I tried again softly. "Come with me. Even just for a little while."

Each day, I watched her fade, a sense of helplessness gnawing at me, as if I was witnessing a slow, painful death I was powerless to prevent. I had watched an already slender Talia wither away during the past few weeks. I often had to prompt her to come to meals, and even then, she seldom came.

She paused, the smallest sliver of hesitation showing through her mask of indifference. I waited patiently, refusing to pressure her, giving space for the silence to coax her decision.

Talia's hand stilled, her eyes flickering briefly toward me. Without a word, she slid off her bed, leaving the splintered pieces carefully lined in formation.

As we entered the dining hall, the usual tension pressed in from all sides. We found seats near the end of a long table, and Talia hunched protectively over her tray, picking listlessly at the food. I observed her, worry fraying at the edges of my composure. She was cracking before my very eyes.

I shivered and rubbed my arms for extra warmth. The dining hall had always felt cold, but now it was frigid, and it was all because of one person's absence—Rowan.

He had been gone for three weeks without a note or whispered word of goodbye. He just vanished. A part of me feared something bad had happened to him, but surely I would have learned that from Renata. Every time I showed up for training, it was Renata on the mat. She was a skilled fighter, but she wasn't Rowan.

Suddenly, a violent cough echoed sharply across the hall, yanking me from my own thoughts and drawing the attention of the room. A boy, thin and pale, lurched forward as blood spilled from his mouth. Gasps and murmurs erupted around us as the poor boy continued to spew crimson. Talia flinched, her eyes wide in fear. I instinctively reached out, gently placing my hand atop hers, anchoring her back to reality.

Healers rushed forward, swiftly lifting the boy onto a stretcher and whisking him away. An uneasy quiet settled once more, whispers rising in its wake.

I clutched my stomach painfully. This was the third time this week the healers had come to the dining hall.

It was in that silence that my gaze lifted, and my heart jolted painfully. Standing near the doorway, looking utterly forlorn, was Rowan. His eyes met mine instantly—wide, filled with unmistakable regret.

He was asking for forgiveness.

I clenched my jaw, irritation flaring inside me.

After weeks without a word, after leaving me adrift in worry and confusion, he now dared to show his face, looking like a wounded animal. The relief at seeing him alive overshadowed the bitter edge of anger—just barely. But I wouldn't let him know that.

With an exaggerated roll of my eyes, I stood abruptly, pushing my chair back sharply enough to cause a scraping sound.

"Let's go," I muttered quietly to Talia, who immediately followed my lead, clinging close as we left the dining hall without another backward glance.

I had barely made it a few steps into the hallway before I heard quick footsteps behind me. Rowan was following behind, and he wanted me to know it. I turned to face a shaken Talia.

I sweetened my voice as much as possible. "Why don't you go ahead? I'll catch up."

Talia glanced back at Rowan, unsure. I grabbed her hand and squeezed it. She looked at me once more and then nodded. I waited until she was further down the corridor before I turned to Rowan. Without hesitation, I shoved him, my anger a palpable force within me.

"Three weeks," I spat my words at him, scoffing bitterly in his face.

"Mavis, please—" Rowan's voice was desperate, almost pleading.

"You disappeared for *three weeks*. No warning—*nothing*. And now you show up and expect me to roll over at the sight of you looking sorry for yourself? No, that's not how this works."

"I don't feel sorry for myself; I feel sorry for having left without leaving word."

I stopped. "Then explain."

I crossed my arms and tapped my foot expectantly.

He hesitated, searching my eyes. "I was handling commander duties."

"Convenient timing," I said sharply. "And what exactly were these duties?"

He opened his mouth to speak, but faltered, his hand halfway reaching for me before dropping weakly at his side. "I want to tell you—but I can't."

"Of course." My voice dripped with contempt. "I almost forgot—you're a Veiler. You were probably off murdering or kidnapping people. How silly of me to assume you were better than that."

Rowan's expression darkened, his voice lowering dangerously. "You knew exactly who I was when you kissed me."

I glared at him, heat rising to my cheeks in anger and embarrassment.

"Apparently not."

He reached for me again, desperation bleeding into his gaze. "Mavis—"

I stepped back sharply, distancing myself from him.

"I have a session to get to."

Without another word, I turned and left him standing there, frustration and hurt still simmering fiercely beneath my skin.

# CHAPTER 43

*"A pure spirit is not without its grief.*
*Without the dark, there is no light."*
- The Old Book

Adina sat in front of me, composed yet expectant, her hands gently clasped in her lap. Her eyes held a patient warmth, though I could sense the intensity lurking just beneath her composed exterior.

It was all fake.

"How have the transfusions been?" Her voice was soft, careful.

I inhaled slowly, trying to calm the residual storm inside my chest. The echo of Rowan's hurt-filled gaze lingered stubbornly.

"Yesterday was my last one. I'm still shaky, but it's manageable."

Adina offered a slight, reassuring nod.

"That's good to hear. Are you ready to talk about Kaven today?"

A heavy weight instantly pressed down on my chest, squeezing the air from my lungs. I hesitated, fingers tightening involuntarily on the fabric of my pants.

"If I do, will this finally be over?"

Her eyes softened further, yet stayed unwavering.

"That entirely depends on you, Mavis."

I released a long, tremulous sigh, feeling vulnerable as memories tugged at the edges of my mind. I just wanted this to be over.

"Kaven was my childhood best friend. Over time, our friendship became... something more complicated."

"A romantic relationship?" she asked quietly, jotting down a note.

"Yes," I answered simply, my voice strained.

"Did you love him?"

"Yes, but not in the way he wanted me to," I confessed, feeling exposed by the stark honesty of my own words.

"What held you back from fully reciprocating his feelings?"

"I don't know," I murmured, frustration bleeding into my voice. The rattling in my skull began—a warning sign I knew too well. A chill crept down my spine, anticipating the pain.

She leaned slightly closer.

"You blame yourself for your father's death, for your mother's worsening condition. Could it be that you believed yourself unworthy of love?"

My breath caught sharply, the rattle intensifying into a harsh sting. Sweat prickled on my forehead as pain flared behind my eyes. I clenched my fists, struggling to maintain composure.

"I couldn't," I gritted out, "love him… it would've caused too much pain."

The stinging ebbed briefly, leaving behind a trembling ache.

"Whose pain were you more afraid of—yours or Kaven's?" Adina's question hung quietly in the charged air.

"Kaven's," I whispered hoarsely.

"Why?"

"Because I was poison to him!" I burst out, my voice cracking with raw, overwhelming emotion. "I'm mold, a toxin that spreads and destroys. He deserved someone better—someone who could genuinely love him. Someone who wasn't broken beyond repair."

Adina sat back slightly, allowing space for my words to settle. "Do you still believe you're undeserving of love?" she asked, gently coaxing me toward the truth I was reluctant to face.

I hesitated, wrestling with the tangled mess of thoughts in my mind, until clarity broke through like sunlight piercing heavy clouds.

"I deserve love."

Pride shone on her face. Whether it was for me or her, it was unclear.

"You absolutely do. If someone else entered your life now, could you lower your walls enough to let them in?"

One face emerged instantly, vivid and unmistakable. It startled me with its certainty, and my heart skipped painfully. Yet I knew my answer, undeniable and powerful in its truth.

"I think I could."

Adina's smile widened, filled with quiet satisfaction.

"Congratulations, Mavis. You've completed your sessions."

# CHAPTER 44

*"By royal decree, the Guild for Religious Conservation is permitted to instruct the Order of the Veil on behalf of the king."*
*- Addendum to Article 1, Section 1, of the Veiled Compendium*

It had been two weeks of pointed silence—two weeks of evading Rowan's gaze, his voice, his presence. Every time he entered a room, I found a reason to leave it. With every glance he offered, I purposely averted my eyes. I was running from him, but more than anything, I was running from myself. Deep down, I knew avoidance wasn't sustainable.

Eventually, I was going to give in.

Rowan must have sensed it too, because after lunch one afternoon, he finally cornered me in an isolated corridor. He stepped in front of me, his tall frame effectively blocking my path, his arms folded resolutely across his chest.

"We need to talk." His voice was firm, though a hint of uncertainty softened the edges of his usual stoicism.

"I disagree," I retorted flatly, refusing to meet his eyes.

"Mavis," he sighed, stepping closer. His scent, warm and comforting—sandalwood and a hint of leather—flooded my senses and sent an involuntary flutter racing through my chest. "Please."

I finally lifted my eyes, intending to snap a biting remark, but the look on his face halted the words on my tongue. He wasn't guarded; not now. Instead, he stood exposed, vulnerability clear in the crease of his brow, the quiet desperation reflected in his expressive eyes. I released a heavy, reluctant breath.

I clenched my jaw, the part of me that still wanted to punish him warring with the one that just wanted to understand.

"Fine," I said at last. "Talk."

He rubbed the back of his neck, visibly uncomfortable. "I wanted to apologize for the way I left so abruptly. I know how it must have seemed."

I arched a brow. I doubt he apologized often, and it meant a great deal, but this hurt couldn't be so easily erased. I had felt rejected by someone I had corrupted my morals for and grown to care about. That couldn't just be swept aside.

"When you kissed me... I was surprised," he continued quietly, his voice barely audible. "Not that I regretted it. I didn't, and I still don't... but I was called away, and honestly, I needed to get away to sort some things through."

"Did you figure it out?" I asked, my voice softer than intended. "Whatever you needed to sort?"

He took a deep breath, stepping even closer. His voice was low, intimate. "I'm starting to."

I pressed my lips together, unwilling to make it easier for him. His hesitation lingered, the tension thick between us.

"I know you're still angry with me, partly because I left and partly because I can't tell you everything yet," he said, straightening slightly, a faint challenge entering his gaze. "Maybe you'd like to take out some of that frustration?"

My curiosity stirred momentarily, overriding my stubborn pride. "You're offering to spar?"

"Yes. I want to see how much you've improved while I was gone." His lips quirked. "Let's see how angry you really are."

A small, wicked smile spread across my lips.

"Deal."

Our journey to the gym was silent, yet tense with words left unspoken. The quiet hum of anticipation was building within me. I had grown to cherish my time on the mat—the burn, the fatigue—it made me feel in control. In a place where nearly everything was out of my control, these moments kept me from breaking entirely.

I rolled my shoulders back and stepped onto the mat, immediately slipping into a fighting stance. Rowan mirrored my movement, the muscles in his arms flexing as he readied himself.

I felt better than last time, steadier. I must have just had an off day, that's all.

"Ready?" he asked softly.

I responded with action, launching myself forward, unleashing every ounce of pent-up frustration, anger, and longing into each strike. I moved swiftly, aggressively, forcing him onto the defensive. Rowan blocked skillfully, but a flicker of surprise lit his eyes as he absorbed the ferocity of my attacks.

"You must be angrier than I thought," he grunted, dodging an aggressive kick. "It feels like you're genuinely trying to hurt me."

I narrowed my eyes, unleashing another relentless series of attacks. "Maybe I am."

In an instant, Rowan turned my momentum against me. He caught my wrist, twisted skillfully, and swept my legs out from beneath me. My back hit the mat, air rushing from my lungs. He followed immediately, pinning my wrists above my head. His body pressed firmly against mine, warm and heavy, as our breathing synchronized. My pulse thrummed loudly in my ears, and I could feel his chest heaving as well.

We stared into each other's eyes. The challenge was replaced by unspoken yearning. Something shifted. My anger dissolved, taken over by a fierce, undeniable need. I lifted my head, closing the small distance between us, and captured his lips with mine.

He responded instantly, his mouth urgent and demanding against mine. His hands released my wrists, sliding slowly down my arms, fingertips grazing bare skin, igniting trails of fire in their wake. He moved against me, his touch bolder, more desperate, drawing me tightly to him. The kiss deepened, heated, breathless, and intoxicating.

I tangled my fingers in his hair, pulling him even closer, feeling as though I might combust from the intensity. Rowan's hand slid daringly along the curve of my waist, thumb brushing the sensitive skin beneath my ribs, sending sparks racing along my nerves. Each touch intensified the ache building between us.

Abruptly, Rowan broke the kiss, chest heaving, eyes dark and hazy with desire. I groaned in frustration, clutching the fabric of his shirt.

"As tempting as this is," he whispered, voice hoarse with restraint, "we can't—not here. Not even if it's empty. It's too risky."

I let out an impatient sigh but nodded. Suddenly bold, I offered a suggestion. "Come to my room in an hour."

His eyebrow arched in surprise.

"Talia will be in the rec room doing crafts. It's the only thing she still takes part in. Trust me—she won't miss it."

Slowly, a mischievous smile spread across Rowan's face, eyes gleaming playfully. "An hour, then."

He stood, pulling me gently up with him. We left the gym quickly, anticipation in every step. As we parted ways, we shared one last glance at each other. It was brimming with promise. I felt feverish, but it wasn't because I was coated in a sheen of sweat. Heat lingered on my skin from his touch, branding me.

I showered, trying to clear my mind and relax my muscles. It didn't work.

I slipped into a simple nightgown, fingers trembling nervously as I combed through my damp hair. My chest tightened slightly, a small pang of discomfort. I rubbed the ache until the soreness subsided. Then, I slid beneath my covers, counting down the moments.

A gentle knock echoed at the door, and my breath hitched.

"Come in," I called out shakily.

Rowan entered silently, the door clicking shut behind him. His eyes immediately sought mine, filled with tenderness and carefully guarded desire.

"You can come a little closer," I said huskily.

He took a step toward me and stopped.

"Hi," I murmured shyly, feeling vulnerable yet emboldened by his heated gaze.

A mischievous smile spread across his face, eyes glowing excitedly in the dim light. My hands trembled as I clutched the covers tighter.

"Hi."

# CHAPTER 45

*"When two souls touch, they do not leave unchanged.*
*Even if the flesh forgets, the spirit remembers."*
*- The Old Book*

Rowan stood with his hands in his pockets, staring at me like I was going to disappear at any moment. Like he needed to memorize my image.

I pulled the covers off my body, exposing my short nightgown that cinched mid-thigh. I pivoted onto my side and rested my head in my hand, enjoying his lazy perusal of my body. His eyes stopped twice on their journey south. Once at the peak of my breasts, and the second time at the area between my thighs.

His throat bobbed, and I *burned*.

"Didn't anyone ever tell you it isn't polite to gawk at a lady?"

"Cruel woman." He smirked.

Rowan closed his eyes tightly, shaking his head and tilting it back. He threw his hands over his face and let out a small guttural groan that made me squirm in equal frustration.

He began walking toward my bed, and when he reached the foot of it, he stopped again. I bit my lip, not in a teasing mood in the slightest. But he didn't move an inch. He placed his hands back in his pockets and studied every move I made, noting the hitch in my breath.

If I kept on with my very obvious flirtation, this was going to end up going somewhere I wouldn't be able to come back from. Rowan was gorgeous, and my body had been annoyingly drawn to him ever since the first moment he put his hands on me in Oak Hollow.

I had ignored my body's betrayal for months because I couldn't fathom ever acting on it. To act on my basic desire toward him would be to forsake my ethical integrity, and who would I be without my morals? But right now, I didn't really care who I was. All I could think about was that aching need.

All I could think about was him.

He tested the waters, dropping one of his arms and lightly circling a finger on my calf. I shuddered at the sensual touch. He watched his finger as it leisurely moved up the side of my leg. He stepped toward me and continued to trail up higher, stopping when he reached my lower thigh. Rowan flicked his heated eyes to mine and kept his finger still.

My heart was frantically attempting to leave my body. I focused on trying to control my breath as it clipped when I inhaled. Rowan watched the flutter of my chest and quirked his lips. I wasn't sure how much more anticipation I could take. I was growing impatient to touch him, but I held myself back. My lips parted, and his eyes darted there.

"What are you thinking, Mavis?" His voice was smooth and dark. His finger began making lazy circles on my thigh. Heat flared in my lower abdomen, and suddenly I felt like I was on fire.

"It's hot in here," I admitted, utterly breathless. He lowered a second finger and then drifted them up and inward, pausing at the edge of my nightgown.

"Say the word," he whispered, "and I'll cool you down."

I swallowed hard. Words were not coming to me, no matter how hard I tried to think of them. My brain was empty of all thought, only feeling.

I nodded, giving him the silent permission we both yearned for.

Rowan grinned and dipped his fingers under the nightgown and hovered them dangerously close to where I ached for him most. I lay my back on the bed and slightly parted my legs in invitation.

His fingers slipped under the edge of my underwear, dragging them slowly down. Rowan kicked his shoes off and then placed one knee on the bed next to my hip. He settled his other knee between my thighs, pushing them farther apart.

In one swift motion, I pulled my nightgown over the top of my head and tossed it on the floor. Rowan's eyes flared with overwhelming desire at my uncovered body. I bit my lower lip in response to his intense stare.

"Gods, you're gorgeous," he said as he spread his hands over my thighs.

He let his hands roam over my curves and up to cup the swell of my breasts. He gently squeezed and then moved his head down to nip at the swollen peaks. I moaned, and he repeated the act.

I clutched his tunic and tugged. Rowan looked up at me and then obliged my unspoken request. He tore his tunic off and allowed me a few moments to enjoy the view. His body was a masterpiece painted by the gods themselves. Every chiseled edge and scar was beautiful.

I followed the dusting of dark hair below his navel down to the tight press of his pants. My eyes widened, and my core throbbed. That was all he could take before he snapped and lowered his lips to mine.

The first time we kissed was soft compared to this. This was frantic and fiercely passionate. He dove into the kiss with a yearning that I matched. He drank from my lips like a man dying of thirst. I opened my mouth wider to give him more access, which he quickly took advantage of and flicked his tongue against mine.

We became a tangle of tongues and teeth, all the while his hands grabbed and massaged my curves and breasts.

I ran my hands down his back, digging my nails in just enough so that the pain was laced with pleasure. He groaned into my mouth, and I unraveled.

My need for him was powerful and all-consuming. I needed him more than I needed air in my lungs. At that moment, I didn't care who he was or what he represented.

It was just us.

I reached for the ties of his trousers, fingers trembling slightly—not from fear, but from the unbearable ache building inside me. Rowan let out a low groan as he leaned into my touch, pressing his forehead to mine.

"Are you sure?" he whispered, voice hoarse, eyes searching.

"Yes," I breathed. "I've never been more sure of anything."

After that, there were no more words—just breath and skin, touch and heat. When he entered me slowly, fully, I gasped, clinging to his shoulders, feeling everything at once: the pain, the beauty, the rush of being so completely known.

He kissed me through it, coaxed me into the rhythm. We were the embers of a fire that could burn for days. One I would gladly let burn for as long as possible if given the time. However, we were constrained in our allotted freedom in this place.

When I finally gave in to the blaze, it felt like being shattered and remade in the same moment. Rowan followed soon after, collapsing against me with a quiet, reverent moan.

We lay tangled together in the stillness that followed, our bodies slick with sweat, chests rising and falling in unison. I traced idle circles on his shoulder, too dazed to move, too full of feeling to speak. I was afraid to move, scared of losing whatever the feeling in my chest was.

The silence between us wasn't awkward—it was heavy with something unnamed. Something fragile and terrifying and precious.

I turned my head slightly, glimpsing his face in the dim light. His expression was soft, vulnerable in a way I'd never seen before.

"What happens now?" I whispered.

He didn't answer right away. Just tightened his arm around me and pressed a kiss to the top of my head.

"Now we breathe," he said. "Together."

# CHAPTER 46

*"To protect is not always to speak.*
*To love is not always to hold.*
*Sometimes the greatest mercy is to remain silent and stay."*
*- The Old Book*

### The Facility - Month 4

A sudden, sharp pain pierced my chest, stealing the breath from my lungs. The room rocked, and the brush slipped from my trembling fingers, clattering loudly onto the floor. Darkness swiftly enveloped me, swallowing me whole.

When I came to, I felt the cold, unforgiving floor beneath my cheek and heard a low, anxious whining beside me. Slowly, with considerable effort, I turned my head. Talia hovered close, eyes wide with panic, tears silently streaking down her pale cheeks. Her lips moved soundlessly—her voice having abandoned her entirely in recent days.

"Talia," I rasped, weakly reaching out to grasp her trembling hand. "I'm okay."

She nodded shakily, unconvinced, and continued to cling to my hand desperately, refusing to let go as I sat upright. Breathing had become painfully labored, each inhale feeling insufficient. The dull ache in my chest intensified, but I pushed the worry down, locking it away.

"See? I'm fine," I murmured, though the lie tasted bitter.

After reassuring Talia enough to release me, I stood shakily and dressed for breakfast. Every movement was heavier than it should've been, each step toward the dining hall more taxing than the last.

As I entered the dining hall, a subtle but tangible shift in atmosphere hit me immediately—a heaviness hung in the air, thick with unease and sickness. Murmurs echoed softly, everyone speaking in low, subdued tones.

Marcum stood at the podium, his face unreadable as ever, voice coolly detached. He recited two names I barely recognized, the monotonous announcement underscoring the somber mood gripping everyone present.

My gaze instinctively swept the hall, searching among the scattered, weary faces for the one person I longed to see. For the third breakfast in a row, Rowan was nowhere to be found. The hollow ache of his absence clawed uncomfortably within me.

I barely touched my food before leaving, feeling suddenly too restless and uneasy to remain seated. My quarters would be quieter, a safer refuge from my troubling thoughts.

But before I could reach my bedroom, the scent of sandalwood enveloped me, sending a thrill of anticipation down my spine. A strong, familiar hand seized my arm, gently pulling me into a side room off the hall.

"Rowan—" My surprised whisper was silenced immediately by his lips capturing mine fiercely. The kiss ignited something deep within, chasing away the lingering shadows of the morning.

Breathless, I pulled back, eyes wide with both excitement and mild scolding. "You're going to get us caught, being this reckless."

Rowan's eyes sparkled mischievously, his lips curving into a teasing smirk. He leaned in closer, his voice a whisper against my ear. "Trust me, Mavis, I can be much more reckless."

The playfulness of his tone made something flutter in my chest—not pain this time, but something perilously close to delight.

I rolled my eyes and stepped back slightly. "We can't."

His brow furrowed. "Why?"

"I'm busy. I'm still trying to figure out where Willam might have ended up."

I still had a collection of books that I'd checked out and never returned. The librarian would probably come after me soon for them, but for now, they were still in my possession.

"I thought you said you discovered he didn't make it here?"

"That doesn't mean he's gone," I snapped, sharper than intended. "Just be-cause he's not in the records doesn't mean he's not out there."

Rowan hesitated. "I just don't want you chasing ghosts."

"Then let me chase them. I need answers."

"What if there are none to find?"

"Then I'll finally stop looking. But I need to know. There has to be someone who knows something."

He stared at me, silent for a long moment. Something moved behind his eyes—something unsaid—but then he sighed, and his hands found their way back to my waist.

"I get it," he murmured. "I do."

"Thank you," I said, appeased. "Where have you been? You haven't been at morning meals for the last few days."

Rowan gave a half-smile. "You've been looking for me, huh?"

I smacked his chest playfully. "Don't deflect. Where were you?"

His amusement faded.

"I can't tell you. Not yet."

"Why?" I asked, exasperated. "Why is everything with you a riddle? Why can't you ever just say something real?"

He furrowed his brow. "Something real?"

"Yes, something honest. Something no one else knows."

He tilted his head, considering.

"I hate cherries."

I blinked. "Cherries?"

"They taste strange. And the pit situation? Absolutely infuriating. That ob-jectively makes them the worst fruit."

I snorted.

"That's your deep, personal truth?"

"It's a start." He shrugged.

I grinned, shaking my head. "Pomegranates are worse."

"Blasphemy," he whispered, mock offended.

"They're bitter and hard to eat. Nothing about them is worth the effort."

"I respectfully disagree."

I nudged him. "Respectfully?"

He leaned in and nuzzled against my neck, and I let out a startled giggle—an honest-to-gods giggle.

"I like it when you laugh. You don't do it nearly enough."

"I haven't had a lot of reasons to laugh in my life."

"Maybe we can fix that."

His voice carried an unspoken weight. I knew what he meant: survival. Hope. The future.

But it hurt—because I didn't believe in any of those things anymore. Not for me. Not here.

Still, I didn't want to steal the light from this moment. So I smiled and leaned into his touch, resting my forehead against his.

He didn't need to know that I had lost hope of ever seeing the sunrise or smelling the scent of rainfall again.

For now, a moment of laughter was enough.

# CHAPTER 47

*"The veil is not death, but the hush that comes before it.*
*A breath unspoken, a thread unspooled.*
*Mourn not the crossing—*
*for even the gods must pass through it to be born again."*
*- The Old Book*

### The Facility - Month 5

The air was unusually still that morning, heavy in a way I couldn't name. I swung my legs over the edge of the bed, stretching stiffly as the cold floor greeted my bare feet. Across the room, Talia remained curled under her blanket.

I padded softly over to her bed and knelt.

"Talia," I whispered, nudging her shoulder gently. "Come on, let's go get breakfast."

She needed to eat, and if I didn't wake her to go do so, then she wouldn't. Talia no longer made crafts, smiled, or even spoke. Her body was a hollow shell—her mind absent. She had stopped taking care of herself entirely—she hardly even got out of bed to shower.

I tried again to shake her, firmer this time.

"Talia. You need to eat," I said firmer.

She still didn't stir. My stomach twisted. I leaned in closer, my pulse erratic. Her skin was pale–too pale. I reached out, my fingers pressing gently against the side of her neck.

There was no pulse.

"Talia?" My voice cracked. I yanked her blanket back fully, exposing her small frame, stiff and too still. Her lips were blue, and her eyes were closed peacefully, as if she'd simply drifted into a dream she never woke from. The faintest smile was on her face.

Panic swelled in my chest.

"Karina!" I screamed. "Someone! I need help!"

Within moments, footsteps echoed down the hall. Karina burst through the door, followed closely by two healers. I stumbled backward as they rushed in. I couldn't look at her anymore. My sweet, broken Talia—who painted flowers on dresser drawers and molded whimsical characters from clay—was gone.

One healer pulled out a device of some kind and scanned it over her lifeless body. His expression was blank, clinical. After several moments, he spoke to his colleague, who was standing by, notepad in hand.

"Heart attack."

I blinked, stunned.

"A heart attack? She's thirteen."

"Fate is mysterious," the healer said quietly, "and not to be questioned."

I recoiled as if slapped. She was only thirteen—the same age as Alona. So young and innocent. I wanted to scream, to rip his words from the air and shove them back down his throat. But all I could do was stand there, chest heaving, trembling.

I watched silently as they took Talia's body away. They had put her body on a stretcher and placed a white sheet atop her still body. It had been respectful, and that tempered my rage—but only slightly.

I was left alone in a room that felt far too large and far too quiet.

I didn't go to breakfast that morning. My appetite had vanished, and I didn't want to hear her name called out.

What even was the point of eating? What was the purpose of keeping my body on the precipice of life, when the edge of oblivion was so near? I was destined to die here, a fate I was no longer running from. I had accepted it fully.

Instead of eating, I wandered through the corridors until my feet brought me to Rowan's door. I hesitated only a moment before I knocked.

The door opened a crack.

"Mavis?" Rowan's eyes squinted at the light, and his voice was sleep-ridden.

I didn't wait for an invitation—I pushed past him and into his quarters. I was beyond caring who saw.

"Where have you been for the last few days?" I asked, my voice brittle.

He had been absent for the past two days—no warning issued and no reason given. Typical Rowan.

He shut the door softly behind me. "I've been busy."

I turned on him, anger and grief a volatile mix in my chest. "Of course. You can never give a detailed answer, can you? Only surface-level ones. Gods forbid anyone ever actually gets to know you."

I let out a choked laugh. I felt the tears wanting to spring free, burning behind my eyes. But I was too scared to let them flow for fear of drowning in them.

His jaw tightened. "Is this really about my being gone, or did something else happen?"

I opened my mouth to speak—but the words dissolved. My knees buckled, and I broke. A raw sob escaped as my entire body folded in on itself.

"I found her," I cried out, tears streaking down my face. "Talia. I woke up this morning, and she was just—gone."

Rowan crossed the space between us in two strides and pulled me into his arms. I collapsed against his chest, gasping through the storm of my grief. His hands steadied me, one cradling the back of my head, the other wrapped tightly around my back.

"I didn't want to be alone," I whispered brokenly. "I didn't come here to fight."

He paused. "Did you come here to forget?"

"No, I came to feel."

Rowan's body relaxed as he pulled me even tighter into his arms.

"You're not alone," Rowan murmured into my hair. "I promise."

He guided me gently to the small couch in the corner. We sat in silence for a long time, his arms wrapped around me as I buried myself in the warm safety of his chest.

After a while, my tears slowed. My breath evened out. I stared at the wall across the room, hollow and raw.

"When I lost my father," I began, my voice low, "I was so angry. The kind of anger that consumes you and turns you into a stranger."

I looked up at Rowan and saw that he was watching me, patiently waiting for me to continue. He looked as though he were absorbing my words.

"He took his own life, and I couldn't understand it—couldn't forgive it. I was just a child, and I didn't know how to properly grieve for him."

Rowan didn't speak. He just held me tighter, letting me unravel.

"My brother had just been taken from us, too—my best friend. It didn't feel fair for him to give up so easily while my mother and I were also going through the same thing. It felt selfish, and I hated him for it—for leaving us and forcing me to grow up faster than I should have. I shouldn't have had to take care of my mother, but I did."

My shoulders tensed momentarily before I forced them to relax.

"But now..." My voice wavered. "Now I understand. There's only so much a person can take before something breaks inside them. Something irreparable. It all becomes too much to bear. So, I get it now. That weight. That kind of grief."

His hand shifted, his thumb brushing slow, soothing circles into my spine.

"Do you feel that way?" he asked quietly.

I paused, considering my answer. The air felt impossibly still.

"I've thought about it before," I admitted. "In passing. When everything feels too heavy and suffocating. But I don't think I could go through with it. Death will come for me like it comes for everyone. I know I'll meet Anam at the end of my days—but I'm in no rush to greet him."

Rowan pressed a gentle kiss to the top of my head. "We'll make sure that day doesn't come too soon."

He couldn't make that promise. My odds of survival were slim. I knew it, and he knew it. I already felt a stirring of something beneath my skin. But there was no point in arguing about it, so I said nothing. There was nothing to say.

I closed my eyes and let myself sink into the comfort of his presence. I never thought that the day would come when I was grateful for a Veiler. But I was.

He made me feel like maybe I didn't have to face this darkness alone after all.

# CHAPTER 48

*"The faithful endure much.*
*But not all suffering is sanctified.*
*Some is simply because of the cruelty of flesh."*
*- The Old Book*

I t had been a week without Talia.

The room felt bleaker now, like the warmth had drained away and taken all the air with it. Her side of the room was barren—only the stripped mattress remained. No blanket. No pillow.

No Talia.

Just an empty bed where a girl used to sleep. A girl who hummed softly as she fell asleep, painted delicate yellow flowers, and offered gentle smiles and acceptance to everyone she met.

They'd removed all her belongings. There were no more clay figurines on top of the dressers and the bathroom sink. The space was plain and lifeless once more.

Some mornings, I still woke up with her name on my lips, inviting her to breakfast with me. A habit burned into my muscles. And for a second—just a second—I would forget. I would expect to hear her breathing, to see her curled up under the covers, paint still smudged on her hands.

Then the silence would slam into me like a stone wall. And I'd remember.

Today was no different.

I dressed sluggishly, as if every layer were a weight. All I wanted was to escape the ache sitting just beneath my ribs. I needed a distraction. Movement. Something that demanded my focus.

The gym lights were already on when I arrived. Rowan stood barefoot on the mat, arms folded, his stance relaxed but alert. He nodded once as I approached, his expression unreadable. We didn't need words.

We never had—not for this.

Our sparring began in silence, movements measured and precise. The rhythm was familiar, almost soothing. But as the minutes wore on, something in me was faltering.

It must have been an off day again.

My vision darkened at the edges, a slow narrowing tunnel. My limbs felt heavier, as if I were moving through water. I tried to push through it. Just one more strike. One more dodge.

Then the floor lurched under me, and the air left my lungs in one violent sweep.

"Mavis?"

Rowan's voice broke through the static just before everything went black.

I awoke to a ceiling too far away and the sterile scent of antiseptic burning my nostrils.

The infirmary.

The sheets were too crisp. The air smelled of bleach and endings.

Was it time for my transfusion already? I thought those were over. Or maybe it was another test. But I had just had one yesterday, I thought, or perhaps it was the day before.

All my days blended.

I turned my head slowly, and there he was—Rowan. Sitting beside the cot, with fingers laced tightly in his lap, his leg bounced in a quiet rhythm of worry. His expression was controlled, calm, but his eyes, which stared off into the distance, betrayed him. Beneath the careful stillness, they were frantic.

"Hey," I whispered, my throat dry as bone.

He looked at me immediately. "You're awake."

His voice was tight, a thread pulled too taut.

"What happened?"

"You lost consciousness," he said, as if saying it aloud made it more real.

Dr. Sinters appeared beside me, tablet in hand. "How long have you been experiencing symptoms?" She asked while scrolling on her screen.

I hesitated. "A little over a month."

Rowan shot to his feet.

"Over a month?!" His voice splintered with disbelief. He paced once, hands flying behind his head. "Why didn't you say anything?"

"I thought it was the stress," I mumbled. "It didn't seem that bad."

He turned away from me, jaw clenched so tightly I could see the muscle twitch in his cheek.

Dr. Sinters was suspiciously unfazed by Rowan's uncharacteristic outburst. She ignored his odd behavior and asked me questions.

"List all your symptoms, please."

"Chest pain," I said, voice small. "Mostly when I lie flat. My breathing's been shallow. Dizziness. Weakness."

"Loss of consciousness?"

"Once before. A few weeks ago."

I felt Rowan's eyes snap to mine. He scoffed—quiet, bitter. "Unbelievable," he muttered, like the word tasted like ash.

She scanned me again, frowning.

"There's nothing out of the ordinary showing on your scan. Vitals appear stable, but that doesn't always mean there's nothing wrong. Sometimes, these things take time to reveal themselves. I want you to come in twice a week so we can monitor it closely."

I nodded, too tired to protest.

Rowan and I left in silence.

Rowan kept a hand on my back, his touch steady. I let him lead me, too tired to argue—but I noticed quickly we weren't headed toward my quarters.

"My room's the other way."

"I know," he said, not breaking stride. "We're going to mine."

I glanced up at him. "People will notice."

"No one will say a word," Rowan replied. "Not to me."

"Because you're their commanding officer?"

He just nodded.

Inside his quarters, he gestured silently to the bed. I sat without protest, not out of fear, but because, for once, I didn't want to fight him.

"Why didn't you tell me?" he pressed.

"You couldn't have done anything. I didn't see the point."

He stepped back as if I'd slapped him. "You didn't see the point in telling me you've been suffering?"

I shrugged and looked the other way, refusing to meet his gaze. If I told him I regretted my actions, it would change nothing. It would also be a lie.

"I didn't want to worry you."

He stepped closer and used a single finger to tilt my face back toward him.

His expression undid me.

He was terrified.

"You think I wouldn't want to know if you were suffering?"

Silence stretched thick with the hurt I had caused.

I didn't argue. I couldn't.

"You're not just a *participant*. You're my business, Mavis Ashbone. If I want to worry, I gods-damned will." He nodded to the bed once more. "Now lie down. You need to rest."

I did as he asked, slipping beneath his blankets. The scent of sandalwood clung to the sheets, soothing me. His presence lingered like a second skin, and for the first time in days, I let myself relax.

Sleep found me before I could think too hard about why I felt safer there than anywhere else.

When I woke hours later, I sat up, limbs stiff with exhaustion. I moved to the door, more out of instinct than intent, and froze when I heard voices just outside.

A man I didn't recognize: "I don't think we'll be ready in time."

Rowan: "We have to be. She doesn't have much longer. I know them—they're lying to stave off any panic."

A pause.

"Then we'll be ready."

I stumbled back from the door as if I'd touched flame.

My pulse skipped a beat, rumbling in my chest. I practically dove back into bed just as the door opened.

Rowan entered calm and collected, the mask firmly in place again. "You're up."

"Barely." I forced a yawn. "Still tired."

He sat at the edge of the bed and brushed a snowy strand of hair from my cheek. "But better?"

I nodded. "A little."

I studied his face, searching for signs—cracks in the mask. But he was unreadable now, smooth as glass.

"I think I want to go back to my room," I mumbled.

He didn't argue. He just nodded and extended a hand to help me up.

He didn't ask what I had overheard.

And I didn't tell him.

But the words echoed in my mind long after the silence had returned.

*She doesn't have much longer.*

And deep inside me, something fragile that had been built began to crumble.

# CHAPTER 49

*"Gods answer to the natural world—for they are created and bound by its energy.*
*Mortals carry that same energy within them, though disconnected."*
*- The Old Book*

It had been a week of stillness.

My hair had turned stark white.

I hadn't left my bed once. My bones ached from inactivity, yet the thought of standing felt like lifting a mountain. Each breath rasped from my lungs as if it cost me something.

Every morning, Rowan brought me breakfast.

He barely spoke. He didn't need to. His silence was steady, like the breeze on a summer day. He set the tray down gently each time, sometimes brushing my hand, sometimes just sitting with me for a few minutes before leaving again. He was always watching me as if he were waiting for something—something he didn't want to happen but couldn't stop.

Today, I could barely eat more than a few bites. The toast tasted of ash. Even water felt too heavy to swallow.

Rowan sat in the chair beside the bed, his arms resting loosely on his knees. I turned my head on the pillow and caught his gaze.

"Have you been paying attention to the death roll?" My voice came out as a whisper, brittle and raw.

He didn't answer at first. His jaw tightened, and he looked away—toward the door, toward the floor, anywhere but me.

"How many are left?" I pressed.

He hesitated. "Four."

My stomach twisted. "Including me?"

His eyes flicked up to mine, and he gave the faintest nod.

The final four. I wanted to laugh, but it would've hurt too much. Instead, I closed my eyes and tried to steady the quiver in my chest.

Rowan leaned forward and kissed my forehead. His lips were warm, but the words that followed were ice.

"You won't have to fight much longer."

The gentleness of his tone undid me.

I didn't respond. I didn't have the strength. Instead, I let the weight of exhaustion pull me under again, drifting back into half-sleep, half-silence, the kind that felt like floating between worlds.

Three soft raps on the door woke me.

I opened my half-crusted eyes to find the room dark, and Rowan gone. Shadows stretched long and unfamiliar along the walls. Only the flicker of light from beneath the hall door offered any anchor to reality.

I stirred only slightly, my body aching with even the smallest shift.

Another knock. Louder this time. Then a voice.

"Mavis."

I knew that voice. It belonged to Thomas, one of the night sentries. But the way he said my name made the marrow in my bones go cold.

The door creaked open, letting wisps of light trickle in.

"Mavis."

The voice was wrong now. Higher. Harsher. As if someone were pulling it from a torn throat.

The hair on the back of my neck lifted as my skin prickled.

Light footsteps padded closer until a figure stood at the foot of my bed, fingers locked on the frame. It was Thomas. His posture was rigid, trembling with some inner strain.

His face slackened. And then, *that smile*. Sharp. Too many teeth, which seemed to glow in the dim light.

His eyes went white.

No pupils. No iris. Just a blinding, moonlit void.

His smile spread wider across his face, almost *inhuman*.

I froze at the sight of it.

My breath caught in my chest. My hand fisted the blanket instinctively.

"W-what do you want?" I stammered.

He tilted his head.

"It's not what I want. Though I have been waiting... such a long time."

"Who are you?"

Because whatever it was, it was not Thomas anymore.

"You know my name." The voice now came from *beneath* the skin, not from Thomas' mouth, but from somewhere far older than the body it wore. "You can feel it."

I did. Somehow, I knew.

It rose in me like an instinct, like a memory that had never belonged to me but lived in my bones.

"Elspeth—The Courier of Death," I breathed.

Her smile widened. "In the flesh."

"So I'm to die, then." My voice was flat. Empty. "You're here to kill me?"

"I am but the messenger," she crooned. "Fate will take you all on its own."

"How much time do I have?"

"Not long," she said, with a chuckle like shattered glass. "You'll be with Anam before the sun rises."

A cold sweat coated my skin. My mouth was dry, but I forced the next question out anyway. "Why are you here?"

She cocked her head. "I wanted to meet you. I've been watching you for quite some time."

"Why?"

"You avoid death like a flame dodges the wind," she said, eyes narrowing with something like admiration—or hunger. "Peculiar, isn't it? Haven't you ever wondered why?"

I swallowed hard, the dryness of my throat scratching like sandpaper. "I've avoided it before. I can do it again."

Elspeth's head twitched. Her smile faltered.

"Not this time," she said, suddenly sharper. "Not even you are powerful enough to evade what's coming. Your name belongs to Him now—and He always comes to collect."

The air grew heavier. My limbs went numb. Her words rang like a bell inside my skull.

The glow in her eyes dimmed, the blinding white fading back to Thomas' hazel.

Thomas blinked, disoriented. He was back in control, and his body sagged as if cut from an invisible string. He looked down at his hands as if he didn't recognize them. Then his eyes flicked to mine; confusion and fear shone there.

"Mavis?" he asked hoarsely.

I said nothing.

I couldn't.

Because the weight of her words sat in my chest like stone.

*You'll be with Anam before the sun rises.*

And for the first time, I truly wondered... not if I was ready to die—but if I were ready to be forgotten.

What if this were it? What if all the pain, all the fighting, all the fractured hope led me here...

Alone. In a borrowed bed. Waiting to vanish like morning mist.

# CHAPTER 50

*"Do not fear death.*
*Death is a friend to life—they walk side by side.*
*There is an end as surely as there is a beginning—it is the course of time.*
*Look now to the light and bear no more hardship.*
*In Anam's name, may you rest at last."*
*- The Rite of Passing (spoken only to death-bound souls)*

I stirred at the sound of the handle turning.

At first, I didn't open my eyes. I thought it was her again—Elspeth. Come to finish what she'd promised.

But the footsteps were too solid, too human. I blinked blearily toward the door and saw Rowan step inside. He wasn't alone.

A man followed him—blonde-haired, broad-shouldered, with a hard face and dark eyes that scanned the room like a predator.

I tensed instinctively.

"Don't panic," Rowan said gently, crossing the room in quiet strides. "This is Sam. He's a friend."

Sam's stern expression gave way to a warm smile as he tipped his head to me.

"Hello, Ms. Ashbone, it's finally nice to meet the woman who's got my cousin all stirred up."

Rowan shot him a look that could've withered stone. Sam grinned brighter and held up his hands in mock surrender.

"I know his voice," I said slowly, staring at Sam. "You're the one from the hallway. I heard you before. You were talking about me."

Rowan gave a single nod. "So you overheard. I thought you might have."

I sat up, wincing. "What are you doing here?"

Rowan met my eyes with a steadiness that rattled me more than if he'd shouted.

"We're getting you out."

The words didn't register at first.

"What?"

"You're leaving the facility, Mavis. Tonight."

My heart skipped a beat.

"You can't just—how? Why now?"

He nodded toward the door. I turned and saw Renata standing watch, Naia at her shoulder. They were heavily armed, still as statues, eyes sweeping the corridor like wolves on the hunt.

"I've been planning this for months," Rowan said. "That's why I've been gone so much. Sam's been helping me gather supplies and clear a path. Quietly. We couldn't risk suspicion."

I shook my head, dizzy with disbelief. "The doors are open... but we'll die in that cold."

Rowan's jaw tightened. "They keep those doors unlocked as an illusion of freedom and choice. They know you'll freeze to death—but only if you're un-prepared. We made it here alive, and I plan on leaving alive. *All* of us."

Rowan crossed the room in a few long strides and knelt beside my bed. He took my hand, and for a second, everything else fell away.

"I won't let you die here."

"You should've told me," I whispered.

He gave a strained smile. "It's not that I didn't trust you. I just didn't want to fail you. If I had given you hope, only to strip it from you later, I couldn't have lived with myself."

I didn't argue. I couldn't. Not when it felt like hope was the only thing holding me upright now.

The halls were a labyrinth of shadow and silence.

Fluorescent lights flickered above, casting thin blades of white across the floor. Each step sent a jolt through my spine. I clung to Rowan, my legs barely obeying me. He didn't rush me—he bore my weight as if it cost him nothing.

We stopped at a door just down the corridor. I didn't recognize it.

"Whose room is this?" I asked, already dreading the answer.

Rowan didn't answer.

The door opened without a knock. The light inside was warm, deceptively so. Dr. Sinters looked up from a datapad in surprise—and then alarm.

She didn't have time to scream.

In a fraction of a second, Sam had a blade to her throat, his other hand fisting her hair and jerking her head back.

"Don't scream," he said coolly. "Not unless you want to drown in your own blood."

Her eyes went wide, and her mouth froze in a silent "o."

Rowan stepped forward. "Sit," he said to her.

She didn't move fast enough. Sam shoved her into the chair.

"We're not here to play games, Doctor. We need answers."

"I-I don't know what you're talking about," she stammered.

Sam pressed the blade tighter. She whimpered.

"Mavis' scans," Rowan said. "What was on them?"

"They were normal—just signs of fatigue, maybe dehydration—"

Sam didn't wait for the signal. He grabbed her hand and snapped one of her fingers backward with a sickening crack.

She shrieked, muffled by his palm.

Rowan's voice didn't rise. It didn't need to. "Try again."

Her chest heaved, face having gone pale, and panic surged in her eyes.

"She has tumors," she whispered, tears brimming in her eyes.

Rowan gave Sam another glance.

Crack. Another broken finger and another muffled scream.

"There's more you're not telling us."

Dr. Sinters' voice was hoarse with tears. "She has dozens of them. All around her heart." She sniffled. "I don't know how she's still alive."

My breath caught.

Rowan's voice turned razor-sharp. "Can they be removed?"

"No. Not now. Maybe a month ago—maybe. But they're too far gone. Cutting them out would kill her."

He went still. I saw his throat move as he swallowed the grief.

Dr. Sinters looked between us, eyes wide with something colder than fear. "You're all going to hang for this. The Guild won't stand for it. They'll find you—and when they do, they'll make an example out of all of you."

Her gaze pinned Rowan. "Even you."

Rowan didn't blink.

He gave Sam a silent nod.

The doctor didn't even scream. Sam twisted her neck swiftly, and she crumpled to the floor with a thud that echoed far too loudly in the small room.

Silence descended, thick and final.

Renata appeared in the doorway, her voice low and urgent. "We need to go. Now."

So we ran.

Or at least—they ran.

Rowan half-carried me, his breath sharp and jaw clenched. I tried to keep up, but the hallway spun beneath me. My chest burned like fire, every inhale a punishment.

"I've got you," he whispered, over and over.

But I was slipping. I could feel it.

Everything went gray. Then black.

The last thing I remembered was Rowan's voice, calling my name

And then—nothing.

# CHAPTER 51

*"Netali's Vow is most sacred.*
*It is only to be uttered with sincerest reverence and purest love.*
*But take caution, for breaking this vow will fragment the soul,*
*sacrificing one's true happiness for eternity."*
*- The Old Book*

I was surrounded by a black void.

But not nothingness. There were sounds. Distant, muffled voices. Footsteps thudded. Strong arms caught me before I hit the floor.

I opened my eyes a crack.

Rowan's face hovered above mine, pinched with panic. He looked like a man unraveling.

"Hold on," he commanded, voice strained. His hands framed my face, trembling. "If you want to know more about me, I'll tell you everything. You just have to live first."

"I'm trying." I coughed. "It's getting harder... to breathe."

He gently shook me, and my eyes re-opened. I hadn't even known they were closed. "Want to know my favorite color? It's blue. Want to know my middle name? It's Rowan. I hate my first name."

His voice broke.

"I'll tell you even more. Anything you want. Just please, Mavis. Stay strong. Fight."

That was all I needed.

I don't know how I stood—only that I did. On shaking legs, breath shallow, and eyes half-lidded. He helped me when I swayed, and didn't comment on how much I leaned into him.

We made it as far as the armory.

Then, my knees buckled.

Rowan cradled me in his lap, his arms tight around me like they alone could keep me from fading.

"No, no, no," he murmured. "You don't get to give up. You're not allowed."

His voice cracked, raw and terrified. "I can get you to a real healer—someone outside this cursed place. Someone who can save you."

Hot drops fell onto my cheeks.

He was crying.

I lifted my hand with great effort, fingertips brushing the tears trailing down his face.

I murmured weakly. "*Your tears do nothing but muddy the Ground.*"

Rowan barked a laugh, choked with grief. "That's the worst line in *The Old Book*. Fuck the idea of you dying, Mavis. I'm not ready to lose you."

I wanted to respond. I wanted to tell him I was still here. But my mouth wouldn't work. My body was betraying me.

Naia crouched down beside us, her hand finding mine. Her thumb made slow, rhythmic circles against my knuckles.

"*Do not fear death. Death is a friend to life—they walk side by side. There is an end as surely as there is a begin—*"

"Don't you dare say those words! She's not dying today!" Rowan spewed out, slapping Naia's hand off mine. "We just need to get her to a healer." His voice broke on those last words, and with it I heard his splintering conviction.

Renata's protectiveness was evident as she positioned herself between Naia and Rowan. "Don't snap at her like that! It's not her fault you won't accept the reality of the situation. Just look at her, Rowan!"

Rowan's soft cries turned into gentle sobs.

"She's all I have."

Renata's face softened, and she put her hand on Rowan's shoulder. "You have us, Rowan. We are your family, too. Don't you miss your freedom? Staying here and getting caught will have made Mavis' death for nothing."

"It can't happen again," he whispered.

Rowan looked at Renata and then shifted his gaze to me. I looked at him half-dazed. He took a deep breath and wiped the tears from his cheek.

"You see, Mavis, I lied to you. When we first met, you told me who you were, and I acted like you were a stranger. But I knew who you were. I knew who you were the moment I looked into those pale blue eyes. In those eyes, I saw a face I have tried time and time again to forget... I saw your brother."

"Willam?" I choked.

Rowan nodded.

"It was my first mission, and I had met your brother along the way. I was in a dark place during that time in my life, and Willam had been the first one to show me kindness in a long time. In return, I promised him I would look out for him. But I failed. He grew ill while on the road, and I couldn't get him to a healer. He died quickly in the night and was buried by morning."

"Sick?" I coughed.

"A fever took him. He burned up before I could find help. Please, understand. I'm so sorry I lied. I just didn't want you to hate me more than you already did. After Willam died, I swore I would never get attached to another destined for the same fate again. But I failed at that, too—I became attached to you.

"I thought maybe I could redeem myself with you. That perhaps I could keep you safe until you got to the facility. Your fate would be tied to the program then, but I could at least get you here in one piece. My feelings for you are something I could never have predicted."

I reached a shaky hand up and cupped the side of his face. He mirrored my action. My heart pounded unevenly in my chest. Tears burned at the edges of my eyes, not for pain, but from a deep, aching sorrow for the years of unanswered questions finally put to rest.

"I don't hate you," I croaked.

"Good, because I love you. I love you, Mavis Ashbone." Rowan lowered his mouth to my ear and whispered. "*I will love you 'till the air leaves my lungs, 'till fire meets my bones and I'm all but dust and a memory. Should you perish before me, a part of me will follow. In this life, the next, and every other. I vow it."*

My breath caught painfully, his words hanging heavy in the space between us. *Netali's Vow.* He had whispered words more sacred than any marriage oath without hesitation.

I knew what it meant. What it had *cost*. His soul had just bound itself to mine. Beyond time. Beyond life. Wherever my soul went, a piece of his would follow—even into the afterlife. The part of his soul that remained amongst the living would never feel complete until it was reunited with mine once more.

A life of mourning.

I lacked the strength and courage to make the same promise.

Rowan, as though sensing my hesitation, softly brushed my snowy hair from my face, the warmth of his touch anchoring me to consciousness. A sad, understanding smile softened his features.

"Don't say it back. Not yet."

I shifted in Rowan's arms, barely, my strength a thread unraveling. My vision was blurring again, the pressure in my chest growing heavier by the second.

"I tried," I rasped. "I really did."

Rowan held me tighter, as if he could stop time by sheer force of will. "Don't say that. You're not done yet. We're so close."

A soft smile curled on my lips. "It's my time, Rowan."

"No." His voice broke, fractured at the edges. "No, it's not."

"I'm not scared," I whispered. "Not anymore."

My eyes found his through the haze. I memorized the lines of his face—the panic in his expression, the desperation swimming in his eyes. "You need to let me go."

"There's no fucking chance I'm doing that," he said, choking on the words. "You're staying alive, Mavis. I need you."

His lips found mine, one last kiss—fierce, trembling, filled with everything he couldn't say. My hand brushed against his chest, over the place where his heart beat furiously.

When we parted, I touched his cheek with the last of my strength.

"This…" I murmured, barely audible now, my hand weakly motioning between us, "…this was all real."

And then, with a soft exhale, my eyes closed.

The stillness that followed was complete.

As if the world had paused.

And there it was—peace at last.

# CHAPTER 52

*"The bond of soul to soul is not broken by death,*
*but the weight of separation will hollow even the strongest spirit."*
*- The Old Book*

When I opened my eyes, I was no longer at the facility—I was somewhere else entirely.

The vast room around me had walls painted the deep blue of midnight, stretching endlessly upward into a swirling mist of darkness. There was no ceiling, only the delicate spirals of shadows high above. Gentle, golden light emanated from unseen sources at the corners of the room, warm and comforting—entirely different from the stark glare of the facility. This atmosphere calmed my restless spirit.

"Where am I?" I asked quietly, to no one in particular.

"The in-between," came a silky voice.

Turning sharply, I saw a stranger seated upon a throne of black and gold. He sat with his legs elegantly crossed, hands clasped neatly atop one knee. His features were striking—tall, lean, with wavy black hair combed into a perfect pompadour. His skin held a warm, golden-bronze glow, exuding an aura that made me pause. He was divine. The truth of it was in his obsidian eyes, the void of death.

*Anam.*

"Though some call it the veil," he added.

I had heard stories and seen depictions of the beauty of gods. But they paled in comparison to reality. Anam was stoic, radiating power and a sense of peace. The kind of peace I had felt only moments prior, when I thought I had closed my eyes for the last time.

"Am I dead?" The moment the words left my lips, embarrassment washed over me. If I were with Anam, the conclusion should have been obvious.

"Yes—and no," he said while studying me, eyes glittering with intrigue.

"What does that mean?"

"It means your mortal body has ceased to sustain life, yet your soul remains here temporarily." Anam tilted his head slightly, considering me as if I were a fascinating puzzle.

"I don't understand."

I didn't feel dead, but I could also recognize that something was different. The feeling of sickness I had was gone. I felt neutral.

"I suppose you wouldn't." Anam's eyes glinted as they shifted to just over my shoulder.

The sound of wind rustling and gentle footsteps approaching caught my attention. A voice, achingly familiar yet untouched by time, spoke faintly from the shadows. "You always were stubborn, Mavis."

I froze at the sound of a voice I never thought I would hear again. Tentatively, I turned around, my eyes rimmed with ghostly tears.

"Willam?" I whispered, hardly daring to believe the sight before me.

He stood there, preserved exactly as I remembered him—thirteen, eyes full of warmth, dark hair tousled as if by an unseen breeze. A small, delicate smile curved his lips as he regarded me fondly.

"Mavis." He stepped forward cautiously, as if he were afraid to spook me. His body may have been thirteen, but his presence was much older. "I've missed you."

My knees weakened, and tears spilled unchecked down my cheeks. "I never stopped looking for you. All these years... I hoped you were alive, that someday we'd find each other."

His eyes eased further, sorrow blending with tenderness.

"I know, but I wasn't meant to make it. When the Veilers took me, I knew I wouldn't see you again, but I didn't want to leave you. I prayed to Our Lady—not to save myself—but to save you."

Anam's voice came softly from behind us, respectful of our reunion. "My sister granted your brother's wish, tethering his spirit to yours, allowing him to watch over you, and protect you until your journey reached this moment."

Realization washed over me. The comforting voice so similar to my own, the shivers—it had always been Willam. "The voice I heard... that was you?"

"I didn't want you to feel so alone. However, exposing my presence outright could have altered your future, so I stayed hidden—secretly guiding you on your path. I'm sorry it was one of loss and bloodshed, but you were strong."

"That's not true." I frowned, remembering every moment of weakness I had.

"Yes, it is. It's you who carried on after I was taken, taking care of mother. You were brave, hunting for food when you needed to. You even got a job as a tanner."

"An apprentice," I corrected.

"See, stubborn," Willam said, rolling his eyes. "My point is, when the situation demanded something of you, you rose to the occasion."

"I couldn't save father," I whispered, my heart breaking on the admission.

"That is not your burden to bear," Anam declared from his throne. "Do not mourn the death of a soul that was not yours to save. You have no say in when the threads are cut."

Anam was right, even though it was hard to acknowledge. The years I'd spent mourning—my life, and the ones I'd lost—had taken enough from me. I had been holding on to far too much, for far too long. Nothing could erase my grief, but maybe it didn't need to disappear entirely.

Maybe it was enough that I made peace with what I couldn't change.

"Why did you ask to protect me?" I asked Willam.

"Because you're my sister," he said, as if it were that simple, "and because I foresaw your future."

"You... you were a seer?"

He grinned.

"I saw the future—one where you shone like a star. And I saw what I needed to do to get you there."

"Wait," I paused, "were you the one sending me visions?"

Willam nodded. "By being tethered to you, I could share my gift. I apologize only for all the close encounters with death that I couldn't prevent."

"Oh, Willam, I could never be mad at you." I reached out, desperate to embrace him, but stopped just inches away. "Can I..."

He stepped forward and wrapped his arms around me. Warmth flooded my spirit, familiar and comforting. I sobbed into his shoulder, holding onto him as though he might vanish again.

"You've been so strong, Mavis," Willam said, stroking my hair reassuringly. "I'm so proud of you. But now, it's time for me to move on."

"No—please stay," I begged weakly, gripping tighter.

"I can't," he murmured, leaning back just enough to meet my eyes. "I've done what I was meant to do. You've grown into someone incredible. Someone important."

"What happens now?" My voice trembled.

"I finally get to rest. And you," he smiled, "have an even greater destiny waiting."

"No," I whimpered, covering my hands over my mouth to keep myself from sobbing.

It was Anam who spoke next.

"It is time. His body has been long buried, and so he should never have stayed in the realm of the living. That was a decision my sister did not have the right to make. His name belongs to me, and his soul mine to judge." Anam's commanding voice left no room for argument.

Willam stepped back, his form growing translucent. "We never really say goodbye. We just find each other again in different ways."

A silent sob escaped as he faded peacefully into the surrounding darkness, his presence lingering warmly before finally disappearing completely.

I stood there, feeling both hollow and filled with profound peace.

Anam's voice broke the silence. "He has crossed over into the Realm of Remembrance. But your journey, Mavis Ashbone, is just beginning."

I wiped my tears and shifted my gaze back to Anam. He still sat on his throne, observing.

"What do I do now?"

"I have judged your soul as well, and I deem you worthy."

"Worthy of what?"

"Of something countless others have sought—and perished for."

With a graceful gesture, Anam raised an open palm, and before me, a door materialized out of thin air. It was slightly ajar, with warm light spilling from its edges. A profound sense of purpose emanated from beyond it, calling to my soul. It was inviting yet intimidating.

"Of course," Anam continued, voice deceptively calm, "you have a choice. If you would prefer to follow your brother, that path is available to you as well."

The air felt charged, crackling around me. I stared at the door, feeling instinctively that whatever lay beyond it was significant—possibly dangerous, certainly transformative. My fingertips tingled as I reached hesitantly toward the smooth golden handle.

"What's on the other side?" I murmured.

Anam's eyes glinted knowingly, but he imparted no more information.

Swallowing my fear, I opened the door wider, the white light enveloping me like a gentle embrace. I felt strangely certain I was making the right choice.

I thought of Rowan's tears. Of his vow. Of the world I might leave behind. But I had to believe this step wasn't an ending, only a beginning.

"Mavis," Anam spoke once more, drawing my attention. I glanced back at him over my shoulder. "When you meet my sister, tell her this: one more soul meddled with, and I'll come calling."

Despite myself, I smiled at the Reaper of Souls. Turning forward, I took a deep breath and stepped confidently into the unknown, embracing whatever destiny awaited me.

# CHAPTER 53

*"Worthiness is planted within virtue.*
*So be virtuous in life, and perhaps worthiness will find you."*
*- The Old Book*

**Rowan**

Alarms wailed through the corridor like a chorus of mourning wraiths. Red lights pulsed across the ceiling in sickening flashes, bathing the icy walls in color that felt too cruel, too loud for the silence inside me.

"She's gone," I whispered, though no one had asked.

I knelt on the floor, cradling Mavis in my arms, her body limp and far too still. My forehead rested against hers, and I inhaled the remnants of her scent—rosemary, old parchment, and something uniquely hers that had never been defined by words.

Sam's voice was distant, like it echoed from behind glass. "Rowan, we have to go! Now!"

I couldn't hear him—not truly. My heartbeat had fractured, split down the middle, and now only half of it beat. The other half had died in my arms.

I had whispered Netali's vow into her ear, binding my soul to hers. And now that hers had fled, mine was unraveling. I felt it—like the universe had turned inward, like the stars themselves mourned her.

"She's all I had," I murmured, unaware I'd spoken aloud.

Renata crouched in front of me, her face both fierce and soft. "I know," she said, her voice barely audible over the alarms. "But if you want to bury her yourself—if you want to lay her to rest the way she deserves—we have to move."

Her words sliced through the haze.

My breath caught. The thought of her being left behind, dissected or discarded was unbearable. They wouldn't bury her the way Anam demands it, to spite me, and so her soul would never know peace. I couldn't allow that to happen.

I nodded once.

We moved quickly after that.

Sam took point. Naia and Renata flanked our rear. I carried Mavis's body close to my chest, wrapped in my cloak, her pale face tucked under my chin like a fragile secret.

Every step was torturous. I had never known true agony quite like this. My heart felt hollow—my soul alone—and yet I was forced to carry on. I was forced to endure.

We were almost to the elevator when they found us.

Marcum's voice echoed through the hall like poisoned honey. "Going somewhere, Commander?"

I stopped.

He stepped forward with a dozen Veiled Ones at his back, each of them armed and alert.

Marcum looked proud of himself, and I bet he was. I wanted nothing more than to rip that smug smile off his face and slit his throat. He was a plague, and the reason I was in this godsforsaken place.

"I was rooting for you, you know," Marcum continued, eyes locked on me. "The two of you. I thought maybe this time, love might be strong enough to keep her alive. How sad." He smirked at my visible flinch. "Did you think I didn't notice the disappearances? Or the way you looked at her when you thought no one was around? How naive of you. I see everything."

I said nothing. He didn't deserve a retort.

Marcum tilted his head. "What am I going to tell your parents? They'll be so disappointed."

I looked up at him through the red haze of the alarm light.

"Then I guess they'll stay disappointed."

The first blade came for Sam.

We exploded into motion. Renata surged forward, blades flashing. Naia used her knives and precision to take two off their feet. Sam parried with brutal grace, his movements calculated and deadly.

I ran.

Call me a coward for not fighting, but my team knew what I had to do. I had to lay Mavis to rest, to give her a chance at a peaceful afterlife. Failure was not an option. It was something I was willing to die over—even though death meant very little to me anymore.

Mavis' weight in my arms was a prayer. I never wanted to let her go. I kept my eyes on the elevator at the corridor's end and didn't look back, even when I heard someone scream.

I reached the panel and hit the button. The doors creaked open just as Renata, Naia, and bloodied Sam came hurtling into view.

I quickly glanced Sam over. It wasn't his blood.

"Go!" Sam shouted, dragging a nearly unconscious Renata in behind him.

As the doors shut, Marcum's voice rang out one last time. "There's nowhere you can hide. We will find you—and when we do—you'll wish you'd died with her."

Our eyes met in a blazing fury.

My next words were low and grave.

*"May the salt burn."*

The doors shut, and the elevator shuddered as it lurched upward. Once we reached the top, I slammed my fist into the control panel, and sparks flew. The damage would buy us time—hopefully enough.

We surfaced into the chilled open night.

The air was crisp and clean, a far cry from the recycled staleness of the facility. Stars blinked overhead, indifferent and eternal.

I was barely two steps out of the elevator when I dropped to my knees.

Still cradling her lifeless form.

The tears came without shame. Silent and savage, I wept for her. For what she had endured. For what she had never been given.

"I'm so sorry I failed you," I whispered. "I tried. I really fucking tried."

I reached out and touched her cheek, my bloodied hand painting her porcelain face with crimson streaks. I brushed a lock of icy white hair behind her ear and kissed her temple. Her skin was cold now, her expression hauntingly serene.

I squeezed my eyes shut, trying to pull myself together. I had a team I needed to be responsible for, one I had to get to safety. Yet I couldn't drag myself away from the sorrow threatening to drown me.

I opened my eyes, wanting to steal one last look—

Only to see a set of familiar blue eyes, now flecked with gold, staring back at me. She was alive.

www.ingramcontent.com/pod-product-compliance
Lightning Source LLC
Chambersburg PA
CBHW020132120726
47903CB00007B/2221